Eye of Truth
Cassie Sweet

Dreamspinner Press

Published by
Dreamspinner Press
5032 Capital Circle SW
Suite 2, PMB# 279
Tallahassee, FL 32305-7886
USA
http://www.dreamspinnerpress.com/

This is a work of fiction. Names, characters, places, and incidents either are the product of author imagination or are used fictitiously, and any resemblance to actual persons, living or dead, business establishments, events, or locales is entirely coincidental.

Eye of Truth
© 2013 Cassie Sweet.

Cover Art
© 2013 Brooke Albrecht.
http://brookealbrechtstudio.blogspot.com
Cover content is for illustrative purposes only and any person depicted on the cover is a model.

ISBN: 978-1-62798-207-8
Digital ISBN: 978-1-62798-206-1

Printed in the United States of America
First Edition
December 2013

To Chris and Margie—Thank you for all you've done to support, encourage, and guide me in this new direction for my writing. It has been most greatly appreciated.

Chapter One

FREEDOM!

Theodyne Thespacian took a deep lungful of the cool, fresh air and let it out slowly. After spending the last four years inside the stale, moldy confines of Pallonia Prison for thieving, the morning breeze that blew down into the valley from the mountains made him choke. Breath sputtered and wheezed out as he tried to gain control of his lungs.

The prison guard looked amused. "Happens to all of you when you leave."

Theodyne nearly told the man that if the conditions were better, it wouldn't happen. But at this stage of the game, standing outside the prison walls, he wasn't about to say or do anything to get sent back inside. At least not at the moment.

The guard reached into his uniform and pulled out a small leather-bound packet. "These here are your release documents. Keep them with you at all times or the city guards will lock you up again."

Theodyne took the packet. The *T* branded into the side of his face proclaimed him a convicted thief. He ran a finger down the telling scar. Tingles erupted under the puckered flesh where it hadn't quite healed sufficiently. Resentment burned up his gullet.

He'd once been considered the handsomest man in all of Lancor. Women and men alike had thrown themselves at his feet and in his bed. And who was he to have denied himself the pleasure? Now the adoring masses would look at him and hide their purses. The pickings, once so bountiful, were going to dry up like grapes on the vine if not plucked in time.

"Go on now. Get out of here." The guard gave Theodyne a healthy shove between the shoulder blades, which almost knocked him off his feet.

Theodyne straightened his tunic and cap, then began the long walk from the prison grounds to the gates of Lancor proper.

As he walked, he kept the marked side of his face away from the road. He angled his cap to hide the top crossbar of the *T*. The rest he concealed with a lock of hair. It wasn't a perfect or even permanent solution, but it had to do.

The closer he drew to the gates, the more traffic he encountered. Wagonloads of fruits and vegetables passed him. His stomach let out a long, miserable growl. The prison officials did not believe in spoiling the inmates by overfeeding. Nor did they feel it their duty to give a released criminal a meal before leaving the walled enclosure. From the moment their sentences were up, prisoners were on their own, which was only a slightly less frightening concept than incarceration.

Word of his impending release had sent an unfamiliar emotion running through his veins—worry. He'd never possessed even a drop of it before. Oh, to be sure, his arrest and subsequent conviction had caused more than a few moments of trepidation, but he knew he'd make it through. Sentences for first offenses carried only the minimum time. The scar on his face, marking him as a thief, was another form of punishment. It was akin to announcing his nimble fingers and quick mind to the world. A more effective method of cutting his earning power had yet to be invented.

The more Theodyne walked, the slower his stride became. There was an ill wind blowing from the east. Each small gust contained a hint of warning, as if something infectious had descended upon the city.

Theodyne stopped for a moment and looked around. Nothing in the scenery had changed since he'd been dragged off to prison. The mountains were where they'd always stood. The tree line leading into the forest remained tall and pristine, untouched by man's progress. Yet the intangible sense of wrongness lingered on the air. As if some harbinger of doom was about to sweep down and give Theodyne an earful, telling him to flee and never return.

Theodyne had never lived in fear. He did not intend to start now.

Pushing the disquieting thoughts to the back of his mind, he started walking again, casting his gaze on the expanse of the city wall.

The gates of Lancor loomed dark in the distance. A line of travelers queued up at the checkpoint. For those traveling by more opulent means than an oxcart or on foot, the left gate was open, with a guard who simply waved the wealthy and noble of Lancor through without the usual stop and search of papers.

The glut of nobility riding past brought a secret smile to Theodyne's lips. The crests on the black carriage doors were blatant and recognizable. There wasn't a house represented that hadn't felt the breadth of his expertise. Jewels, paintings, silver, crystal—all had been lifted and taken away into the night. Anything small enough to fit into a satchel, a pocket, or down his pants had been fair game. Theodyne did have standards. The item also had to have a generous resale value or be of interest to an awaiting party who paid for his specialized skills.

His services had sometimes been retained to take items that had only sentimental value to family members, but they had been willing to pay dearly to obtain the object from a rival member of their house. Theodyne provided an important service. The city *prolate* had taken extreme exception to the way he chose to earn a living. For that he was truly sorry, but it was the only vocation he knew.

It was a damn good thing he'd hidden several chests full of coins and jewelry in a couple of places around the city in case he was ever in dire need.

Theodyne glanced around at the slowly shifting lines of people. His situation had not gotten to the point of desperation. Judging from the amount of goods moving into the city, the bordering farms were prosperous. More money in the hands of the peasants meant more spending in the city, and thus more need for workers of varying skills.

In prison, Theodyne had learned all manner of tasks he'd not had the wherewithal to learn before. He had been a successful thief—why did he need to learn to plant and harvest crops, cook a meal for thousands, or dig ditches in the heat of the Sadonia summer? Yet, he had done just that. There hadn't been a choice in the matter.

The line shifted. The sun beat down on Theodyne's head. The pungent scent of farm animals and dung baked on the hot dirt. The warning breeze that had swept through the valley earlier in the day had died away, leaving the city to the sun's mercy.

Sweat ran down his back and pooled in the tops of his loose breeches. When he moved his arms, he got a strong whiff of body odor. It was no way to present at the gates of the city, but he had only the clothes on his back and the letters of his release.

Glancing around, he didn't even see any fountains or streams he could use to wash some of the stink away. Theodyne had always prided himself on maintaining the utmost standards in grooming. The clothes he'd worn had been of the latest styles and richest fabrics. All had been confiscated upon his arrest.

It was common practice for the *prolate*'s men to come in and seize all valuable property to pay for the accused's trial and subsequent incarceration. No one was ever found innocent in such proceedings. And even if by a miracle they were, all their lands, clothing, gold, jewels, paintings, and other items were already gone.

Theodyne often wondered what happened to the riches taken by the greedy city officials. Obviously they were not sold off to provide for the infirm and destitute. Those poor bastards were left to beg in the streets if they could find no alternate means of support.

Before his arrest, Theodyne had contemplated breaking into the *prolate*'s villa in the heart of the city just to see if all the treasures remained there. One of his friends, Damonino, had recently been sent to a prison ship to serve his sentence for breaking into the Medovin family vault, stored deep in the catacombs that ran under the city. It was rumored they hid pure gold coins in the vaults, guarded by their long-dead ancestors. All of Damonino's precious belongings had been taken from his home and had never surfaced again. Theodyne had a running bet with their mutual associate, Menarch, that all goods confiscated remained in the hands of the *prolate*. Menarch maintained only the most valuable things were kept, all others were shuttled out of the city to the *prolate*'s other holdings throughout the country.

The line shifted again, and Theodyne was next to face the guards. He had the papers ready, but feared they would not allow him back into the city—not a city that knew him as an infamous thief. One who made his fortune by stealing from the wealthiest and noblest of families.

The oxcart in front of him was allowed through the gates, and Theodyne stepped forward. He handed the guard on his right the papers and looked directly at the man, daring him to say anything that would prevent his entrance.

The guard glanced up and studied Theodyne's face. "You know it's an offense to hide or alter your badge."

"Can you see it?" Theodyne challenged.

The guard narrowed his eyes. "Watch your mouth or I'll have you taken back to Pallonia for unlawful conduct."

"Things have changed since I've been away if the merest of questions is considered unlawful conduct. I shall have to watch what I say." The tone in which Theodyne spoke brought a confused look to the guard's face, as if he didn't know whether he was being made a fool of or not.

"You'll have to watch more than your words." The guard folded the papers and placed them back into the folder. When Theodyne reached for them, the guard held them away. "I don't understand why they allow you criminals outside the prison walls. You should be locked up for the rest of your days or simply executed so you're not a drain on the dole."

Theodyne canted his head. "So you would have our property seized to pay for our keep and then just kill us outright anyhow, no matter the offense?"

"It's better than what you lot deserve."

"Freedric, leave him be." The other guard shook his head. "Where would we be if there weren't criminals in the city? Out of work and begging for day labor."

Freedric made a face and shoved the leather folio back at Theodyne. "Go on. Get inside, then. But don't let me catch you loitering about anywhere or I'll arrest you for vagrancy."

Theodyne made no reply, but touched the pouch to his cap in a salute of thanks to the helpful guard.

As he stepped through the gates of Lancor, his eyes opened wide and he stared in mute disconcertion. The city had changed so much in the four years he'd been away. New construction dotted the square. Scaffolding rose into the sky like hulking skeletons. Stonemasons scurried over the structures with all the agility of monkeys in trees.

One of the new buildings was attached to the Cathedral of St. Paulo Marín. As if that august bastion of greed needed another wing. Theodyne shook his head and started the journey to his sister's home on the other side of the city.

Lisette lived in the merchants' quarters near the open stalls of the market. She helped one of the local produce sellers man one of his many booths spread throughout the square. Theodyne had always done his best to try and provide for her, but she'd wanted nothing to do with his ill-gotten money. There had been no letters or support from her when he was arrested. He doubted she'd be overjoyed to see him freed, but as she was the only family he had, there were limited places he could go for help.

As Theodyne made his way to the market square, the buildings became thinner and smaller, with three levels at the most and each floor housing a different family. The brown mud bricks were of the same shape and size no matter the building, making each home indistinguishable from the next. However, the area was tidy, the streets clean. Even the common fountain at the center of the *plazo* shot pristine water in sparkling splendor from the underground aquifers. There was no place where pride of ownership did not show in this tiny haven of the city.

Theodyne passed under the archway, which served as a walk between two upper stories of the buildings, and into the cool shade. The sun had begun its downward descent in the afternoon sky, and the buildings cast long shadows across the square.

The heavenly scents of baking breads, cakes, and roasted meats filled the air with a mouthwatering aroma. Theodyne's stomach let out a ferocious growl. Hopefully his sister had supper on the table and would invite him in.

Lisette's cooking was beyond compare. The things she did with meat, vegetables, and flour were sublime. Theodyne's stomach growled again in anticipation.

He quickened his steps and came out from under the crosswalks and into the main promenade. A fountain designed like a large basket of fruit sprayed water high into the air. Wind blew across the top, sending a gentle mist over the milling people gathered in the square.

Theodyne paused for a moment to let the refreshing air cleanse his face and fill his lungs. His sister's home was on the opposite side of the square. From where he stood, he could see her door. It looked as if it had a fresh coat of bright paint. Window boxes were filled with colorful flowers and herbs. The house looked cheerier than when he'd left, the mood lighter.

Theodyne made his way across the square. Children ran and played, cutting off his progress and making him stop short. His sister's door opened, and a squat woman with blonde hair and a doughy face flicked a rag at the boys.

"Get away from here with your noise. You'll wake the baby."

The boys screeched in laughter and ran away.

Baby? Did his sister have a baby now?

Theodyne hurried to the door before she shut it again. "Excuse me. Could you tell Lisette her brother is here."

The woman made a face and looked him up and down. Her gaze landed on his face, and her eyes narrowed. "There's no Lisette here. Go on with you."

He put his hand on the door to stop her from shutting it in his face. "My sister lives here. This is her home. Who are you?"

"This is *my* home." She pointed to the thief's badge on his face. "You must be that no-good one she spoke of. Theocant."

"That's Theo*dyne*." He bit the words out. "Where is my sister?"

"She moved south. Married a merchant from there and sold the house to me."

Married? She'd never told him such. Never bothered to let him know she'd left Lancor. It was as if he'd ceased to exist for her after his arrest.

Resentment filled his gut. No matter how much she'd condemned and railed against his vocation, he'd never once thought of turning his back on her. For all his sacrifice and risk-taking, this was all the thanks he was to receive.

"Did she leave a message for me, then?"

"Ha! Only if you were to come looking for her to tell you that she no longer considers you her family." The woman took great pleasure in revealing that bit of news. Her eyes danced when she said it, as if the pain was hers by right to inflict.

A hollow pit opened in Theodyne's belly. He was rudderless, disconnected from the world. As long as he had at least one family member left, he'd felt he had an anchor. Now he was left as a castaway without a home, shelter, or connections.

Bereft of his only family, he was at a loss. He had to go somewhere to wait until the sun went down so he could attempt to dig up his hidden fortune.

His belly let out another loud growl.

The woman looked down at his stomach. Was it his imagination, or did her features soften a bit? With nothing to lose, he decided to play on her sympathies.

"Do you have any work for me to do? Errands I can run? Letters you need written? I'm well versed in several languages and good with figures. I only ask for payment in a small meal."

She made another snort and tried to shut the door again. Theodyne did not remove his hand. She glared at his arm preventing her from closing him out. "What? So you can rob me blind when my back is turned? I'm not a stupid woman. And before you think me uncharitable, I'll have you know I am to those who deserve it."

Theodyne shook his head. "And what have I taken from you? You have no reason to resent me. I've done you no harm." He lifted his hair away so she could fully see the thief's badge. "I earned this by stealing from those who have more than enough to give, yet refuse to help those less fortunate. You call me thief and stick your nose in the air as if you smell something bad to have me in your presence, yet you pay your taxes and tithes to a *prolate* and church who rob you through both laws and canon.

"Oh, they are worse than me and any thief I've ever known. They sentence a man to prison, then take his belongings while he's gone so he has nothing to return to. Yes, there are thieves all around you, madam, but I am not the worst you'll encounter."

Anger burned Theodyne's throat and made his heart beat hard against his breastbone. He shook his head in defeat. People like her would never understand that they were all just one step away from the same fate he'd suffered. All it took was a neighbor or guard to hold a grudge against some perceived offense and all they worked for would be forfeit.

Theodyne turned to leave.

"Wait." She took a few steps out of the door, starting after him. "Maybe I can help in a small way."

He turned back around. "It will be much appreciated."

"My Uncle Guiseppan is foreman of the cathedral expansion. Tell him Marghette sent you for day labor. He is always looking for men to haul debris away at the end of the day." She fanned a hand at him. "If you hurry, you might catch him before they break for meal."

Theodyne doffed his cap and hurried away from his sister's former home. He'd probably earn just enough for a meal at the tavern. That was all he needed. A place to sleep he'd worry about after he collected his treasure.

GUISEPPAN WAS a worse taskmaster than the overseers at Pallonia. By the time Theodyne finished hauling away the day's debris and laying out the materials for the next morning, his back hurt, his eyes stung from sweat running into them, and his hands were caked with white dust.

Theodyne stuck his hands in a bucket of cold water and rinsed them off. The water turned to a cloudy mud. The rest of the workers had lined up in front of Guiseppan to receive their daily wages. Theodyne dried his hands on his shirt and hurried over to get in line.

Thoughts of sweetbreads and tasty stews filled his head and made his mouth water. He was so hungry he could have eaten a wagon wheel and been content.

When he stood in front of Guiseppan, the old man held out an empty purse. "You'll have to come back tomorrow. I pay nothing on the first day."

"You'll pay me what you owe me."

"Off with you, or there'll be no work for you in the morning."

"This is how you treat a man who has done as you asked and made no problems for you? Is this the integrity of a man who helps build a cathedral?" Theodyne shook his head. "The walls will be tainted before they are even built."

Guiseppan narrowed his eyes. "You lecture me on integrity? You who wears the mark of his crime for all to see?"

"Yes. *All* can see my mark. It's plain as the sun in the sky." He pointed his finger at Guiseppan. "But at least mine shows."

People walking around the cathedral stopped to listen to the argument. They pointed and whispered behind their hands, their shocked faces condemning both men.

When that failed to get a rise from the foreman, Theodyne started to walk away. "It's a poor excuse for a man who believes he is justified in cheating another out of a day's wages because of a past crime he's already paid for." He was across the square when he turned and yelled, "May you one day know the hospitality of the fine people of Pallonia. Cheating a man out of his rightful pay is still a punishable offense, is it not?"

With that, Theodyne donned his cap and walked under the arch toward the lower-rent district.

As he made his way out of the square, he heard the plaintive cries and requests for Guiseppan to pay the poor bastard his due.

Whether he did or not was really immaterial at this point. Theodyne's pride would not let him accept money he had to force a man to pay him, even if owed to him. Plus he doubted Guiseppan would back down, no matter how much his name was sullied in the streets of Lancor. There was one thing for sure—the workers were going to check their coins carefully the next day to make sure they weren't shorted.

It would serve the man right if he had no day laborers come morning. If they all heard that Guiseppan had taken to withholding pay from workers who offered an honest day's labor, they might not be so inclined to show at the job site. Granted, Theodyne had only worked half the day, but that was enough to put a few coins in his fist.

He made his way to the area of the city known as the Downs. It was so called because water from the underground drainage ran downhill, forcing the reeking spill to rise from the sewers until a heavy rain came and washed it to the river.

The fountain here was modest, a simple urn in the middle of the pedestal. The people of the Downs were lucky to have that for their water supply. He drew closer and noticed the bottom of the fountain was coated in a brackish sludge. It was a shame no one bothered to clean it out. Of course, if one stirred the water in order to clean the bottom and sides, the motion would swirl up silt, lifting it to the top. It was probably better to leave it be.

But the idea did pose a tempting option to him.

Hunger was a strong motivator, and Theodyne really wanted a hot meal before he attempted to dig his treasures out of their hiding places.

He scanned the streets. Few people remained outside at this time of night. Most were inside enjoying a quick repast before retiring for the night, or they were in the tavern drinking to forget the day that was past and the one ahead.

He made his way to the fountain and bent at the waist, as if he meant to cup water in his hands to wash his face. If anyone was watching, Theodyne wanted his act to be convincing. He stuck his hands in the water, surprised at its coolness, and felt around on the bottom for some coins. It was a fool's gamble to think anyone in this quarter could spare a coin for a wish, but then, the superstitious often paid more for a lot less.

Theodyne's first pass didn't reveal any coins stuck to the bottom. Damn. He brought his hands out, patted his face with the water and rubbed it over his neck. During the second pass he felt a few small coins. Probably copper or brass, not enough to buy him a bed for the night, but it would be enough for a bowl of stew and a glass of cheap wine.

He held a lifted coin with his thumb to his palm and made a show of running his hands through his hair. He repeated the action a few more times until he had enough to sustain him for the evening. When he finished he placed his cap back on his head and made his way out of the square and to a small tavern he'd passed on his way to the Downs.

Chapter Two

THE TAVERN was low lit with candles in sconces along the walls. The pungent scent of tallow nearly overrode the aroma of spiced meats and fresh breads. Theodyne's belly let out another rumble. He sat at a table near the back of the tavern and pulled his hair over his cheek to hide his mark.

On his walk he'd cleaned the grime from the coins. They remained dirt encrusted and a bit eroded, but they'd spend all the same. He'd seen some in worse shape pass hands. The serving girl came to his table, pulling her dress down in the front to better show her generous cleavage.

Theodyne ordered his meal and drink. There was no way he could afford any bed partner for the night, though the thought of having a willing body under his stirred his sex.

"So the prodigal thief returns." The voice was low, scratchy, and spoke eloquently of the years of hard work and abuse suffered at the hands of an oppressive ruling class.

Theodyne turned to address the man. "Keep your voice down, Menarch. I don't want the whole tavern to know. They can guess for themselves from the mark on my face."

Menarch stood and tottered over on bandy legs to sit across from Theodyne. He reached over and lifted the hair from Theodyne's face before letting the curtain fall once again. "They didn't do that pretty face any good."

"Or my earning potential. Men see me and they hide their purses. Building foremen think it's a sign they can cheat me out of a day's hard-earned wages. Not even one full day out of Pallonia and I am disgusted with the lot. I haven't been away long enough that the world has changed so much in my absence."

"No. It's as cruel and unfair as always. Even more so for men like us now the new *prolate* has taken over."

"There is a new one? I hadn't heard. Who is he?"

"Estobán Medovin."

Theodyne's heart gave a great lurch at the knowledge. Estobán and he had been lovers for a time. It had been fun and exciting to bring the Medovin heir to his knees in pleasure while knowing he was robbing the family blind. Then Estobán had wanted to install Theodyne in an apartment away from the family villa, make it their secret love nest. Theodyne had refused. He was no man's hidden secret. Not on that scale. An affair where both men stood on their own feet was one thing, but a relationship where one had the advantage was a situation he'd not wanted to place himself in. Much to his detriment, as it turned out.

Menarch rolled his bulging eyes skyward. "The man is a menace to his own office."

"That man is the reason I was sent away in the first place," Theodyne said between clenched teeth.

"Ah, yes. I remember now." Menarch chuckled. "Well, there is one way you can get back at him for the injustice."

Theodyne laughed. "As far as that is concerned, he caught me dead to rights. I did break the law. So there was no real injustice, save the fact if I'd taken him up on his offer to install me in his apartment, I'd have been untouchable."

Menarch gave a nod. "So you are both a thief and a fool."

"And if you had been a true friend, you'd have told me of Estobán's anger."

The serving girl set his food and drink on the table and lingered for a moment before Theodyne looked up. "Is there something you want?"

"Payment. The landlord says you need to pay up front due to your...." She let the words trail off, but her gaze strayed to his thief's badge.

He stuck the coins on the table and slid them over to her, not even wanting to get close enough to her to place them in her hands. She'd probably scream that he'd made an overture and refused to pay for her services.

She scooped up the coins and moved away from the table.

"This is intolerable."

"Then have your revenge." Menarch took out a rolled piece of tobacco and stuck it into his mouth. He struck a flint on the stone wall and lit the tip of the cigar, puffing hard to keep the burn. A gray ring of smoke rose, pungent and fragrant on the air. It circled Menarch's head like a tainted halo.

An odd glint filled Menarch's eyes. Old and otherworldly. Menacing. Theodyne glanced down into his bowl to break contact. A shiver passed over him.

"I can ill afford revenge. I could barely pay for this meal." Theodyne dug into the thick stew with appreciation, keenly aware a stolen wish had provided for him.

"Very well." Menarch blew out a cloud of smoke. "Estobán's ascension to *prolate* isn't the only change in the area. On the edge of town, outside the south gates, is a new villa. The Villa de Valencia. It is a fortress of paradise, with riches to rival that of the Medovins."

Theodyne picked up his wine and took a sip. It had been watered down significantly. "If you meant to tempt me, it won't work. You see before you a man reformed."

"Once a thief, always a thief."

"Says a man who has yet to be caught."

Menarch gave a mischievous smile—there was definitely evil there, but of a nature Theodyne had never seen. Theodyne remained hunched over his bowl and studied his old friend from the tops of his eyes. There was something off about that gaze, but for the life of him, he could not put his finger on just what or why.

"It is rumored that the Count de Valencia has a treasure in that villa. An arcane symbol of power and mystery: the *Eye of Truth*." He leaned forward. "It is said that he who possesses the *Eye* will hold untold wealth."

Theodyne affected a conspirator's pose and leaned in. "It is said he who steals a second time is condemned to death."

"Oh, baaah. You've lost your sense of adventure."

"I've lost my freedom. I'll be damned before I lose my life as well."

Menarch waved his hand in the air. "I'll wager you'll be at the villa before morning."

Theodyne held up his hands, palms out. "I have nothing to wager you."

"I can float you a marker."

Theodyne gave a rusty laugh. He knew all too well about Menarch's markers. Failure to pay when they were called in usually resulted in grievous bodily harm or worse. "No thank you. I'll find other means to support myself than wagering with you."

"Suit yourself."

Across the tavern someone strummed a *guitern* while another sang. It was a plaintive tune that tugged at some lost corner of Theodyne's heart.

He finished his meal and took his leave. All he wanted from this night was to dig up his treasure chest and find an inn, have a bath and some clean clothes, then sleep.

THEODYNE MADE his way through the darkened streets of Lancor until he came to the area known as Aterary, so named for the family who owned most of the block of houses along the lane.

There was a breathtaking fountain in the center of the *plazo*. A beautiful man and woman carved from a single piece of marble frolicked forever in the water. Where the *plazo* had once been open to the public, it was now closed off behind large iron gates. Guards patrolled the area with lanterns held aloft. They weren't dressed as the city guards, but in the Aterary house colors of deep purple and crimson.

Theodyne would not get in there anytime soon. Not with armed guards marching in intervals through the *plazo*.

Damn.

He studied the patterns the guards made and tried to calculate if there was time to sneak in and make it to the hiding place before they detected him. He doubted it. There were too many of them. Too many sets of eyes on the area.

Temporarily defeated, Theodyne made his way to his second hiding place. This one was on the south side of the Arch of Darium. It was a monument dedicated to a fallen warrior during some long-forgotten battle. The Darium family had once been one of the richest and most powerful in Lancor and the whole city-state of Sadonia, possibly the entire country of Dominicál. Like many other ancient families, their downfall had been hard and fast.

Potted trees and climbing flowers lined the boulevard where the arch stood. At the seventh tree on the right, facing the arch, was where Theodyne had hidden the second treasure. He searched the area for any passersby who might alert the city guards to his activities.

He hunkered down under the tree and began to pull away the heavy blanket of grass from the base. Most of the grass plots in the city had been brought in from local farms in squares, then put down to complete the landscape after construction. Only the most exclusive projects could afford this harvested sod.

Without the help of a trowel or shovel, Theodyne was forced to dig with his hands. Luckily the ground was soft and easily excavated. He'd made his way down almost a foot when panic set in. His heart pounded in a frantic rhythm. His breath came in short gulps between his lips. Perspiration broke out on his forehead and upper lip.

Where was it?

His memory was so clear on where he'd hidden it. He'd never have forgotten where he'd placed a treasure, the location engrained in his memory as indelibly as the mark on his face.

Theodyne had used the lowest branch as a guide. Direct center and straight down. He ran his hand through the sides of the hole he'd made and found no telltale edges of the box he'd placed the items into before burial.

He rocked back on his heels. It was hard to swallow. Hard to breathe. He had to open his mouth to get in enough air. Nausea rose.

Oh Gods.

The dinner he'd just eaten rumbled in his stomach. It was not going to stay put for long.

The treasure was gone. Someone had taken it while he was in prison.

Theodyne sat there dazed in disbelief for a few moments before the reality of the situation set in—the once rich and infamous thief, who had moved in the highest circles of society and rubbed elbows with diplomats and artists, was now destitute and alone.

With a halfhearted attempt, he shoved the dirt into the hole and sat back. The aroma of rich soil and greenery smelled of defeat.

He hung his head. There were few options left. He dared not return to the day work. Not with Guiseppan as the foreman. If Theodyne looked into a mirror, he'd not see a bigger thief than that man.

After filling the hole and replacing the grass, Theodyne stood and brushed his dirty hands on his pants. Out of choices, he made the trek to the south gate, cursing Menarch with every step.

The bastard had read Theodyne's fortunes as if through a crystal ball or scrying glass. Perhaps he'd known of the treasure's location and helped himself to it after Theodyne's incarceration? Whoever had taken it hadn't left even a splinter of wood or a golden *tonza*.

The gates were closed and locked for the night. The only way through was to climb the vacant guard hut and stand on the roof to get over the wall. Once up on the wall, it was a long drop to the other side. He'd done farther ones in his time.

Theodyne stood under the overhang of the hut and jumped to catch the side. He swung up first one leg to catch the roof, then the other one. Slowly, so as not to roll off the steep slope, he got his feet under him and walked up to the peak.

Going over the wall was easy, but first he needed to get his bearings. It was a short climb to sit on top. About fifty feet away was a tree he could use to climb down the other side.

Theodyne walked with his head down, one foot directly in front of the other, until he made it to the tree. The problem was his poor estimation of how close the tree stood to the wall. Now he was close up, he could see it was not a matter of him reaching out to grab the nearest branch. It was going to take a bit of maneuvering on his part to make it to there. A jump at the very least.

Between the full moon and the lights dotting the city, Theodyne had just enough illumination to get a good sense of exactly how far the nearest branch extended. He wiped his sweating hands on his breeches and jumped.

There was a moment of weightlessness, and then his hands caught the branch. Uneven bark bit into his palms, cutting painful rents along the center. He bit back an oath and moved hand over hand until he was able to hug the trunk. From there it was a matter of shimmying down.

With feet firm on the ground, he set off to find the Villa de Valencia.

Chapter Three

COUNT NICODEMUS de Valencia gazed at the porous pieces of gray limestone bound along a length of string. Desdemona diGarza watched in rapt attention as he whispered words over the rocks and blew a fine breath across the top. He waved his hand over the surface of the makeshift necklace a few times. The more pageantry he showed the client, the more convinced they became that he held arcane powers.

He did. But it was more a learned craft than an innate one. Years of study and practice had made him into the magician his clients believed him to be. But it was all deception. Everything in this dimension was, in part, a deception.

Nico picked up the necklace and held it in a closed fist. He blew in one end, then opened his hand. Where there was once nothing more than twine and rocks now sat a beautifully fashioned chain of gold and diamonds.

Signora diGarza took in a sharp breath. "It is exquisite. Perfection."

"I warn you to get this to your cousin quickly. It will only stay in this form for so long before it reverts back to the elements from which it was made." Nico tapped the largest stone in the necklace. The woman had only enough to pay him for a temporary transmutation.

The original necklace had been lost during a night at the theater. Signora diGarza had come to Nico to create a necklace to replace the one she'd borrowed from her cousin, the Countess de Rivo.

She set a bag of coins on the worktable. "I will not forget what you've done for me."

Carefully she placed the contrived piece into the box and closed the lid.

Nico gave a salutatory nod and watched as she walked from the workroom. It was a service he provided for people who were desperate enough to pay his price. The money kept him in a villa the size of Valencia and allowed him to continue to pursue his studies and perhaps one day build a school in Sadonia. It wasn't the perfect arrangement, but it was damn close enough.

One of the house servants, Cassius, came into the room and bowed low. "My lord, there is an intruder in the vineyard."

"An intruder? Are you sure it isn't merely a pilgrim traversing the fields in order to save steps on his journey?"

Cassius scrunched up his weather-beaten face and considered the question. "I don't know. But I know he doesn't belong. He's lingering. A traveler would make his way through and be done with it. This one slept in the fields all night."

"Perhaps he was called to rest by the sweetness of grapes on the vine."

Cassius stared.

"Very well, bring him here." Nico leaned back in his chair and folded his hands in front of him. It was some time before there was another knock on the door and his most trusted and loyal servant Pedraus ushered in a golden god of a man to stand facing the desk.

Nico tried not to react, but it was damn difficult. Though the man was dressed as the lowliest of peasants, his bearing was of the noble class, and his haughty gaze met Nico's in defiance. The thief's badge on his face told another story entirely.

"You were trespassing." Nico steepled his hands and looked over them at the man.

"I am looking for work."

"Then that is a different matter altogether." Nico gave the man a fleeting smile. "What is your name?"

"Theodyne Thespacian."

Nico had a hard time not reacting to the name. The man before him had been the subject of gossip, fable, and innuendo since Nico had arrived in Lancor. The once celebrated and charismatic thief had fallen very far and hard to come to the villa begging for work.

"What can you offer the villa that I don't already have, then, Theodyne?" It was a question he normally wouldn't ask, as his servants had all come to him when a specific position came open. He'd never hired just for the sake of hiring, but there was something in this Theodyne's expression that was different. It was worldly. Wary. Angry. That combination intrigued and moved Nico. As did the man's plight. No one should ever have to live looking as if they were haunted by their sins.

Theodyne met his eyes directly. "Stealing is my one true skill. I learned many others in Pallonia."

This man was more than mere façade. No thief, no matter how skilled, could have possibly gotten away with his crimes as long as Theodyne Thespacian had. There was something different there—other. It would not surprise Nico in the least to know that Theodyne had more than a drop of elemental blood.

And it was a known fact that elementals made for some of the best alchemists.

"Have you ever considered an apprenticeship? Something to occupy your time and give you a vocation so you don't have to steal for your sustenance?"

"Never considered it, but it is a fair question."

And insolent. The man was full to the brim with it. "And how do I know you won't rob me blind?"

Theodyne glanced around. "You don't. But I fail to see much of a challenge here. Your valuables are out for all to admire. Even your current servants could make off with them. No skill required."

Nico laughed and stood. "A truthful and bold answer."

"Why lie? You can tell by the mark on my face that I am already on a watch list. My next such offense and I lose my life, not merely my livelihood."

Nico came to stand in front of Theodyne and took his chin in his hand. He moved Theodyne's face to better see the heinous mark. "A barbaric practice if ever I've seen one."

Theodyne jerked his chin away from Nico's grasp. "Is there any work here, or should I keep moving?"

"Do you want an apprenticeship?"

Pedraus made a sound of disapproval from his place by the door.

Theodyne narrowed eyes just as golden as his hair. "Depends on the discipline. Suppose I have no affinity for the vocation?"

Nico crossed his arms over his chest. "I have no doubt you will prove very adept."

"You aren't going to tell me until I agree, are you?" Theodyne's gaze moved over the room and then stopped at Pedraus before moving back to Nico. "Judging from the instruments and arcane symbols, I'd say you're one of those rare men gifted in the arts of alchemy."

Pleased that Theodyne recognized the symbols of Nico's craft, he gave a nod. "And have you known many alchemists in your experience?"

"Not a one."

"We are not all that uncommon, but I can understand, if you hail from Lancor. The Medovins are intolerant of anything that could possibly usurp their hold on the city." Nico made his way to the tall black-lacquered cabinet with the mother-of-pearl inlayed sigils along the front.

With a flick of his wrist, the locks disengaged and the door opened. He glanced over to Theodyne, who watched him intently. It was evident by the look on the thief's face he'd noted Nico had opened the lock and the door without ever touching the mechanism.

"There are more things within this room than you can see with your eyes. More things than you'll ever know by using any of your natural senses."

"And I'll be paid for my time?"

"Will you need payment?" Nico posed the question with a lift of his brow. "If you agree to become my apprentice, you'll live here at the villa. You'll be fed and clothed from my coffers. I suppose we can arrange for a small sum to be paid, depending on your progress."

"I won't be kept like a pet."

"Who said anything about keeping you as a pet? I make those who live here work very hard for their pay. You'll earn every morsel that passes your lips and every thread that touches your body."

Theodyne gave a quick nod. "As long as we understand each other."

"You are quite decided for a man who has limited options."

"I may be limited, but I also know what I *won't* do for money."

Nico smiled. "Very well. Go with Pedraus. He'll show you where you can bathe and give you a change of clothes. I'll expect you in the dining room for afternoon meal in one hour. Are we clear?"

"Yes."

"Very good." Nico fanned his hand in the direction of the door to get the man moving toward a cleaner body and brighter future.

He'd not contemplated taking on an apprentice, but now the decision was made, it was perfect. The Gold School needed new recruits, and he had not taken on a student himself in a very long time. Not that he particularly enjoyed teaching his craft to others. It was always difficult for him to explain to an outsider those formulas and applications he found second nature. Growing up within the school and being a direct descendant of the Gold School's founder, Mercurian Dante, gave Nico an advantage over other students. The way of the alchemist was as much a part of his blood as the cells that flowed through his veins.

There was much more to Theodyne's story than needing a way to support himself. Very few thieves were redeemed even on the threat of death. Not many knew any other way to be. It was the thrill of the act that drove them, not the actual item stolen. Theodyne had confirmed it was so when he'd dismissed the contents of Nico's study as not enough of a challenge to steal.

Nico pulled a book from the cabinet—a primer. The small tome held all the symbols and definitions of the practice along with a few simple conversions of materials from their compounds to base substances. It was always easier to break down an article than to build one. That came with time and attention.

Thumbing through the book, memories assailed Nico from the depths of the musty pages. The ink had faded in places. Others were stained by candle wax and various chemicals, where they had been spilled during a lesson.

He'd hoped one day to pass the books on to his son, but that seemed an unlikely proposition. The call of a woman's flesh held no sway over him. Not even for the sake of procreation. Often he'd thought to take a foundling into his home and heart and raise the boy as his son. Perhaps he might still, but for now, Nico would wait and see how Theodyne worked out.

"Theodyne." He said the name aloud, tasting the syllables on his tongue. They were musky and filled with spice. It was a flavor that bore savoring.

Nico spent the hour before the midday meal straightening out his work area and collecting those materials appropriate for an apprentice-level practitioner. After they ate, he'd bring Theodyne in to show him the prime matter and discuss basic theory. He didn't want to overload the man on the first day, but give him enough to stew on while he read the primer.

A bell over the door tinkled, letting Nico know the meal was served. He washed his hands in a basin and dried them on a soft cloth before making his way to the dining room.

The dining area was a long, cool room with a beautiful mosaic floor depicting the sun and celestial bodies moving in sacred order around it. A heavy wooden table sat as the focal point. The sun gleamed off the high-polished surface, highlighting what appeared to be golden flecks in the wood grain.

The meal was set out along the length of the table. Durgin, the dining servant, stood midway down the table, ready to assist with the passing of platters to the diners.

Theodyne sat at the near end of the table. He stood when Nico entered. The effects of a good bath and grooming were devastating. Nico gritted his teeth and kept walking to the head of the table. He motioned for Theodyne to follow.

Nico heard the soft footfalls of Theodyne's feet as he walked behind. When they were at the far end of the table, he pointed to the chair at his right hand. "Sit here. I do not intend to shout to be heard during the meal. It's bad for digestion."

Theodyne pulled out the chair and sat. He watched as Nico took his seat as well. There was something in those golden eyes that was unsure and almost afraid. It was easier to read now all the dirt and neglect had been washed away.

Nico lifted the hand linen and placed it in his lap. "You may serve, Durgin."

The servant removed the lid from a steaming platter of seasoned vegetables. A distinct noise came from Theodyne's stomach.

Nico smiled. "Wait until you taste it." He kissed the tips of his fingers. "There really is nothing like Molari's cooking. He has a way with food that makes you realize paradise is an epicurean concept."

Theodyne watched the food going onto his plate. "It smells good."

The next platter was opened, and a roasted game bird sat in all its golden-brown goodness. Fragrant steam rose to fill the room.

"I want you to eat hearty. You will learn better on a full stomach." Nico pointed to Durgin and out into the field where the workers could be seen sitting at a table, eating their meal. "I believe in fueling the body as well as the mind. You need both nutrition and education to feed your soul."

Theodyne looked bewildered. "I guess I never thought of it that way."

"No? Well maybe today is the day you start."

"AS ABOVE, so below." Nico lifted his arms, then brought them down in demonstration. "In all the world, in all the universe, there is but one substance." He lifted his right index finger, pointing it skyward. "This is the basis for alchemy. Everything you see and feel and touch comes from the same source."

Theodyne frowned. "The church would disagree with you there."

"Only with the terminology, not the concept."

"And you'd be sent to death for heresy." The handsome thief picked up a small marble crucible off the table. "Do you ever worry the church officials in Lancor will hear of your work?"

Aw, so the man thought to blackmail him. "The officials tend to look the other way when someone as rich and generous as myself is involved. You have seen the construction on St. Paulo's."

Theodyne's gaze snapped to Nico's. "You paid for that?"

"*Am* paying for that."

"Then you owe me a half day's wages." Theodyne set the crucible on the table with a *thunk*. "Your foreman Guiseppan refused to pay me as a day laborer. Said that I didn't deserve it due to my thief's badge."

"Hmm." Nico gave no outward appearance that he cared, but inside he raged and burned. How dare the foreman cheat a worker out of pay for a debt already served? He made his way to a small hidden drawer, recessed into the underside of a desk. "How much are you owed?"

"Two copper *slews* and a *gint*."

Nico raised a brow. "For a half day's wages? What did you do?"

"Hauled away debris and cleaned tools." Theodyne raised his chin, nose out. Proud and beautiful.

Nico went tight all over. Desire kicked him low in the gut. He took out a small coin purse and counted out the amount. What was a few *slews* and a *gint* to a man who could always make more? "Here. Consider the matter closed."

Theodyne closed his palm around the tiny sum. "Nice to know there is still some honor among thieves."

Nico threw his head back and laughed. "Thief? No. I'm a practitioner of an ancient art. I don't steal to create or change substances; I merely manipulate what is already present. There is a vast difference."

Theodyne placed the coins back on the table. "Then turn these to gold."

Seizing the challenge and a way to turn the tables, Nico leaned over the work surface and leveled his gaze on Theodyne. "If you want those coins turned to gold, then I suggest you study, learn the craft, and change them yourself. We'll consider it a test to move you from journeyman status."

"Not from apprentice?"

Nico lifted the corner of his mouth. "I'm not that easy a master."

He slid the primer across the table to Theodyne. "The first order of business is to read this book. Cover to cover. Memorize its principles and recite them to me."

Theodyne picked up the book and flipped through the pages. "The script is atrocious."

"It was handwritten by a master dead some five hundred years now."

"It should have been recopied to make it more legible."

Theodyne had a dry wit and cynical tongue. How Nico longed to hear something sweet and soothing pass those lips.

"One of the aspects of using a book penned by a great master is that the pages are imbued with some of his wisdom and power." Nico held up his hand so the outside edge near his little finger faced Theodyne. "Imagine Master Krutarch's hand touching the pages as he wrote. Now yours will touch that same page as you read. His loving guidance reaching through the centuries to you as you learn."

Theodyne glanced up from the book. "I think you have a bit of the poet in you."

"And you have a bit of the cynic."

"Prison does that to a man. Makes him realize the world isn't full of second chances unless he makes them himself."

"That makes me sad for you." Nico slid another book over to him. This one empty. "In your room you will find a desk outfitted with ink and quills. Use this book to write down any notations, observations, or questions you have regarding the reading. I will check it each morning for progress. We will review those concepts you find difficult first thing before moving to the next lesson."

"Do you really believe I can do this?"

"What have you got to lose at this point? You came here looking for work. I have none. All my domestic positions are filled. What I didn't have was an apprentice." Nico came around the table and placed his hand very gently on Theodyne's shoulder. There was heat and tense strength there in Theodyne's bunched muscles. "It beats getting cheated out of money you rightfully earned."

Theodyne worked his jaw back and forth as if Nico had asked to keep the thief's soul in a trunk under the house. "All right. I'll do it. If it helps you out."

So that's the way it was going to work? Theodyne had to think *he* was the one in control. The one to bless Nico with his presence.

"Not for me. For you."

With that, he dismissed Theodyne. There were some other matters Nico needed to tend to before the end of the day. Item one was to reprimand Guiseppan for daring to withhold pay due a worker. Such despicable behavior had no place in an operation funded by Valencia money.

He penned a particularly scathing and threatening letter that Guiseppan would no doubt have to have someone read to him. Nico also informed Guiseppan he was withholding that amount of money from his pay to make up the difference.

That would make the foreman angry, but Nico didn't care. He was beyond the reach of someone like Guiseppan. The man had only the power he was given through his position, and even then it was only enough to extend to the men on the build site. Any other transgressions and Nico would see him permanently removed.

The world was often an unfair place. It was Nico's duty to even the gaps in social class a bit.

Chapter Four

THEODYNE SAT in the sun on a very beautiful *plazo*. The bench seat was padded with the finest cloth, making it comfortable against the hard wood from which it was constructed. The sweet scent of exotic blooms filled the air, along with the fruity tang of grapes on the vine. The occasional creak and squeak of the winepress filtered into the air from one of the villa's outer buildings.

It was as if he'd fallen asleep and awoken in a foreign world surrounded by luxury. Theodyne had once traveled in such circles, but only as a pet for a rich patron who'd wished to secure his services.

Even sounds were different here. The small hum he'd always heard when near a treasure had grown in volume and intensity. Theodyne had to concentrate extra hard to push it to the background.

Count Valencia seemed to be of a different breed than any other man Theodyne had ever met. Certainly he was a far cry from Estobán Medovin. But then, Theodyne and Estobán had been lovers. The rules governing such associations were different.

This relationship was of an adept to an apprentice. Teacher to student. Count Valencia had the power to turn him out on a whim and have him returned to prison. Though, in all honesty, he doubted the man would do something so drastic. Theodyne's initial interactions with the alchemist showed the Count to be a fair and just man. At least on the surface.

Theodyne's heart tripped and began to pound. The man was simply the most beautiful person Theodyne had ever seen. Not only in the physical sense of the word. There was powerful charisma and presence there. It was hard to look directly at the Count, and yet he found himself drawn into not only doing that, but staring as if hungry for the sight of the Count.

Odd and fanciful thoughts raced through Theodyne's mind. It wasn't as if he'd ever met the Count before. No, a man such as Nicodemis Valencia, he would have definitely remembered.

He opened the book. The sun glinted off the ancient ink, giving it an iridescent quality. Depending on the angle of the light, it appeared purple, pink, or black. Oh, there was power infused in the words all right. One had only to pick up the small volume to feel it radiate from the pages.

As above, so below.

The first words of the book lodged somewhere in Theodyne's sacrum. In his mind he heard the Count's deep, resonant voice rumble out the phrase. It was a sound that stripped away the layers of his body and went straight down to his soul.

Desire swam in Theodyne's veins. It was going to be hard to keep focused on arcane principles when his teacher had the face of a fallen god.

The reading came easy. None of the principles contained within the first chapter were difficult to comprehend. Not for someone who was raised in the church and had heard the teachings of how the Gods had made the heavens and the world from nothing more than a thought. The Count was correct in that respect.

The sun had started to fall across the western horizon when the sound of footsteps against the tiled *plazo* brought his head up from the book. The Count stood with his hands clasped behind his back. A sensuous smile played across his lips.

"You've done quite a bit of reading for one afternoon. Come inside and enjoy a light repast with me."

Theodyne closed the book and stood. "If you don't mind, I think I'll pass on the meal. My belly is still full from earlier. I will, however, indulge in a beverage."

"Then that is what you shall have." The Count placed his hand on Theodyne's shoulder and steered him in through the *plazo* door and down a short hallway. They entered a room Theodyne didn't remember seeing from the outside. The outer wall appeared a solid piece of glass. The vibrant sunset was visible beyond in all its spectacular colors.

"I've never seen anything like it." Theodyne moved to the wall and placed his hand on it. The surface was warm after absorbing the sun's rays.

"No doubt." The Count lounged on a long, low-slung sedan, his arm thrown elegantly over the headrest. "It's all brick and mortar. I partially transformed the visual aspects of the substances so I could have an unobstructed view of the vineyards."

"Why not use glass?"

The Count shook his head. His dark hair shone in the light from the few sconces lit around the room. "Too many imperfections. This way the wall is even and without blemish. It's superior to anything a glassmaker could fashion."

That much was true. It was a remarkable piece of alchemical ingenuity.

"What other miracles do you perform? With such power at your disposal, how do you keep from getting bored? I'd think you have nothing left to work for."

The Count frowned. "That's where you're wrong, Theodyne. Improvement of the mind and perfection of the soul, those concepts are what make it worthwhile to keep seeking knowledge. My prime goal is to expand and advance the Gold School. As long as I hold to that, there will always be a need to work harder."

Theodyne had never possessed such a goal. He'd made his living and existed through a series of crimes. There were never any personal desires beyond wealth and fame to even consider. No plans as to what lay beyond that. Now his fame had turned to infamy. His face ruined beyond redemption. There was no escaping his past, no matter how much he improved his mind.

Theodyne fingered the scar on his cheek as he turned back to watch the last fading rays.

The door opened and the servant Durgin entered, wheeling a small serving cart.

"Thank you, Durgin."

The door closed again and Theodyne felt the acute intimacy of being alone with the Count. He rubbed a hand over his heart. If it pounded much harder, he was sure it would give out on him. It had not beat so hard when he'd nearly gotten caught robbing the *desan's* residence five years before.

"Come, Theodyne. Sit and enjoy your drink." The Count leaned forward on the red velvet cushions. He poured two glasses of a deep-red wine and took one, then lounged back in the corner of the furniture. One arm rested on the back of the seat. Dark eyes watched Theodyne.

Should he take a seat by the Count or take a drink from the tray and retire to a spot across the room? That way seemed safer but cowardly.

Theodyne took his wine and made his way over to a series of shelves that held an assortment of exotic glass orbs. Inside each sphere were tiny storms that churned with violent energy.

"What are these?"

"Experiments." The Count gave him a lazy smile and rose. He made his way to the cabinet to stand beside Theodyne. "Be careful. They can be quite dangerous if dropped."

Theodyne had no doubt. The storms rolling inside looked vicious. "You keep bad weather in a bottle like the wines made from your vineyards? What do you use it for?"

The Count ran his thick fingers over the surface of one of the globes. "To see if I could. You never know when it might be of use."

The Count hovered somewhere between madman and genius. Intense intelligence shone in his eyes as well as the curiosity of a child. Yet he seemed as stable and good as any man Theodyne had ever met. It was a remarkable combination, and it captured Theodyne's attention in no small measure.

Suddenly, Theodyne knew he wanted to please the adept, that doing well in the arcane arts of transmutation might be just what he needed to save his life and turn his fortune.

"How long did it take you to learn how to capture storms in glass?"

The Count frowned. "I have no idea. The vision came to me one night in a dream, and I began the process in the morning when I woke. I thought it a divine challenge."

"The priests would call you a blasphemer. Only Gods can create weather."

"If I listened to the priests, I would forgo the pleasures of the flesh as well, but I have no intention of doing that in this lifetime or the next." A sensuous smile lifted the corner of the Count's mouth. He turned and made his way back to the tray and speared a tiny square of meat with a silver fork.

A fever spilled inside Theodyne's body. It spread through his veins like quicksilver. He tried to look away from the Count but was trapped by the spell of the adept's eyes.

"You enjoy pleasures of your own, Theodyne." It was not a question, but a statement of fact. As if the Count had intimate knowledge of Theodyne's innermost thoughts.

"Before my imprisonment, I enjoyed many different pleasures. Physical and otherwise."

The Count's smile widened. "I shall remember that as we go through your studies."

There was a brief, uncomfortable silence. Theodyne had no idea what to say. It was a unique experience for him. There were very few instances in his life when he'd felt as if he had no idea what waited on the horizon. His ability to read a situation and act accordingly had been both intuitive and useful. The Count had thrown Theodyne off-balance and made it hard to regain his footing. Maybe that was part of the risk of taking a place as an apprentice. The master had to retain an upper hand at all times or fail in his teachings.

"Did you have any questions from your lessons?"

Theodyne brought his wine back to the table and set it on the tray. He'd barely taken a sip, which did not speak well of his manners. "Not as yet. I haven't come across any concepts that are new or foreign to me."

"Good." The Count kept his gaze on Theodyne's. "Did you not care for your wine?"

"It's rather potent. I make it a habit not to drink too much of such spirits."

The Count raised a brow. "A habit learned during your years of thievery?"

"Too much drink makes it difficult to open safes or pick pockets. A man needs to keep his wits to survive in those circumstances."

The Count nodded. "A good policy. Commendable, even. It is said that the wine from my lands can instill inner vision and foresight into those who consume it."

"Is that so?" Theodyne looked at his abandoned glass on the tray. "I prefer to live my life without knowledge of what is to come. It makes it more interesting. Take today, for instance. When I came here, I had no thought that the job I sought would turn to an apprenticeship."

"And had you known, would you have avoided the villa or come to demand what you felt was your due?"

"Neither. I would have seen the advantage of making the journey but approached it in the same humble manner you met me."

The Count let out an incredulous laugh. "Humble? I have never seen such arrogance in all my life as you displayed in my office."

Slightly taken aback by the Count's reaction, Theodyne frowned. "You must not have found offense or you wouldn't have offered me the position."

The Count swirled his wine around in his glass. He raised it to his mouth, hesitating before taking a drink. "You've got me there. I can see your value, even if you do not."

Theodyne's heart skipped. He'd always known his own value, though it was measured in the goods he'd stolen. No one had ever wanted to be around him for the sake of his own heart. Not even his sister. She'd left as soon as he'd embarrassed her with his unfortunate incarceration.

He swallowed and looked down into the Count's smiling face. There Theodyne saw things he'd only dreamed of—or had been afraid to aspire to in dreams. Not even his acquaintances among the other thieves could be called friends. No, it was more of competition and rivalry. Even Menarch had treated Theodyne with a kind of friendly contempt, but there were no real fond emotions there. Menarch would throw Theodyne to roast in the pits of hell before he'd lift a hand to truly help him.

Eye of Truth? Indeed. Menarch wanted to find it for himself, but he wanted Theodyne to take all the risk. Theodyne doubted the Count even kept the relic where any visitor to the villa could see or steal it. So much the better. Out of sight, out of temptation's way.

"Is there something more you wanted, Theodyne?" The Count raised a dark brow in query. His sensuous lips were lifted at one corner. The way he had his arm thrown over the back of the settee looked as if it were placed there in invitation.

From this angle, Theodyne noted the strong pull of muscle in the Count's upper arms. The splay of it down the side of his chest tapered to a trim waist. Looking lower, Theodyne cast a lingering glance on the fold of material gathered at the Count's lap and wondered if the bulge in the fabric was material or flesh.

Heat burned Theodyne's cheeks, and he turned his face away from the sight. In doing so, he hid the ruined side in lengthening shadows. His own body had begun to stir, but shame forced him to deny his growing desire.

Theodyne cleared his throat. "No, Count Nicodemus. I believe I will retire for the night."

The Count motioned with an elegant yet powerful hand, releasing Theodyne to go to his room.

As he made his way through the villa, Theodyne peeked into the other rooms, wondering what the *Eye of Truth* looked like and where it was kept. Not that he intended to steal it, but out of simple curiosity.

Only a fool would steal from someone like the Count. The power Theodyne had witnessed today was surely only a fraction of what the man possessed. Not that anything had been overt or even awesome. It was the subtlety, the graceful movement of his hand that made the act awe-inspiring. It was as if the Count thought no more about the actions than he did about breathing.

If Theodyne learned to execute transmutation, he'd never have to worry about stealing again. He'd not have to worry about digging in the ground for a treasure someone else had taken from him. He'd be able to support himself in the manner to which he had become accustomed and not have the discrimination of his thief's badge to give a master the chance to cheat him out of a day's wages. Instead, Theodyne could be *the* master. Hire his own domestics and perhaps one day possess a vineyard like here at the villa.

It was a worthy goal.

But what about the swirl of desire that flowed through his veins whenever he looked at the Count? Keeping that emotion in check was going to be infinitely difficult when every move the man made spoke of a deep, innate sensuality.

He had been through one disastrous affair with a man of a higher social class—he didn't want to do so again. Not with someone of the Count's powerful nature.

Theodyne entered his room and staggered back a step. Colorful tendrils of light danced in intricate patterns on the ceiling. They cascaded down like luminescent waterfalls.

He stood watching them in awe. Never had he seen anything quite as beautiful—not to mention oddly calming.

He crossed the room to the small cot and sat down. The wood and ropes let out squeaks of protest under his weight. The lights danced over him. How was he supposed to sleep with that show going on above his head?

But he supposed he had slept through worse. Echoes of his first nights in prison came unbidden to his memory. The screams of terror and pain as men were repeatedly raped. Then there were the cries of those who had gone insane in the confines of solitary confinement. The sounds of their panicked shrieks would forever live in his soul.

Theodyne kicked off his shoes and lay back, placing his hands behind his head. Slowly, his eyes began to grow heavy. The gentle sway of the light ribbons moved him to a state of total relaxation.

As he drifted off into sleep, words of some arcane alchemist danced before his eyes. The sentences and concepts began to twirl like the lights above his head. His dream self lifted a hand, bringing the principles closer to him to examine.

Then Theodyne knew nothing but the feeling of complete euphoria.

NICO FINISHED his drink, staring out at the black velvet night. Lights coming from the workers' cottages on the other side of the vineyards speckled the hillside like grounded stars. He wondered what had been Theodyne's reaction to the light show Nico had provided above the small bed.

He'd expected his apprentice to come back down the stairs to ask for an explanation. The man was more accepting than he appeared. But then, as a thief, he must have had his fill of unusual and harrowing situations. A display of fanciful lights to welcome him to the villa probably went unnoticed in the grand scheme of things.

Slightly disappointed, Nico returned to his workroom. There were other projects pending that he needed to tend to. His contacts at the Gold School were becoming increasingly concerned about the growing element within the church that sought to suppress all alchemical knowledge. Then there was that damn unsettling feeling on the wind…. Nico sensed trouble, but not the direction or form it would take when fully manifested.

The next few weeks would prove to be a hard row. Nothing he couldn't counter with a few well-placed gold *tonzas*. Money in the right hands always went further to clearing the way for his particular discipline than trying to work in the shadows—at least for the problems on the material plane. It was the trouble on the ether that worried him.

Nico opened a portfolio filled with all his most important documents and letters, preparing to begin to work on some correspondence, when a loud pounding began on the front door.

Nothing good ever came of night visitors when they tried with all their might to bash in a solid wooden door. Durgin was only a step or two ahead as Nico came out of his study.

"Hold your water. There's no sense breaking it down!" Durgin shouted as he reached for the lock in order to slide the mechanism free.

Nico stood behind and a little to the right of Durgin—a position that afforded him the ability to see who had come, but did not allow them to see him.

After a quick nod from Nico, Durgin opened the door. A messenger, tired and covered in road filth, stood panting as he held out a missive. "For the Count."

The man did a slow crumple into a heap on the doorstep. Nico took the missive and stuck it under his belt, then bent over the messenger to feel for a pulse. It was there but weak from the man's exhaustion. Gently, Nico rolled him over and there found the insignia for the Gold School emblazoned under layers of mud.

"Merciful universe! Help me get him to a bed in the servants' quarters."

It took two of them to carry the man to a bed. With the turn of a hand, Nico called forth fire and lit a lamp beside the bed to better examine the poor, unfortunate servant.

Those who worked in service to the Gold School were themselves members of the elite brotherhood. This man had to be at least a journeyman to be entrusted with carrying a missive to an adept such as Nico.

As much as Nico wanted and needed to read the words sent by paper and courier, instead of through one of the other methods adepts used to communicate, the brave man lying before him needed his attention more.

Nico stroked the man's sweat-soaked hair away from his face. "Bring me cool water and a cloth. He's burning with fever. And have someone see to his mount—that poor animal has to be near death as well."

Though Nico kept a limited amount of his staff in the house, there were still enough to do what needed to be done at the moment.

Hair rose on the back of his neck in a pleasant tingle a second before Theodyne filled the doorway. "What's happening?"

"A messenger to the door one step ahead of death." He called Theodyne forward with his hand. "Help me get him undressed. These filthy, stinking clothes are not going to help him heal."

Theodyne didn't hesitate but knelt on the other side of the bed and helped Nico strip the messenger's jacket and tunic. Then they started on the grubby shoes and blood-encrusted stockings. The stink of sweat and fear rose up from the offensive garments.

The insides of the man's legs were bruised and lacerated, suggesting he'd ridden hard for a great distance. Even a man used to riding could not endure the abuse the body took under such circumstances.

Nico shook his head. "The poor man must have held on only as long as it took to get here."

"Do you know him? Does he live here?" Theodyne held the man's thighs apart, inspecting the wounds. "This one is deep. He might need it stitched. It's already hot and angry. He'll probably need it bled first."

Nico glanced up. "You know about these things?"

"In prison we often had to take care of each other's wounds. Heaven knows the guards would have let us rot to death. You learn quickly if you want to survive."

A well of desperate longing filled Nico's heart. Thoughts of the once-infamous thief brought to such a pass made his admiration grow.

Theodyne hadn't succumbed to his trials, but had risen above them and took those lessons with him into the world.

"You have water coming?"

Theodyne looked around the room, Nico supposed for something useful as medical supplies. "Yes, but only cold."

Theodyne shook his head. "We'll need hot water and soap to draw the poison out of the wound."

"That might take time."

"I know. Do you have a very sharp knife?" Theodyne rolled up his sleeves.

"Not in here."

Nico rose to go find one, but Theodyne placed a hand on his arm to stop him. "Make sure it's the sharpest one you own. The cut needs to be quick and clean. Also a bottle of your strongest spirits. Preferably not wine."

As Nico was leaving, Durgin returned with the cold water. Nico halted the servant. "Theodyne wants hot water as well. If Molari is not awake, wake him. Tell him to put the cauldron on the fire."

Durgin hurried back to the kitchens while Nico made his way to his workroom. There he had an array of bladed tools sharp enough to cut the wings from a bird without the bird being the wiser.

Shouts erupted down the hall as he hurried back to the servants' quarters.

"Quit fighting me. I'm trying to tend your wounds." Theodyne had his arm across the man's chest, holding him to the bed. Theodyne glanced up. "Hold him down while I get to work."

Nico handed Theodyne the bottle of spirits, which he uncorked with his teeth, then spit the cork across the room. It was a movement as fluid as a dance and done with experience.

"Hold him good. This is going to burn like a bitch."

No sooner had Theodyne said that, than he poured the spirits into one of the wounds. The man screamed and bucked. How he had any energy left to fight, Nico had no idea.

Theodyne pressed the thigh open wider. "Here, hold his leg exactly like that, so I can get a good angle."

Nico did as told and watched in fascination as Theodyne pierced the flesh with the knife tip. Dark-green pus, purulent and foul, rolled out of the incision. Theodyne made a face and backed up a bit but kept his hands firmly on the area around the injury, milking the infection from the site. His handsome face was drawn in complete focus. He worked the wound as if performing some arcane ritual. It was that look of total concentration that made Nico know, without reservation, that he'd made the correct decision in offering Theodyne the position as apprentice.

When the exudates ran with blood and serous fluid, Theodyne turned to Nico. "I need the hot water."

Durgin came into the room, carrying a pail with steam rolling from the contents. "Right here. Where do you want it?"

"Next to me. On my right side." Theodyne stuck a finger into the pail and nodded. "Good. I need some clean cloths."

Nico handed one to him, watching carefully as Theodyne worked. His movements were competent, his actions confident.

With the wound dressed and the others cleaned, Theodyne stood from the bed and washed his hands. "That dressing will need to be changed every four to six hours until the area looks normal. I think we might have saved his leg. We'll know in the next day or so."

"We have some herbs to make a poultice. That should help draw more of the infection out and promote healing."

Theodyne nodded. "That will help." His mouth drew down at the corners.

"Come into the study and have a drink with me." Nico gave Theodyne an encouraging grin. "Let the man sleep. Durgin can watch him. In the morning, I'll send for one of the field workers' wives to tend him."

Theodyne nodded and followed him into the study. "Are you going to read that letter the messenger almost died to bring you?"

Nico touched the letter still shoved into his belt. "Yes."

The letter would keep until he poured them both a drink. A feeling of wrongness made him seek fortification before he opened the letter. The timing of the messenger's arrival was not lost on Nico.

He handed one of the snifters to Theodyne and kicked back the liquid in his own. It burned down his throat and spread warmth throughout his body.

He set the glass on the table and pulled the missive from his belt. The wax was embossed with the signet of the Headmaster of the Gold School.

Nico split the seal and unfolded the thick parchment. It was signed by Rhone, a man Nico had known since they were both children. Both of them had learned the ways of alchemy as they grew into manhood. Many rites of passage had been taken together. It was a bond as deep as brothers.

Rhone was requesting assistance in the Delaneux region. A group of clerics there had stormed the school and taken Headmaster Donando to prison for consorting with spirits. How could such a thing even be proven, let alone supposed? Alchemy had nothing to do with such things, unless one expressed the change in forms of energy. When a person passed on to the other side of the veil, they changed forms. There was nothing untoward with the process; it was part of nature—the ascension to the next plane of existence.

The quiet clink of a glass against the tabletop invaded Nico's thoughts, but he didn't look up to see what Theodyne was doing. The only thing he knew next was the room felt empty. When he finally looked up, Theodyne had gone.

It was probably for the best. Decisions needed to be made that would affect the course of the Gold School long into the future. *If* the school was to survive.

Once the church decided it had to take a stance against the alchemical discipline, there was little could be done at the governmental level to protect themselves. Most of the Dominicál city-states' *prolates* were in the pockets of local clerics. Nico doubted, with the substantial contributions he made to the cathedral, his connection to the school would be called into question in Lancor. Not many people knew of his commitment in the first place. They thought him a wine maker.

It was probably best that it remained so, at least until he came up with a way to help Rhone. For now, Nico had enough money to pay for Headmaster Donando's release. If that was possible.

It was hard to tell exactly how the Delaneux *prolate* would rule on the case. The situation might be made all the harder, depending on how much the clerics put into the *prolate's* coffers. He needed to get a message to Rhone, let him know the wheels were at work. Though the fact Rhone had sent a paper missive, rather than communicate in the normal way between school chapters, worried Nico in no small measure.

The question was, why? Had the clerics been monitoring the practitioners in some way? It defied explanation.

Nico would write the response and send it via a paid courier to Delaneux. There was no other way to handle the situation. It would take too long for one of the special messengers to arrive at the school. The closest Gold School chapter was located in the town of Braeton, still a day's hard ride away. And it was at least a week's ride to Delaneux.

No, he'd be best to pay a courier and hope like all the hells the man had no way to read invisible ink.

Chapter Five

THEODYNE MADE his way down to the servants' quarters. The night had been full of strange experiences. The twirling lights above his bed, the half-dead messenger—he didn't understand a bit of it. The activities of the villa were much harder to explain than the concepts of the alchemical primer he'd been given to read.

Was every day as chaotic as yesterday? If so, he didn't know how long he'd last in the villa. Not that his life had ever been structured, but at least he'd been able to take his leisure and move on his prey as he saw fit.

It was such a different environment than he was used to. So many new things to learn—and that didn't include the alchemy.

The Count was in the messenger's room when Theodyne arrived. He stalled at the door, listening to the soft rumble of their voices. At least the man was conscious now. That boded well for continued health, as long as those the Count assigned to care for the wounds were diligent in their duties.

Theodyne started to leave. No matter how badly he wanted to hear their conversation, to know what was so urgent a man had almost given his life to deliver a message to the Count, he wasn't going to be guilty of listening at doors. This was no longer prison, where information meant survival. This was the residence of a nobleman, and whatever the Count and the messenger discussed was none of Theodyne's business.

"Come in, Theodyne. Our guest wishes to thank you." The Count's voice came from the room's dark depths.

Theodyne shook his head at being discovered so easily. He stepped over the threshold. The room was stifling, with little ventilation. He hurried to the window and threw open the shutters. "For a learned man, you know nothing about healing."

Sunlight poured into the room, bringing with it the power to heal. This was no arcane magic or alchemy at work, but the observations he'd obtained while imprisoned. Those prisoners kept inside the dark, dank confines of the prison proper did not fare as well as those who had managed to go outside into the yard to bask in the sun's healing rays.

The Count raised a brow, but his expression was amused. "And so you shall teach me your secrets while you learn mine."

The words were a hot river down Theodyne's spine. They lodged in his groin with the promise of long lessons that had nothing to do with transmutation.

Theodyne pretended he'd not noticed the heated subtext of the Count's words. He nodded to the messenger stretched out on the bed. "You look much better in the light of day."

The messenger's gaze went directly to the thief's badge. "I… I thank you for your assistance."

"Not even this convicted thief is hard-hearted enough to watch a brave man die of injuries sustained while carrying out a service. Doubly so when that man is sent as a special courier to my master." Theodyne bowed slightly. "I'll go see if Durgin has made any progress with that poultice." Anything to flee the room and not look as if he did so.

The appearance of industry hid a multitude of sins. At least, Theodyne had found that during his years of thievery. No one looked twice at a man hard at work, with concentration on his task absolute.

Murmurs resumed from the room as he moved away from the door. He'd not caught even the odd word. It was best to not intrude on their discussions. Given he was most likely the immediate topic, Theodyne didn't want to hear what was said. Questions about bringing a convicted thief into the villa, no doubt.

The kitchen was a scene of complete chaos. Molari shouted orders to hapless workers who didn't seem to work fast enough to suit the cook.

Molari turned to Theodyne. "You there. What are you doing in my kitchen?"

"I came to see if the poultices were ready. We need them to dress the messenger's wounds."

"Here not even a day and already you think you run the house." Molari pointed a particularly nasty-looking knife in Theodyne's direction. "You are his apprentice and nothing more. You got that? You do not give orders to me and my staff."

"I ordered no one. I merely inquired if the medicinal was ready. Is that forbidden as well? Perhaps we should meet later and you can go over what I am allowed to inquire about and what is outside my scope as an apprentice."

"Insolence!"

"Arrogance!"

All motion in the kitchen stopped. Molari's face turned red as the crimson robes of the *prolates*.

"I have been abused and ill-treated by any manner of men since my imprisonment, but I'll be damned before I'll be talked to by a cook as if he were king and I a lowly peasant." Theodyne advanced, daring Molari to make good on his implied threats with the butcher's knife. "Now, I'll ask again. Are the poultices ready?"

Molari stood his ground, eyes narrowed. "You'll get none from me, you beggar."

"Very well. I'll inform the Count you failed in your duties." With that, Theodyne turned on his heel and started back through the house. Perhaps it was unwise to provoke the man in charge of making one's meal, but Theodyne spoke the truth when he stated he'd not be spoken to in such a manner. If he let the servants get away with such arrogance now, they'd see him as subordinate and he'd never earn his place.

Sometimes one had to demand respect.

Truthfully, he had no intentions of running to the Count like a spoiled child. He climbed the stairs to his room to retrieve the primer before going back down to the messenger's room.

He tucked the book under his arm and rapped his knuckles against the door.

"Enter."

Theodyne pushed the door open to find the messenger seated in a chair, facing the sun. He looked better than first thing that morning. "Your restorative powers are miraculous."

The messenger swallowed. "I… it's that way with our kind."

"Alchemists?"

The messenger said nothing, but frowned and then continued to stare out the window.

"Has anyone tended your wounds?"

The messenger nodded. "A woman from the fields."

At least someone had done what they were instructed. "Very good. I'll leave you to your contemplations."

Theodyne turned to leave but stalled at the doorway, then turned back to study the messenger's profile. There was no discernible difference between the man seated in the sunbeam and any other. He looked like a man with the weight of the world pressing down on his shoulders. It was quite a different portrait than the one he'd made last night, lying in the putrid stench of infection. Still, Theodyne was curious as to what had happened to him on the road and how he'd come to be so sick.

"Were you set on by bandits? Or simply not used to riding such distances?"

The messenger glanced at Theodyne with a frown. "I don't remember. I only know I had to make it here quickly. It was the only thought in my head as I rode."

Odd, but Theodyne let it go. It might be completely true. If the messenger had been focused on duty, the miles might have slipped by without him being conscious of them doing so. At least Theodyne hoped it was so. There was something deeper there that Theodyne dared not poke at—for fear he wouldn't like what he found.

The sounds of servants moving around the villa while discharging their duties echoed softly through the halls. There was a quiet kind of peace and comfort in the sound, one Theodyne hadn't felt in a long time. Perhaps it was wrong to think so. After all, he'd not even been here a full day. Twenty-four hours was not long enough to judge how well he was going to like or hate a place. Caution and observation would serve him better than anything else.

He passed the hallway that led to the kitchen and heard the bellowing rants of Molari rolling forth like a tidal wave. Most of the words were garbled but for the ones that painted the air blue with their profanity, followed closely by Theodyne's name.

There were definite times when throwing caution to the wind had its rewards. Theodyne had walked in higher circles than the cook had ever aspired to. He'd brushed shoulders with kings and princes. Discussed art and philosophy with religious elders and *prolates*. There wasn't a social stratum he hadn't infiltrated. To be dressed down by a cook—even a trusted member of the Count's household—was the worst kind of offense. One that made Theodyne burn to avenge.

Theodyne passed out of the house and into the same garden where he'd sat the day before. The sun shone on the east side of the vineyard, bathing the land in a soft, golden glow. Winds blew in from the surrounding mountains, bringing with them the sweet scent of grapes on the vine.

The book lay across Theodyne's lap, the pages turned to the place where he'd left off without the least encouragement. It was as if the tome knew instinctually where he had quit.

As the pages fluttered open, sigils rose from the parchment and danced like golden butterflies on tiny currents of air. He blinked a few times to clear his vision.

It was simply one of the most magnificent displays of power he'd ever seen. Lights above his bed was one thing, but infusing the pages of the primer with power that remained locked inside five hundred years later was absolutely breathtaking.

The alchemic nuisances continued to fly around his head like symbolic pests. What did they want from him? If it was merely his attention, they'd gotten it.

A formation began to take place, hovering before his eyes in a gold-streamed equation. He wasn't quite sure what it meant, and on his second day of study, it wasn't even clear if he had enough knowledge to sort out the hidden significance. Perhaps it was used to spark interest. To make the reader strive for greatness—to one day be able to apply the principles in order to perform such miracles.

Instead of ignoring the sigils, Theodyne studied them very carefully and committed them to memory. If he ever saw them in such a configuration again, he'd know it and remember.

Feeling he was no longer alone, Theodyne looked up to find the Count watching him. There was a crooked smile on his face as he came to take a seat on the bench across the way.

"I should have mentioned the special annotations in the lessons."

Theodyne glanced over at the Count and gave a shrug. "In the extremely short time I've been under your roof, I've learned to expect the fantastic."

The Count looked down at his hand as if inspecting his fingernails. "It would be a shame and a sin to run a boring household."

Theodyne stuck his fingers in the pages of the grimoire to hold his place. As he did so, the golden symbols faded from sight. "I have a question to pose to you about the messenger."

The Count's expression changed, grew serious. Grim. "What about him?"

"When I commented on his miraculous healing, he said it was so with his kind. What did he mean by that? He gave me no answer even when I asked if it was due to his knowledge of alchemy. So I ask you, what matter of man is he?"

The Count put his hands in the air. "What *matter* are any of us?"

It was a trick question, taken directly from the text. Theodyne didn't care for the fact the Count turned a simple question into a lesson. "Do not play as if you do not know what I mean or that I'm looking for some ethereal answer to my query. Because if the answer was as simple as we all come from the same material of the Grand Matter, then I'd have no need to ask in the first place. I would find the answer under my own skin. And I assure you, I do not heal as fast as your guest."

The Count let out a long breath and stood. He took a turn about the garden, seemingly deep in contemplation. Here and there he'd stop to smell a bloom or pick a dried leaf from the foliage. When it appeared he would not answer Theodyne's charge, he came to stand in front of his apprentice.

"His secrets are not mine to tell, but I will divulge a mystery to you that is not known by most of the populace. I do not consider this a violation of any sacred trust because you will learn about it later in your lessons. Much later—at journeyman status—but since you've brought up the topic now, I see no reason to hide it until then. Knowing you, even as little as I do, I have a feeling you'll not take the news well if I should withhold it from you until such a time as you advance." Here his smile broadened, became sensual. His eyes danced with an inner fire. "Besides, I have the distinct impression you'll advance very quickly through your studies."

Theodyne wished the Count would get on with it.

"We are not alone as intelligent beings who inhabit our world. All around us are others, elementals who govern disciplines of fire, water, air, and earth. Sometimes these elementals fall in love and breed with humans. The products of these unions have powers inherent in both species."

If the Count had just informed Theodyne he'd taught a toad to dance, Theodyne would not have been more shocked. The problem was not to look as if he'd been caught off guard. "And these elementals exist because all matter comes from the same source."

"Correct."

It was as esoteric an explanation as he'd ever heard. He glanced around the garden, trying to see if he could catch a glimpse of one or more of the elusive beings, but saw nothing but the known material world.

"I've never heard of such before. Not in any of my teachings or in any of the gatherings I have been to." And the great Gods above knew he'd been to enough of those, with all the great thinkers and artists of their time. "I'm surprised the church doesn't rail against them or warn us from falling prey to their influence."

"They do, but they call them by very different names." The Count took a seat next to Theodyne. "There is more you should know. Trouble directed at the Gold School."

"From what quarter?"

"The church, but I have my suspicions it started elsewhere. Most of our collectives are very careful to give generously of their funds to the local *prolates*. They in turn give the money to the clergy to see that new cathedrals are built, or it's used to spread the word." The Count rubbed around his mouth and behind his neck. A worried expression drew his brows together. "I am afraid our mission to deflect attention may have given way to some unexpected consequences."

"Such as?"

"I'm not yet certain. An investigation into the matter will have to take place, but in the meantime, the headmaster at the Delaneux branch of the school has been taken into custody. Assistance has been requested to obtain his freedom. It is a delicate situation."

"What will you do?"

"I fear I must go there myself and speak for my colleague. He has no advocate. None who will touch him, given the religious and political climate in Delaneux."

Loneliness was an unexpected pinch to Theodyne's heart. "How long will you be gone?"

"I cannot anticipate such a thing. It might be over quite quickly, or it may drag out, as these things sometimes do." The Count placed his hand on Theodyne's knee. Heat from his palm penetrated the loose weave of Theodyne's homespun breeches. "Come with me. Learn on the way to Delaneux."

Theodyne swallowed down the desire that had risen at what must have been intended as innocent contact. "I may hinder your case."

The Count's gaze lingered a moment on the thief's badge before coming to rest on Theodyne's lips. "If the case is to be lost, then that has already been determined by the powers in Delaneux."

"I thought your colleague needed an advocate."

"You mistake my use of the word." The Count chuckled and removed his hand from Theodyne's leg. "I meant it as a clever word for bribe."

"Oh." There had been no such person to speak for him or to slip money into the *prolate*'s coffer when Theodyne had been arrested. No one had cared. Not even his sister. Instead, they had seized his riches, but never used them toward his release.

"Will you travel with me?"

What better things did Theodyne have to do? At least with the Count he'd be protected against the harshness of the road. No one would dare to turn him away from a warm bed or meal because of the brand on his face. Besides, it might be good to get away from Lancor for a while. To see city-states other than Sadonia. After such a long incarceration, it might be the balm he needed to heal his soul.

"I will. When do we leave?"

"In the morning. Pedraus is packing my things as we speak. I'll alert him to prepare your things as well."

Theodyne laughed. "What's to prepare? I have this one set of clothes and the threadbare ones I arrived here in. Pedraus threw those in the rubbish pile during my bath."

The Count joined in the laughter. "Did you not check the chest or the wardrobe? I'm afraid you will find more than enough to outfit you properly in both places."

With that, the Count rose and made his way from the garden. Theodyne remained. Speechless and humbled by the generosity of a man he'd only met the day before, he sat for a moment and contemplated his good fortune. It had been much too long since anything like benevolence had smiled on him. Longer still since someone had cared for him as a man, a person. The one he'd believed loved him had wanted to keep him in a gilded cage, and then turned against him when he'd wished to be set free.

A twig snapped in the foliage on the other side of the *plazo*. The bushes rustled with movement. Eyes twinkled from the shaded area, though Theodyne couldn't tell if they came from man or beast.

Despite the heat of the sun, chills broke out along his arms and neck. He set the primer down and chafed at his goosefleshed skin. "Is someone there?"

Another crack of a dry stick, and Menarch eased from his hiding place.

"What are you doing, skulking around out here?"

"Listening to your conversation with the Count. If you are going to steal the *Eye of Truth*, now would be a good time, while his mind is focused on other matters."

"You're hiding gold balls in your britches if you think I'm taking anything from that man."

Menarch made a rude noise at the back of his throat. "You used to have more nerve than you've got now."

"I used to think I was invincible, too, but prison robbed me of that notion. It taught me just how vulnerable a human body can be." Theodyne turned on the seat, presenting his back to his unwelcome visitor, trying to give Menarch the hint to leave.

"The *Eye* will give you power and riches beyond your wildest dreams."

"Sorry, but I can imagine quite a bit."

Menarch came around Theodyne's side to face him again. That odd glint returned to his eyes. The background sounds in Theodyne's head grew louder, as if thousands of tiny voices were trying to warn him of danger.

"The world is changing, Theodyne. It is best that men like us change with it or get swept away on the tides of others."

Theodyne held up the primer. "I am planning to change, though not in the way you may think."

"You are a fool. Always have been and always will be. That, my friend, will *never* change."

Theodyne waved his hand in dismissal. When he turned around again, Menarch was gone. There was no sign he'd ever been on the *plazo* or moved through the foliage to leave.

There were odd forces at work. Theodyne had seen more unexplained things since his release from prison than in all four years inside.

A hint of warning skittered across his consciousness. The voices receded again.

Why would a man with everything to give—and much more to lose—risk it all on an apprentice he couldn't even be sure would remain loyal? Had the Count looked inside Theodyne to the naked need to belong? Had he stripped Theodyne's flesh to the bone and laid his soul bare?

And what had he seen beneath the surface? Something worth saving?

Theodyne had no qualms that his life was precious. It was the rest of the world that needed convincing. And Menarch? Why didn't the old man just make a play for the *Eye of Truth* himself and leave Theodyne out of the equation? Theodyne had no doubt that if that particular artifact went missing, the Count would realize it was gone before it ever left the property. There was some elusive quality in the Count's eyes that made Theodyne never want to see disappointment in their dark depths.

It was best to leave the thieving part of his life behind. That way lay nothing but trouble.

NICO HAD so much to do before they left for Delaneux. He had to secure the villa with bindings and wards. Not so much against theft, for he could obtain through alchemy anything he lost as a result. All but the *Eye of Truth*. That was one thing that could never be duplicated, fabricated, or pulled from the ether. However, that particular artifact would travel in the wagon with them. He'd never risk leaving it behind on a journey. It had not left his family's possession since it was penned centuries before, directly from the legendary Emerald Tablet, and the hand of one Akabar Kolhen

The main concern was to ensure there would be no uninvited guests of the clerical persuasion making their way inside. Not that Nico had reason to fear suspicion from that quarter, but it paid to be cautious. Who knew if the pestilence that had spread to the walls of the Delaneux school had sent feelers out to Lancor.

The bell announcing the midday meal chimed throughout the villa. Workers in the vines would pause in their labors to feed their bodies and nourish their souls. Servants would retire to the kitchen to eat once the meal was placed on the table. It was the quiet ebb and flow of a day at the villa that brought comfort to Nico when the outside world seemed to spiral out of control.

Nico made his way to the dining room. Theodyne stepped in from the garden. Sunshine haloed him as if he wore it on his shoulders like a cloak.

Breath choked up in Nico's throat as he watched Theodyne walk with his attention planted firmly in the primer. There were no words for the strength and beauty of the man. He moved like a shadow, but glowed like the sun. Not even incarceration had dimmed the inner light that made up Theodyne's essence.

Nico swallowed down emotions too heavy to speak of and followed at a sedate pace behind his apprentice.

Suddenly Theodyne stopped and turned to Nico. "I know you're trailing me, I just can't figure out why."

Nico smiled. "Nor will you."

"Oh, I think I'm catching on."

They entered the dining room. Individual platters were already in front of each place setting. Odd. Things were usually not done in such a manner.

Theodyne took a place at Nico's right arm. They looked to each other before pulling the domed lids off the plates.

Fragrant steam wafted up to Nico from the squab and vegetables presented. He caught the silent tension coming from Theodyne and glanced at his apprentice's plate. It was empty.

Nico frowned. "What is the meaning of this?"

Theodyne gave a self-deprecating lift of his mouth. "Molari and I had words this morning. I think I'm being punished."

Anger flooded Nico's bloodstream. He motioned for Durgin. "Tell Molari I wish to see him immediately."

Dugin visibly swallowed and hurried from the room.

"Count Ni—"

Nico didn't allow Theodyne to finish his words. "No. I will not have you treated thusly. It is not the way things are done here."

Molari came into the room, with his apron removed to meet with the master of the house.

"Yes, sir."

"This is an absolute outrage. I have no notion what words you and Theodyne exchanged this morning, and I do not rightly care, but when you insult me by withholding food from a person dining at *my* table, you have overstepped your bounds."

Molari threw his shoulders back and looked at Nico with contempt. "He ordered me about in my own kitchen. Called me arrogant."

"And this display disproves him how, exactly?" Nico challenged.

Molari flapped his mouth a few times, but no sound came out.

Nico set about cutting the small bird in half. He set the two pieces away from each other, then said a few words over the dissected squab. Out of the two halves grew wholes. Nico plucked one up and set it on Theodyne's plate, and then he divided up the vegetables and did the same, making a mountain of potatoes, carrots, and candied beets.

"In the future, all food is to be divided up equally among all diners or served in large dishes so we may take what we want. Is that clear?"

Molari, white-faced and large-eyed, nodded in assent.

"You may return to your own meal."

He left the room without as much as a mumbled thank-you. Nico started cutting into his dinner and felt the weight of Theodyne's gaze on him.

"Did you expect me to allow you to starve? I'm afraid you've known too much of that these last few years. Not while you're a member of my household."

"It's not that. Why was Molari so afraid? Surely he knows you have powers he can never fully understand."

"It's because now he realizes I can get all the food I want by the turn of a hand. I do not need to employ a cook to see to my needs." Nico stuck a bite of squab into his mouth. It was delicate and succulent.

"Then why do you?"

"Why should I expend the energy to do those tasks when I can as easily employ others?" It was a simple solution to a good many problems with owning an estate the size of the villa.

Theodyne seemed to consider the answer and quietly tucked into his meal.

"We never perform a rite or spell without giving something of ourselves into the work. Our essence clings to everything we touch. When we change a substance, it takes away from us. We have to then replenish what we've lost."

"How do we do that?"

Nico speared a potato with his knife. "By using food as our fuel, by standing out in the sunshine and letting the radiance of the solar body nourish us. By prayer or music to fill our soul and raise our state of consciousness."

"And that's it? That's all we have to do to make ourselves full again?"

Nico nodded. "It's energy transfer. Nothing more secret or miraculous than that."

"And for this reason the church fears you?"

"The church has always feared what it can't control." He picked up another potato, this one rounded on one side, flat on the other. He lifted his hand, and with a movement of fingers and an invocation, the flat side rounded out, making it whole again, as he'd done to the bird. "It doesn't matter the substance, all is made of energy. The Grand Matter."

"And so we are back to that."

"We never left it." Nico popped the potato into his mouth. "It never leaves us. Now eat up. We have much to do after the meal."

THE *MUCH to do* ended up in frustration, aggravation, and tears. The latter Theodyne hid from Count Nico. The principles of alchemy might read easily enough on paper, but they sure as hell didn't work so in practice. There was a lot more involved than met the eye.

The Count glanced up from across the worktable at Theodyne; the man looked as if his last nerve was close to the point of fraying and there was no use trying to smooth it down. Theodyne might yet prove he had no aptitude for alchemy. Then where would Theodyne be?

Back out on his own with no way to support himself and the mark of a thief on his face. He'd probably encounter the same problems no matter where he traveled in the city-states. Judging from the Count's expression, it was going to be soon that Theodyne would discover if the supposition was true.

The Count let out a long breath and hung his head. He braced his arms on the worktable and stretched them out to his sides. "Forgive me. It's been a very long time since I've taken an apprentice, and I must remember that these principles are not innate to you."

"I understand them, I'm just having trouble putting salt with body, mercury with spirit, sulfur with soul, and seeing it in my head."

The Count looked up. "It's more about *feeling* the concepts than *seeing* them." He came around to stand behind Theodyne. "Make your body loose."

Confused, Theodyne turned to see the Count hovering over his shoulder. "What?"

"Make your arms and torso loose so I can control them with my own movements. Once you get the ritual motions down, you can bring the other aspects into play." The Count took Theodyne's hand in his and twined their fingers.

Theodyne's heart kicked hard. His breath caught. Heat ran through his body like rivers of lava. All around him a deeply sensual scent of spice and forest filled his head with erotic thoughts. Theodyne's eyes closed of their own volition. There was no escaping his desire for the Count or the danger this forced nearness put them in. He wanted to moan, but swallowed it down along with regret.

"Loose, I said. Not stiff." The Count's breath was a warm brush against Theodyne's ear.

Easier said than done with the Count's groin pressed against his backside. At least it answered the question from the night before—that was definitely flesh and not fabric between the Count's legs.

"Most of the motions are to bring into play certain aspects of our bodies and brains," the Count instructed as he manipulated Theodyne's arms and hands in a series of graceful movements. "They help to center your mind and assist in concentration."

There was not enough centering or concentration in the entirety of Dominicál that would allow Theodyne to focus under such conditions.

"Do you dance?"

Theodyne didn't understand why the Count asked such a question, but nodded. "I was considered quite a good dancer by all accounts."

"Then pretend we are in a ballroom and I am your partner, leading you around the floor."

"I always lead."

"Not this time." The Count pulled Theodyne's arm out to the side, nearly unbalancing both of them. "Do not fight me. Relax."

"I don't want to fight you." Theodyne barely recognized his voice; it was so thick with desire and longing.

Behind him, the Count tensed. He smoothed his calloused fingers along Theodyne's. The location of the hardened skin suggested he played a stringed instrument. "Then give control over to me."

Oh, how Theodyne wanted to do just that—to release all his power into the Count's capable hands and see where it led. He curled his fingers around the Count's and held on. The Count's breath caught in Theodyne's ear.

"I don't think I know these steps."

"You do." The Count drew closer. His lips grazed Theodyne's cheek. "Let it flow into you."

Theodyne's heart was in danger of bursting from his chest. The temperature in the room reached inferno level. Desire had never been so torturous. So acute.

"You aren't concentrating, Theodyne."

"It's difficult when I don't know what you expect of me."

"You do. Just follow my lead."

The graceful motions were undermined by fits and starts. It must have looked more like a puppeteer trying to control a resentful marionette. "Close your eyes, Theodyne. Feel the movements. Let your body commit them to memory."

"My eyes are closed."

"No, they aren't." The Count leaned forward a bit more, pressing his chest into Theodyne's back. Their bodies touched along the entire length. "You're looking at my hand."

Mesmerized by the rough texture of the Count's palms, Theodyne had not even realized he'd opened his eyes again or that he was staring down at the hand holding his.

"By Dante, you're a hard fellow to get to relinquish control." Tension filled the air on the heels of that statement. The Count stepped away and hung his head. He shook it back and forth before he glanced back up at Theodyne and met his eyes. "I am so terribly sorry. That was both insensitive and indelicate of me. Please forgive me."

Lost, Theodyne simply nodded. "I'll try harder next time."

The Count made a shooing motion. "No. It's time we took a break. We will meet back here in an hour and try again."

Theodyne left the workroom bewildered and more confused than he'd been in the Count's pedagogical embrace. What had made the master call a break when only moments before he'd pressed Theodyne to concentrate harder?

Frankly, how did *he* expect Theodyne to concentrate when he stood so close and smelled so good? It was more than any man should be asked to endure. Then to stand behind Theodyne, so close their bodies brushed, and guide his hands in the simple movements of the first experiment.... It was not to be tolerated.

It was a good thing the Count *had* called a break. If the Count had stood groin to ass with Theodyne a moment longer, there would have been embarrassing and devastating consequences as a result.

Theodyne walked around the villa and then found himself in the little *plazo*, soaking up the sunshine and going over the details of the experiment in his head. Half of them he didn't even remember; the other half he retained in the form of tingles where they had touched.

He let out a moan and closed his eyes, resting his head against the warm wall of the house. In the full day he'd been here, the *plazo* had become his favorite place. He felt drawn here for some inexplicable reason. As if the fresh air and sunshine on his skin would cleanse him in a way no bath ever could.

This entire situation was probably as futile as it was ridiculous. How was Theodyne supposed to hold fast to his conviction never to become involved with a superior again if the Count continued to teach in such an unconventional manner? Perhaps after the break he'd have to make it a point to stand on the opposite side of the table and ask the Count to demonstrate one more time, all the way through—but from a distance. There was no way he'd be able to complete any kind of lesson if the Count insisted on touching him in a manner that, in other circumstances, might be considered intimate. In any other situation, Theodyne might be the seducer.

He glanced down at his hand where the tingles continued to travel over it like tiny golden needles. A few pumps of his fist and the sensation eased. Strange forces at work indeed. It was as if the world had materially changed while he'd been in prison and the general order of the cosmos altered.

If one was to believe in the Prime or Grand Matter, that was entirely possible. While everything had changed states, it had also stayed the same. Everything that was here before remained; it had just manifested in a different way.

Even the constant voices in his soul—the whispering he'd always assumed was intuition—had grown in volume and urgency. It must have to do with all the exotic and rare pieces the Count had in his collection. There was a vase from the Fourth Paralong Dynasty sitting in the entranceway for anyone to stumble along and knock over. That one rare jade work, shaped like a large bud waiting to open, was worth more than any other treasure Theodyne had ever seen. And it was not a copy or a transmutation. Theodyne had stopped to look at it, had held it in his hands and acknowledged its authenticity.

Whether for the betterment of his soul or the protection of his body, Theodyne needed this position as an apprentice. There were no other choices open to him—not any that he'd accept. He'd not repay the Count's kindness by stealing the *Eye of Truth.* Though that was one treasure Theodyne had yet to see. It made him wonder what form the artifact took. Was it a painting, a statue, a chalice, or a seal? It could even be a stone tablet engraved with the teachings of alchemists from the beginning of civilization and man's rule. Perhaps it was a collection of laws passed down from the Gods on high.

Did he even want to know?

No, probably not. If he refused to even look for it, then if it ever did meet with the hands of a thief, Theodyne could say he had no knowledge of the item with a clear and unfettered heart. That was undoubtedly the best course of action. Forget the *Eye of Truth* even existed or that it promised untold wealth and power.

That was a crock of shit right there. Seeing the few demonstrations of power the Count had displayed made Theodyne think there was no need for an eye, truthful or otherwise. The Count had not seemed to need an elaborate ritual to perform any of the feats he'd managed. He merely concentrated on the item and bent it to his will.

No—manipulated its current state and elicited change.

As if a tiny lock inside his head had clicked in place, Theodyne suddenly understood what the Count had been trying to exhibit.

Theodyne pushed up from the bench and hurried back inside and to the workroom. He stood over the crucible and moved his hand over the liquid widdershins. What was the quickest way to extract salt from liquid? To boil it down.

He closed his eyes and imagined the crucible heating. The liquid inside belched as the temperature rose. Soon steam dampened his palm. The belches turned to burbles. With the faster movement, more energy was released. Theodyne felt the result sink into his skin and infuse him with a strange power even as it drained from his other hand and dripped like melted candle wax onto the floor.

He knew not how long he stood there working, but the final hiss of transforming liquid heralded the end of the experiment. Slowly he opened his eyes and looked into the crucible. The only thing that remained on the bottom was a white, dusty residue.

The sound of applause came from behind him. He turned to see the Count leaning against the doorjamb, watching. His expression was one of guarded praise. As if he wished to tell Theodyne he'd done well but wasn't sure if the accolades were warranted.

"That is one way to achieve results, Theodyne. However, the test of this experiment was to divide the component parts, leaving them all intact as separate substances." The Count came fully into the room and stopped to stare down into the crucible. "You have managed to leave some salt behind."

"Then I haven't exactly failed, since that is all you instructed me to extract."

The Count narrowed his eyes for a moment, and then his expression eased out as if he'd just gone over the conversation in his head. "And so I did."

Theodyne's knees felt suddenly weak. He pulled over a small three-legged stool and sat down.

"Are you all right? You've gone pale."

"Only a little light-headed." It was more like the world had decided to spin like a potter's wheel. If working alchemical experiments made one feel like this, it was no wonder there weren't more practitioners running around.

"You've not prepared properly, nor centered your mind correctly." The scold was as gentle as the Count's voice. "When you feel able, go to your room and sleep. You've done too much today, and we've an early ride ahead in the morning."

Theodyne rubbed his hands down his face and lowered his head to the worktable. "Will I ever get used to this feeling?"

"In time." The Count squeezed Theodyne's shoulder. "You came to this much later than most. Younger students are a bit more resilient."

Theodyne glanced up, annoyed with the implication. "I am not *that* old."

The Count chuckled. "No. You aren't. You are, however, older than most apprentices. By your age, most students have advanced to journeyman or one of the master-level practices."

"Oh, so once I reach master there are more levels to go—more training and study."

"There is always training and study. That never ends no matter what level of practice you achieve." The Count struck an elegant pose against the worktable, crossing his arms over his wide chest. "I've been an adept for almost ten years, and I still study every day."

"You must have been a very young adept." Truthfully, Theodyne didn't care. He only wanted to discover the Count's age. There were rumors the alchemists had ways to cheat death—that they were immortal.

"Younger than most, older than some."

As an answer, it was evasive.

"That was entirely too coy for a man of your experience. I'd expect some aging countess in a ballroom to give such an answer, but not a man of the world." Theodyne studied the Count closely to see if there was any way to determine his age by looking in his dark eyes.

Silence stretched out like a string on the point of snapping. Theodyne dared not look away first. He had no want to give in to the fear of his desire for this man. It overwhelmed and overshadowed any emotion he'd ever felt for another. That was more power than he'd given even the mighty Medovin *prolate*—and look where that had landed him.

The whispers in his head began to grow again. If Theodyne didn't know better, he would swear they urged him to take the Count into his arms. He tried to ignore their auditory harassment.

The Count's gaze skimmed over Theodyne's face and landed on the scar. Shame ignited along his nerve endings.

Heat rose to his face. "It's hideous. I know. Would you find it odd if I said I sometimes forget it's there? Not having looked in a mirror for the last few years, I tend not to notice until I smile or speak, and then I feel the tug and pull of the flesh."

The Count appeared embarrassed to have been caught staring at the damning mark. "I meant no offense."

"I feel no offense." Truly, it wasn't that which sank his heart into his belly. It was the knowledge he was not the example of male perfection he'd been in the past. That one touch of the brand to his face had disfigured him for life. It was the understanding that he would never look in the mirror again and see the same man he had before.

A thought struck him and he laughed. "It is odd that, in prison, there were so many of us with the badge we could tell by the scar left behind who had wielded the iron."

A look of complete and utter horror passed over the Count's face. He took a seat next to Theodyne. "I never had any idea the problem was so widespread."

"Thieving?"

"Branding prisoners with the mark of their crimes."

Theodyne shrugged. "Nothing like making a man pay for his mistakes for the rest of his life, even after his sentence is served."

"It isn't merely barbaric, but vengeful."

"I did steal from some very important Lancoran families. There was no way, even with my connections, I was going to escape this fate. Not in this lifetime." The fact he'd gone so long without getting caught was cause for some pride.

"What made you stay in Lancor, or even Sadonia for that matter?"

"What was there to go to? It is not a stretch to think that I'd not have traveled anywhere in the world where my badge was not recognized for what it is. Might as well stay in familiar territory." In all honesty, it didn't matter much to Theodyne where he traveled, he only knew he was tired of living a life that continued to come back and haunt him. The debt had been paid. The ghosts of the past needed to rest.

"You could have gone to the port cities and hired on as a crewman on a ship."

Theodyne raised a brow and regarded the salt-encrusted crucible before he caught the Count's gaze. These questions were too pointed not to have a purpose, or draw blood. "If you would rather I leave your tutelage for not following instruction, please tell me now and I will leave your home." He dug the meager coins from his pocket and stuck them on the worktable. "This is to pay for the clothes I am wearing. If they are worth more, I do not have it to give, but ask that you allow me to send the balance to you later."

"Your pride and your pain will be your downfall, Theodyne." The Count took the coins off the table and then reached for Theodyne's hand. Gently, he uncurled the clenched fingers. His calloused hands cradled Theodyne's wrist. "Keep it. I have no intention of releasing you from your studies unless you decide alchemy is not something you wish to pursue."

Theodyne didn't realize he'd been holding his breath until it came out of him in a long rush. "No. I don't wish to leave. I've spent too many years trying to make my way but not really knowing where I belonged. I think it's time I stopped long enough to realize if it's here."

"Fair enough." The Count nodded toward the door. "Go on up to bed. Read some of the primer before you sleep. We leave at first light."

Theodyne took the exit when offered. It was the most graceful way of bowing out of what had been an agonizing conversation. He cared not to repeat it again, but at least he felt the Count understood him better. That alone was worth the pain.

Chapter Six

PEDRAUS MET them at the wagon the next morning. The old servant had insisted on accompanying Nico. Four of his most trusted guards rode point around their wagon.

The messenger, Jolen, was lounging in the back on a bed so he would not have to ride the distance and reopen his wounds. Both Nico and Theodyne rode on horses alongside the wagon as it made its way over the uneven eastern roads to Delaneux.

The sun was past halfway in the sky, starting on its downward arc toward the horizon as they entered a forest known to be a favorite haunt of bandits. Nico had not wanted to attempt the forest at night. No one in their right mind would—even protected by guards, alchemy, and the strange little bottles Pedraus insisted on bringing.

Truthfully, Nico had seen the contents of those bottles in action over the years and knew they were potent indeed.

Nico tried valiantly to keep his attention on the road and not the handsome man riding beside him. Theodyne sat a horse as if he were a born equestrian. There were not many men Nico felt looked as natural in the saddle, especially on an unfamiliar horse.

"You have much experience riding?"

Theodyne looked down at his hands holding the reins. "I've acquired skills when necessary. In my former life, I consulted with men of power and position. You'd be surprised at the number of them who like to use the hunt to conduct business. To hunt in those circles, one must be proficient in the saddle."

"And are you as skilled with the bow?"

"Fair. It was never politic to bring down bigger game than your host."

Nico laughed. "It sounds as if you learned that lesson the hard way."

An odd expression passed over Theodyne's handsome features then. "I've spent my life learning lessons I'd rather not have known."

Pain started as a slow, dull ache in Nico's heart. It spread down to his belly and up to his arms. Sympathy for Theodyne was as visceral as if the experiences had happened to *him*. However, Theodyne would not take kindly to having that emotion voiced, or to be offered condolences for opportunities lost. He had too much pride for that. Nico didn't need to be an alchemist of any great power to know that. It was there in all their interactions so far. That still didn't stop Nico from asking the questions or attempting to sketch Theodyne's character in greater detail.

"You haven't told me much about yourself," Theodyne pointed out after they had ridden about a mile in silence.

"My story is unremarkable for one having been born into a family with a long tradition of practicing the higher arts. I've held the belief that by tapping into the Grand Matter, all humankind benefits, and I've lived my life accordingly." Nico took in a deep breath, appreciating the tang of earth and sweetness of grass on the air. "All around us is the miracle that is life. You have only to open your true eyes to appreciate it in all its varied glory."

"True eyes?" Theodyne sounded skeptical. "If I had those, I might not have gotten caught on my last theft."

Nico chuckled. "True eyes is a metaphorical expression for being in a state of enlightenment."

Theodyne gave a disgruntled huff. "Then I've definitely seen through them before. No one released from Pallonia could ever claim they've not been *enlightened* to the world."

The pain in Nico's heart increased. It was time to try a different tactic. "Consider this: If you hadn't been caught, convicted, and incarcerated, you'd never have come to the villa in search of work. What comes before sets the path to experiences that come after. It all leads to what some call destiny."

This time the huff was a scoff. "I'll never pretend or be convinced that my conviction and incarceration didn't stem directly from my refusal to be kept as Estobán Medovin's pet."

Nico nearly lost his seat at that tidbit of information. He managed to hold his dignity and countenance by the barest of threads. He turned a raised brow at Theodyne. "You were the new *prolate*'s lover?"

"You find that hard to believe? That the esteemed leader of our city-state would dare to consort with the likes of a lowly thief?" The hardness returned to Theodyne's eyes. There was nothing but challenge in every line and angle of his body. Nico had definitely struck a very sore nerve.

"I meant no offense, Theodyne. Only that if he was lucky enough to have you, he was a fool to lose you."

Their gazes met and held for a long moment then Theodyne glanced away to the road ahead. It was another few miles before either of them did much more than move with their horses. Tension hung in the air between them, thick and potent.

Pedraus stuck his head out of the wagon flap. "Master, Journeyman Jolen wishes to speak with you."

Nico called a halt to the procession and dismounted. He climbed on the wagon and opened the flap. Jolen sat back against a mound of pillows. He looked drawn and weak again.

Nico hurried to him. "What is it?"

"The motion of the wagon is making me feel quite ill. Can we stop for a while? If you must go on, leave two of the guards with me and Pedraus. We'll catch up."

"Can you wait until we reach the other side of these woods?"

Jolen frowned in misery. "How long?"

"About another two hours." Nico was sorry for it, but their safety had to come first. "I'd rather call a halt for the day and pick up again at first light once we're there. We travel together or not at all. Understood?" Nico reached out and ran his hand down Jolen's face. It was cold and clammy. "I think you need to get out into the sunshine and fresh air for a while."

Jolen gave him a weak smile. "That would do me very well."

Nico opened the tent flap. "Theodyne, can you assist me?"

Theodyne dismounted in one smooth move and jumped up onto the wagon, as nimble as a cat. "How?"

"Help me fold the tent flap back off the top of the wagon to let in more sunshine."

Theodyne moved to the other side and reached up for the canopy. "On three."

Nico counted down and they rolled the heavy drapery back, giving just enough room at the front of the wagon for Jolen to lie in the sunshine as they traveled. Though the tree coverings were thick enough to send the forest floor into deep shade, there remained areas where dappled light reached the ground. It wasn't a great deal, but it was enough to tide Jolen over until they made camp in a less densely forested section.

Next he moved Jolen's bed to the open section of the wagon, making sure he was comfortable before taking to the road again.

Nico mounted his horse and called for the team to move out.

Theodyne guided his horse alongside Nico's and then glanced back at the wagon. "What is it? Why didn't you want to stop for the night so he can recover?"

"We need to find a better spot to camp. I don't want to do so in these particular woods, and I don't want the wagon visible from the road."

Theodyne went still. "Because of thieves?"

"Bandits. They are a different breed of outlaw." It was important Theodyne know the distinction the way Nico meant it. He'd never place a sophisticated thief who stole from hidden coffers and safes inside palatial homes in the same category as a cutthroat that plied his trade on the roads—they'd as soon kill as leave witnesses.

Theodyne turned his face away and studied the horizon as Nico studied him. There were little nuances in his expression, the tilt of his head, and the way his shoulders were back that told Nico very clearly he'd annoyed the former thief.

"Then we should probably press on at as fast a pace as we dare."

"My thoughts exactly." Nico gave his mount the signal to move a bit faster. It wasn't exactly a trot, but nor was it a sedate walk. He feared jostling Jolen in the wagon too much might bring on the symptoms faster. He'd be damned before he'd lose the journeyman on the road to Delaneux.

Nico grew quiet. The deeper they traveled into the woods, the more he felt that persistent tension in the air. He glanced at Theodyne. It wasn't coming from the apprentice. No, this was the feeling of being watched and studied. He rested his hand on his sword in case they were set upon.

If bandits watched them, they hid their positions well. Nico had a hard time believing a band of desperate men who stole for their sustenance was capable of spreading a pervasive evil through the forest. This was a sick feeling that went down to the soul and imbedded there. No mere man had that ability, no matter how ruthless.

The sensation persisted for the remainder of the trek through the forest. Not a single person challenged their progress. The birds did not call alarms from the trees. Perhaps it was all in his head or a product of fear for his brothers of the order.

They finally came out of the heaviest tree cover and into a clearing. The road traversed the landscape, curving through the hills. The sun headed toward descent. It was time to call a halt and find a place to set up camp for the night.

"Do you see a place that will afford us cover?"

Theodyne pointed to a thick copse of trees past a sharp fork where the road split three ways. "If we stay to the eastern fork, in that stand of scrub oak, we should be fine."

Intrigued by Theodyne's decided opinion, Nico leaned over his horse's neck and pointed in the opposite direction. "Why not to the south or west?"

"Because the southern road leads to Bellor, Romanta, and Pliern, all city-states of vast wealth and prosperity. The western road leads to the ports of Gila, Rhun, and Farrisi, all of which import and export goods worth more than most men make in a lifetime. Either road is ripe with travelers whose purses are heavy with coin. It's not so with the east." Theodyne raised a brow as if waiting for Nico to challenge the observations.

Nico turned his hand in a releasing gesture. "Then the decision is made. Lead the way, if you please."

Theodyne clicked his tongue and his horse started off at a slow walk, leaving Nico behind.

Logical, astute, and helpful—an adept could not ask more from his apprentice. It was a sad state that they were on the road so soon after entering into the arrangement, but lessons could be conducted during the long hours of travel. Now, with Jolen in need of rest, Nico could instruct Theodyne while the others took their leisure. Never let it be said that Nico did not take advantage of a prime situation if presented with one.

Theodyne tapped his heels into his horse's flank and gave it the signal to trot. He made his way in front of the forward guards and had them fall in line behind him. A few minutes later and they were situated off the road a good bit, hiding under a stand of trees, invisible from the road.

"Very well done, Theodyne." Nico dismounted and patted his horse in gratitude for carrying the burden of man. The horse whickered and nodded its huge head up and down. "You too, Ambrosia." Pleased with the praise, the horse nuzzled Nico's neck, huffing a stream of air into his hair.

In silence, the party tended their horses and made them comfortable before seeing to their own needs. There was a stream, edged by thick grass for the horses to graze. With that taken care of, Nico climbed up into the wagon again.

Jolen looked much worse than he had when they'd stopped the first time. Nico touched the messenger's cheeks and found them still cold, but flushed with color. It was an odd symptom that made no sense given the situation.

"Can you move?" he prompted Jolen.

"I'm afraid to. Just turning my head or blinking my eyes sets off waves of dizziness. I don't know what's wrong. I've never felt like this." His words were weak, halting.

Nico turned to Pedraus. "Get Theodyne."

"No. Please. I beg you. Don't let him touch me."

Pain and anger ripped through Nico like a storm front. "He won't hurt you. I promise, he's a gentle soul under all his arrogance."

Jolen started to shake his head, then winced as if he'd forgotten about making sudden movements. He gripped Nico's hand tightly. "No. Get me off this wagon and to the river."

"Pedraus cannot help lift you. Will you allow me to send for one of the guards to assist me?"

"Yes." Jolen's lips pulled back to form the word, but his teeth were clenched.

"Stefon. Garrick. Attend me." The two guards put down what they'd been doing and rushed over. Theodyne followed at a discreet distance.

"Yes, my lord," Stefon answered for both of them.

"Help me move Jolen to the river."

"Yes, my lord."

Nico took the bottom blanket of the pallet where Jolen lay and pulled it to the edge of the wagon. "Lift the entire bedding, it will make transport easier. On the count of three."

Nico counted down and the guards lifted as one. Jolen had a wiry strength, but he'd not filled out as yet. Shades of the man he would become were there in the cut of muscle and strength of bone. For now, his lean weight served him and the guards well as they carried him with ease to a spot near the stream bank, where sunlight bathed him in a golden brilliance.

Theodyne stood near Nico's shoulder. "Is he worse?"

"I'm not sure. I admit I'm out of my depth here. I can heal clean wounds and diseases with a touch of my hand, but I have to know the source."

Theodyne stared. "A useful skill. We could have used you in Pallonia."

"I'm sure." Nico watched as Pedraus leaned over the messenger and urged him to drink.

"What's in the cup?" Theodyne moved to the bedding where Jolen lay and held out his hand, silently demanding Pedraus give over the drink in question.

"A remedy mixed up by Molari." Pedraus handed Theodyne the cup when the apprentice wiggled his fingers at the old man.

Theodyne raised the cup to his nose and sniffed. "I don't know what's in there, but it's noxious. I'd bet my left nut it's poisoning him."

"I doubt Molari would poison him." Nico grabbed the cup from Theodyne and sniffed. He pulled back as the nausea-inducing stench hit him full force. "Oh, that's awful. Still, Molari is a trusted member of my household, despite the problems you have had with him."

"I never suggested he did it willingly." Theodyne snatched the cup back and poured the mixture onto the ground. "Reactions can occur differently in certain people. Just because this tisane may be safe for one individual does not mean it is safe for all."

The grass turned brown almost immediately where the offending medicinal hit. Theodyne pointed to the area. "I rest my case."

THEODYNE LEANED against a tree. The primer lay open and propped against his bent knees. He might look as if he was studying the arcane arts, but he was surreptitiously watching the messenger from the corner of his eye.

He'd heard the man tell the Count not to let Theodyne touch him. The words had cut, left marks, especially after having saved the man's life a few nights before. What did he think, thievery was a contagion that infected the mind and made sensible men fill with the lust to steal goods without conscience? If he thought like that, no amount of tisane in any configuration was going to help him.

And yet, Theodyne had been moved to help him regardless. He might have been an untrustworthy soul around a pile of gold and jewels, but he'd never stooped so low as to harm a person physically. Not even his fellow inmates had suffered at his hands, and the Lords above knew some of them deserved harsh treatment.

He blew out a sigh and settled more comfortably against the tree trunk. No use in making himself uneasy over the opinion of one Gold School messenger he'd probably never see again after this journey's end. And if he did, well, the man would have no just cause to say Theodyne did wrong by him. He'd saved his life—twice—and kept his distance thereafter.

The Count made his way over to the pallet where the messenger lay, taking in the elements. The soft rumble of their voices carried over to where Theodyne sat, but not the exact words. Those were lost to the winds.

The cold steel point of jealousy sliced his gut. It was as painful as it was unexpected. The Count could talk with anyone he wanted, and in truth, as an adept, he was the messenger's master as well as protector. The upheaval in Delaneux would be foremost in both their minds.

There was no sense in getting his emotions roused because the Count shared a conversation with a man who served him and the school—had in truth, almost given his life to relay valuable information. It wasn't worthy of either Theodyne or the Count. Not to mention that even though the Count's mysterious eyes and seductive gazes suggested he might be interested in something more with him—Theodyne—he'd not come out and said so. The Count might be naturally flirtatious and not even realize he'd started a tentative seduction. Maybe it was the nature of the alchemical practices?

Theodyne ran a hand down his face. He was getting nowhere fast. Sooner or later the Count was going to come over, sit down, and start asking questions on the lessons. So far, he'd managed to get by with only brief discussions and one disastrous experiment that had left Theodyne wondering if he'd made the correct decision in becoming an apprentice.

The Count squeezed the messenger's shoulder, then stood and came toward Theodyne. Instantly his heartbeat picked up pace and throbbed in his neck. Heat shot down to his groin, stirring him to an erection.

No longer able to look into the Count's eyes, Theodyne glanced back down at the book as if he found it infinitely more interesting. Better to act unaffected by the power radiating from the adept than to appear to have fallen under his spell. That way lay pain, he was almost sure of it.

The Count took a place under the tree next to Theodyne. "You haven't progressed very far."

The man was too observant by half.

Theodyne shrugged off the criticism. "Too many distractions. My mind is too busy to study properly."

"Have you written any questions or observations in your journal?"

"No. I've asked you all the questions I've had so far."

"It is not only important to write down questions, but those things you see manifest on a daily basis. All around us are examples of alchemy. As you find them, write them down and study them. We learn as much through observation as we do through reading."

Theodyne smiled. "You are telling this to an accomplished thief? The majority of the act is not the actual taking of an object, but observing actions and movements in order to obtain it without being caught."

"Then your book should fill up quickly." The Count made it sound like a challenge.

"I haven't come across anything interesting enough to observe."

The Count lifted a dark brow as if to say he didn't believe Theodyne. "Is that right?"

"It is. If I find anything worth my attention, I'll write it down." Theodyne turned his head to glance at the messenger. "So far he's the most interesting thing I've observed."

The Count frowned and looked at his hands. "He does present a bit of a conundrum."

"How sheltered do you keep students at your school? He acts as if I were convicted of grievous bodily harm and not liberating a few items from those who could afford to give." Theodyne hadn't planned to turn the conversation to that quarter, but it really bothered him on a soul-deep level that the messenger feared him. Too bad Guiseppan hadn't, for then he might have paid Theodyne what he was owed.

"I have no idea what is going through his mind. He does realize you've helped him."

Theodyne held up his hand. "It's of little importance. I'll not see him again after we return to the villa, and any opinion he has of me will fade."

The Count gave Theodyne a skeptical look. "But the opinions of others matter to you or you wouldn't have come all the way out to the villa looking for work."

"I tried the villa because of the prejudices of the people in Lancor. It became obvious very quickly I'd not earn money to live on while still inside the city walls. Leaving to seek work outside the gates was prudent."

"And resourceful."

If the Count only knew how resourceful Theodyne had been in order to get enough money for a meal that first night, he'd not trust him around the silver.

"He looks better than when we set up camp." The Count nodded in the direction of the messenger. "You may have been right about the tisane."

"You learn a lot about remedies living so closely with others. There was always somebody with an ailment, either naturally occurring or inflicted by the guards." For a while there, it had seemed as if Theodyne and his cell mate were in charge of caring for the entire prison. An outbreak of a deadly intestinal malady had swept the confines and laid up entire wings of prisoners. The stench had been horrific. Even now the remembered scents and sounds of prisoners in agony haunted him.

The guards had only been moved to violence against those afflicted. Theodyne had watched in horror as a couple of them had savagely attacked a man who writhed in pain on a dirty bedroll. They'd kicked him in the head, back, and genitals. Ali, Theodyne's cell mate, had held him back from charging the guards and having their anger turned on him.

The man had later died from the combination of his illness and injuries. Soon those same guards were picked off one by one, and the culprit never uncovered. Theodyne had not felt sorry for them, nor mourned their bitter passing. As far as he was concerned, it had been a bit of justice in a system that saw very little of that particular grace.

Theodyne cleared his throat against a growing gorge. "Sometimes it was as if despair had taken a shit in Pallonia and no one bothered to clean it up."

The Count looked uncomfortable with the assessment.

Theodyne shrugged it off. "The truth is not all multicolored lights dancing over our beds, or spells fluttering up from the pages of a book. It's harsh and dirty and sometimes it kills without mercy."

As if sensing his pain, the Count slid his arm around Theodyne's shoulder and pulled him close. The Count rested his mouth against Theodyne's hair, and he knew more than a moment of panic and a desire so acute it ached deeper than his soul.

"You never have to worry about that again, Theodyne. You are a member of *my* house now. No matter what. Always remember that." He slid his mouth to Theodyne's ear and buried his nose in his hair. There was a deep intake of air, as if the Count wanted nothing more than to remember Theodyne's scent forever.

Theodyne's cock became painfully erect. He longed to feel the Count's hands stroking him, deep and firm.

With little more than a whisper, Theodyne would succumb to temptation. It was there like a fire under his skin. Want. Need. At that moment there was nothing he wouldn't do to ensure he and the Count became lovers. It wasn't, however, a position he wished to push. Things seemed too precarious, even if the Count assured him to the contrary.

A low, sweet moan came from the Count as he pulled Theodyne even closer. "You are a dangerous man, Theodyne Thespacian, and you don't even know it."

Theodyne's heart hammered and the blood pulsed loudly in his ears. Gently, he disentangled himself from the Count's hold. "I might have believed that at one time."

The Count ran his thumb along Theodyne's jaw. There was a definite scrape of stubble against skin. The erotic sound and feel sent Theodyne's senses into a spin. It was all he could do not to grab the Count by the ears and kiss him—long, hard, and hungry. The Count's dark eyes were heavy-lidded and seductive.

"I'll let you get to your lessons."

Before Theodyne could comment, the Count was up and walking away. That had not gone the way Theodyne had envisioned. His stiff cock was in need of attention. He shifted on the hard ground in order to sit more comfortably.

The Count's scent was all over his shirt and skin. The slightest breeze lifted the fragrance to dance around his head.

It wasn't fair.

The attention only made Theodyne wish for things that might never come true. His last true lover had rolled him under the cartwheels and let him be taken away to prison. He'd be damned before he'd let another man in authority hold that much power over him. And yet, there was nothing he wanted more than to lie with the handsome Count. To learn every crest and valley of his perfect physique. To pay homage to the tenderness he saw lurking not too far under the surface.

He swallowed.

It was getting very hot sitting under the tree. He snapped the unread book closed and jumped to his feet. Just a little cooling off in the stream, to help him get his head together and passions in check, would set him up right.

Theodyne rolled up his pants and kicked off his soft boots. Next, he removed his shirt and set it on the stream bank. He waded into the water and bent down, cupping his hands to make a bowl.

The water was cool and clear. Every rock and grain of sand was visible on the bottom. Fish swam by on their way downstream. He splashed a handful of water on his face, then scooped up more to wet his upper body. By the time he was finished, he had both his thoughts and body in control.

Wind blew over his shoulders and back, leaving him with an odd feeling over his bare flesh. Tingles erupted along his spine. He turned and found the messenger watching him from his bed. When he caught Theodyne looking back, the messenger turned his head.

Theodyne grabbed his shirt and dried off, then dressed while keeping his gaze fixed on the man. Jolen. That was his name. He looked a few years younger than Theodyne. His hair was a dark blond, shot through with gold as if fingers of sunlight had touched the strands and brightened them. His blue eyes called to mind the sea off the coast of Farnum. Not that Theodyne had ever been to that port, but he'd seen paintings of that legendary seacoast done by the masters.

It was said that the great sea king, Desrali, had nearly been killed in a shipwreck as a babe. He'd floated on a broken piece of wood all the way to the coast, where he was found by a fisherman and saved. Kissed by the Gods, he'd grown to rule over Farnum and her seas with an iron fist. And the oceans rose and fell by his command.

A powerful legend and mythology used to describe the origins of a mighty king, but hardly plausible. Though, taking into account what the Count had told Theodyne about elementals, perhaps King Desrali had been a bit more than a child nearly lost to a shipwreck.

Could it be that Jolen was more than a mere man? The Count had suggested as much when they had spoken in the garden. If that was true, why did he feel threatened by Theodyne?

Or did he simply hate those beneath him, as did the populace of Lancor?

Theodyne made his way over to the blanket where Jolen lay. He flopped down on the grass, then leaned back in a casual pose. He plucked a piece of grass from the ground and stuck it between his teeth.

"Tell me about this Gold School we're going to."

A quiet tension hung on the air. A quick glance at Jolen proved he was pretending to sleep.

"Come now. That act doesn't fool me a bit. Not when you were staring at me not a moment ago."

"Why should I tell you anything of the school? You'll only think to rob us blind."

Theodyne ground his teeth together, biting down on the blade of grass. The sharp bitterness of the leaf filled his mouth. "Hardly worth the effort of your worry, since you and your masters can only make more."

"It isn't like that. You are too ignorant to understand. Too contaminated with corruption to learn."

Theodyne raised a brow. "You speak so decisively for a young man who knows nothing of my life or my story. Who are you to judge? One who has lived inside the hallowed walls of your precious institution?"

"I've lived plenty. So do not make assumptions of my kind."

"And don't make assumptions of mine," Theodyne warned.

Jolen turned toward him. Those blue eyes were like an angry sky. "Then why do you want to know about the school? I warn you, I'll defend them with my last breath if you mean to rise up against them."

Unable to hold back the laughter at the absurdity of the notion, Theodyne let loose with a guffaw that scattered birds from the trees and echoed through the glade. When he'd finally gotten himself under control and wiped the tears from his eyes, he turned to Jolen. "You? Who can't even ride across the country without succumbing to your injuries? That is no kind of threat to me. I've been up against much heartier souls than yours and lived to tell the tale. No, Jolen, you do not scare me."

"That is Journeyman Jolen to you. I have given you no leave to drop my title."

Theodyne jumped to his feet, then bent over, looking down into Jolen's face. "Not when you haven't even grown a convincing beard as yet."

He made his way back to the tree where he'd abandoned his primer. He picked it up from the ground and walked downstream a ways. Far enough to not be seen by the makeshift camp, yet close enough to make it there in a hurry if the need arose.

He dug back into the book and read for an hour or so. The words were hard to decipher in places, the penmanship sloppy where it seemed the author had gotten excited by the concepts he imposed on the reader.

There were a few passages Theodyne couldn't make out no matter how hard he tried. The letters seemed to move and swirl on the page. Tired from reading so long, he rubbed his eyes and tried again. Not even blinking helped clear the dancing images.

This time nothing actually achieved flight. It was the words themselves that rearranged in sequence and meaning. Each loop and curve of letter morphed into something unrecognizable. The language no longer resembled the local dialect, let alone what he'd been reading for the past few hours.

Wait. There were ancient languages spoken by the first alchemists during the birth of civilization. Could this be what they spoke and wrote?

And why did the book alter the words to something incomprehensible to modern man? There was no telling with the grimoire. Theodyne wondered how much the ancient adept really knew and how much was just fanciful thoughts that adhered to the page as he wrote.

Theodyne placed his finger on the line and followed it along to the end of the changing words as if he could stop them from morphing. A light tingle shot through his fingertip, not unlike a spark of static before a storm.

Suddenly all the words became clear. Not that they had once again arranged themselves into a familiar dialect, but his understanding of them was immediate.

Shocked and more than a little unnerved, Theodyne set the book down for a moment. He never took his gaze from the pages. Wind kicked up, turning them one by one, until they stopped on a page with the heading "Air."

HOURS HAD passed and there had been no sign of Theodyne. He'd stalked off into the woods farther upstream after speaking with Jolen. Nico didn't dare go looking for him again. Not with the call of the hidden grove and the romantic burble of the water. It was too dangerous to his peace of mind.

As it was, he'd been unable to shake the musk of Theodyne's skin or the sunshine in his hair when he'd held him. Powerful currents were at work. Above and beyond what the Grand Matter threw his way on a daily basis. No, this was even more ethereal than that hard-to-harness substance. More potent than the power of the elements.

Nico sat on the edge of the wagon and watched the bend in the stream, waiting for Theodyne to reappear. He hoped he made it back before nightfall. It wasn't good to be spread out so far during travel. Wild animals hunted these woods for food, some of them large enough to kill a man. The only protection Theodyne had with him was his charm and the alchemy primer. Hardly enough to subdue a boar if one wandered so close to camp. Then again, the charm might just do the trick after all. The heavens above knew it had worked wonders on him.

Nico leaned back and pulled out the letter from Rhone again. There were certain elements of the script that could not be deciphered by an untrained eye. Secret coding in the swirls and sweeps of the letters told the underlying story the words did not convey. So it had been with the alchemists since the founding of the Gold School.

Had he missed some of the message in his haste? Was there a hidden warning or clue of how best to use his powers to free the headmaster? Cleverness and lots of coin. The *prolate* of Delaneux was a greedy man with a big family of legitimate and illegitimate children to feed. There were also wives and concubines and only the heavens knew what else inside that palace. And the man had the audacity to call the Gold School a bunch of heathens?

Nico had to put on his humble face while meeting with the man. That might be the hardest magic he'd ever performed. Being a man of title, he didn't cow easily before those who bought their positions of power, or those who stole from the needy to make it there. It had a way of leaving a bad taste in the mouth and sickness in the gut. Such men were beyond immortal redemption, their souls too corrupted by the mortal world and material things.

A quick glance to the stream bank to check on Jolen, and Nico noticed the journeyman appeared to be sleeping comfortably. At least that was good. How would he have faced Rhone with the news of Jolen's death?

Too many young men had been lost to the wrath of the *prolates* lately. There wasn't one city-state where the alchemical schools were located that wasn't overrun with the tyrannical rule of a local *prolate*.

Nico folded the letter and placed it back in his shirt lining. His mind was restless and his body in turmoil. Should he go and look for Theodyne or let him stew until he decided to return to camp?

The sun sat heavy in the sky now. The day was fading steadily into night, and there was still no sign of Theodyne. Perhaps he'd decided to walk back to Lancor. It wasn't all that far. Nico had imagined Theodyne made of thicker skin than to let Jolen scare him off or make him angry enough to leave. So not seeing Theodyne for hours felt wrong.

Nico's heart fell. He jumped off the end of the wagon and started running the way he'd seen Theodyne go hours before. What if he were lying injured? What if he couldn't call for help?

A million and one ugly scenarios fed through his mind as he followed the stream into the glade. He found Theodyne hunkered against a tree, as he'd been earlier, with the primer in his lap. Light glowed from the open pages as if lit from within.

Master Krutarch had been a clever man, indeed.

"Theodyne? Are you all right?"

The apprentice looked up, holding his place on the page with a finger. "Yes. Fine. And you?"

Nico wanted to tell him he'd worried when Theodyne had not returned to camp, but the words wouldn't come. Too many turbulent emotions stirred in Nico's heart with just a look from Theodyne's beautiful golden eyes.

"Come back to camp now. It's almost dark."

Theodyne looked around him. Awareness dawned. "Oh, I hadn't noticed. I started reading this passage on Air."

Nico stalled. "You can read that?"

He'd not told Theodyne about the trap. It had to be unlocked in order for one to advance through the lesson.

"Not at first." Theodyne stood and brushed the dirt off his pants before starting back to camp.

Nico fell into step beside him. "What was difficult about it?"

Theodyne offered a smile that cut right to Nico's desires. "You know already, so don't pretend you don't and make me explain."

"That is not the point. The trap is set to disarm differently for each student. I only wondered what you had to do."

"If that is the case, then it is a matter between myself and the author."

"Exasperating man." There was no malice or force behind the words, however heartfelt they were.

"I would never presume to think I knew more than an ancient master or to tell you how to conduct my studies. If he wanted you to know, then he'd have made the seals the same for everyone."

There was a certain stamp of wisdom there. Not that Nico was surprised. Theodyne had that in abundance. "And what did you learn about our elusive friend the air?"

"As with most things, there is more there than meets the eye." He gave a low rumble of laughter. "Or as much as one can see when observing the air."

That laugh went all the way to Nico's gut. His blood ran hot. Just being near Theodyne was proving a lot trickier than the most complicated transmutation.

They entered the camp. Jolen and Pedraus were asleep near a little bubble of light Nico had placed there to keep them warm and protected. The guards were taking turns watching over the camp. The ones not on watch leaned against the front of the wagon with their hats pulled down over their eyes. Loud snores came from under the fabric.

"We're leaving early, so get a good night's sleep." Nico crawled up into the wagon, where he'd spread a bedroll.

Theodyne made a face. "I could have stayed by the tree and slept there."

"And hurt your neck and back in the process. Nonsense. Come up here where it's comfortable. There is no reason to sleep on the ground when you can rest easily up here."

Theodyne took a step forward, then stopped. "Are you sure?"

"Yes. Of course. You are my apprentice. Why would I not wish to share my luxuries with you, especially when out on the harsh road?"

Theodyne made a grunting sound in the back of his throat. "You don't know harsh, Count Valencia."

Nico made himself comfortable in his bedroll and rose up on his elbow to stare at Theodyne in the dim light from the glowing orb hanging in the wagon. "None of this Count Valencia. Call me Nico."

Theodyne crossed his arms. "That's much too intimate for a student to address his master."

"Then when we are around others, call me master. No one will find fault in that. However, once we enter the school, you'll have to refrain from speaking to me unless you are spoken to first."

Theodyne climbed up onto the wagon bed. "Then I'd best leave you to your own devices and stay with the horses."

Nico laughed at the bewilderment in Theodyne's voice. "Why is that?"

"You've only known me a short time, but you should have realized by now that I'm not good at keeping my thoughts to myself if I think they need heard."

"And I appreciate that." Nico sat up slightly. "Understand that this particular school adheres to very strict standards of behavior and comportment. If you step out of line even a little, you'll be severely punished."

Theodyne froze. His face became impassive. "I've been in that position before and promised myself when I was set free I'd never allow it again. Perhaps when we arrive, I *will* stay outside."

Nico's heart bled. "I can't let that happen either. You must come inside. I won't allow you to loiter about the grounds."

Theodyne turned away. "Why? Afraid I might make you look bad?"

"Theodyne? Please turn around and look at me." He waited quietly, believing his request would not be granted. Light shone off Theodyne's golden hair, creating a halo around his head. More than anything, Nico wanted to reach out and stroke the silky strands.

"Did you not tell me to get some sleep?"

"Yes, but I don't want you to fall into slumber with any misunderstandings between us."

Finally, Theodyne turned and looked at Nico. "We don't have to go back over this again. I promise I'll behave when we arrive at the school. I do know how to behave myself."

"I never thought you'd embarrass me. There will be questions about your scar. I just want you to be prepared."

There was a moment of intense silence. "Nico, I've been scorned and tormented and treated like refuse since the mark was placed on my face. I bear the burden of it because I have no alternative. The crimes I've committed were done with free will. I've never made excuses for that. It was a way of life for me. A chance to rise above my circumstances and walk in higher circles."

"And then you fell."

"As do we all. Eventually." Theodyne placed his hands behind his head. "You let me worry about how to handle any comments that come my way. You just help your friend regain his freedom."

Chapter Seven

THE SCHOOL was like nothing Theodyne had ever seen in his life. He'd seen paintings and etchings of castles with less grandeur than the structure that rose from the mountains before them like some great, hulking giant.

They rode under a bridge whose intricate rail design spelled out arcane words in the language of the ancient masters. Magnificent.

Tall cavern walls protected them on either side as they rode beneath the bridge. A river cut through the mountains on their right. The waters were a torrent of chaos and anger, as the river rushed by on its way down to the valley below.

Gates towered over them. Fog slid down the mountainside to cascade over the edifice. The builders had incorporated all the elements in the structure's design. There was nothing shy or subtle about the school. It was as grandiose a statement as Theodyne had ever seen.

Theodyne's horse stamped and started backward. He raised his brow to give Nico a look meant to chastise him for owning a mount that spooked at the first sign of unusual currents in the air.

But Nico wasn't looking at him. He'd gone on alert along with the guards. They drew their swords. Unfortunately, Theodyne had no weapon to defend himself against attack, nothing to help keep the others from harm. The only thing he had was the horse under him and a cunning talent for getting in and out of tight spaces that served him no purpose in a battle.

"Can you handle a crossbow?" Nico leaned back in his saddle and made a subtle gesture toward the wagon. "There's one back there near the luggage. Get it."

Theodyne turned the horse around and headed back to the far end of the wagon.

Pedraus stuck his head out of the flap. "What is going on? Why have we stopped?"

Theodyne shook his head as he rummaged through the packs for the crossbow. He finally found it under an elaborate robe and a pair of the ugliest shoes he'd ever seen in his life. Hell of a way to treat a weapon.

A quiver of arrows sat next to the crossbow. Theodyne picked up both and held them in one arm while guiding the horse back up to Nico with the other.

"Identify yourselves or die." The voice came from the guard tower at the top of the gates. It rumbled down on them like thunder.

Theodyne glanced at Nico. "You want to answer that challenge? Because I don't think they'll care who I am."

Nico cupped his hands around his mouth and shouted out a sentence that had no basis in any language Theodyne had ever heard.

There was a short pause, and then the voice from the guard tower returned. It, too, spoke in that odd language. Whatever was said made Nico laugh. His eyes twinkled in delight and his mouth held a wicked curve.

He cupped his hands around his mouth again. "Yes."

The gates slowly began to open. The sounds of old metal gears and pulleys grinding together were enough to send a shiver down the spine. The mechanism creaked and groaned as if the process were too much for the system. The gates grudgingly opened and the way was clear to the front of the school.

Whoever stood at the gates must have had some way to communicate with the inhabitants. A greeting party met them at the front steps. A man in robes similar to the ones Theodyne had found in the wagon came down off the steps with his arms spread wide.

"Nico. I did not expect you to make the journey here."

Nico jumped off his horse and into the man's arms for a backslapping hug. They kissed each other on both cheeks. Jealousy speared Theodyne under the ribs. It was obvious the men were old friends. True affection shone in both their eyes and smiles.

"And why should I not? You are in trouble and it is my responsibility to see you safely out." He nodded his head back toward the wagon, where Jolen was being helped down by one of the guards. Pedraus stood behind them, hovering like a doting mama.

"I see you've returned our journeyman to us in one piece."

"A little worse for wear. It was my apprentice, Theodyne, who came up with an excellent treatment plan that saved his life." Nico indicated Theodyne, who had yet to climb down off his horse.

The other alchemist leaned into Nico. "Why is he still seated in the saddle?"

Nico gave Theodyne a look of consternation. "You can dismount."

Theodyne did as instructed as a groom came to lead the horses away. He stayed rooted to his place and folded his hands behind his back. He neither acknowledged the alchemists nor pretended to hear what they said. If Nico wanted him to remain silent and obedient, he would. No matter how much it killed him.

"Theodyne, this is Master Rhone. He is the under-headmaster here at the school."

Theodyne nodded his head in greeting.

Rhone leaned into Nico once more. "He's a somber sort of fellow."

Nico gave a brief smile.

There was an awkward moment where no one spoke, then Rhone clapped his hands and two young men came forward. "Please show Master Nico and his apprentice to their rooms."

Theodyne fell into line behind Nico, following at a discreet distance. He doubted Nico needed to be shown to his room. He most likely had permanent lodgings at the school. However, being the dutiful apprentice he was pretending to be, he kept the question unasked.

The inside of the school was as grand and immense as it appeared from the outside. There was something of the haunted cathedral about the place. The spirits of dead alchemists had not left the building—they'd simply gone to live their eternal existences in the walls or furnishings.

Paintings and sculptures lined the walls as high up as the ceiling. The priceless treasures all had that mystical quality that made Theodyne want to stop and study them until he found that one elusive element that separated it from other paintings hanging in lavish homes. But there was something, almost as if the air, water, fire, and earth had been poured into every stroke of brush across canvas. The work was simply breathtaking.

"I'll take you on a tour of the gallery later."

Theodyne blinked. This wasn't the gallery? It sure looked like one to him. And wouldn't the *prolate* of this city-state just love to get his grubby hands on all this immense wealth? He'd never have to incarcerate another individual as long as he lived. The proceeds from the entranceway alone would make him a wealthy man.

The farther into the interior they walked, the lower Theodyne's heart sank. These men were under attack, and they didn't even realize the significance of their peril.

NICO BIDED his time after being shown to his room. There was so much to discuss and plans to make to secure Headmaster Donando's safe return. However, Theodyne had to be properly attired or run the risk of causing more heads to turn than already had.

The assessing look in Rhone's eyes had not escaped Nico's notice. There would be plenty of questions about Theodyne and the feasibility of taking a man of his age and experience as an apprentice. Not that Nico had to answer to anyone from the Gold School. He did as he wanted. Familial ties with the founder did have their privileges. That was not to say Nico wouldn't be asked by some of the masters in attendance.

A knock sounded on the door.

"Enter." Two first-level apprentices came in, carrying his belongings. "You can put them near the wardrobe. I'll tend to them myself later."

There was a chorus of "Yes, master" as the boys dropped their burden and scurried from the room, as if afraid to be in Nico's presence.

Theodyne's accommodations were a small annex room connected to Nico's. It was often so with visitors to the school. The apprentices or journeymen were used as servants for their masters. He smiled, wondering how long it would take Theodyne to figure it out and what he'd say on the matter. Whatever it was, it was sure to be entertaining.

There was a thud and a shuffle from the annex. Nico crossed the room and opened the connecting door to see what mischief Theodyne had managed to get up to in so short a time. Theodyne stood on the bed, turning a painting of Festus Giaus around to show the back of the canvas and frame.

"What are you doing?"

Theodyne turned around, hands still on the painting. "I don't like the way he's staring at me, as if I've brought the stench of the prison with me."

Nico canted his head. "Actually, Festus there was an *aerothant*—an air elemental. So, if you did bring a particular scent with you, he'd know."

"I don't want him watching me while I sleep or change my clothes."

"It's a painting. He can't see you. Not to mention he's been dead for four hundred years."

Theodyne turned fully and walked across the bed. He stepped off the end in front of Nico. "And the author of the primer you lent me has been dead longer, and that hasn't stopped the ink from dancing and odd little lights and flying things from coming off the pages."

"That's the nature of the primer. It demonstrates as it teaches."

Theodyne pointed at the portrait. "And that? Is it supposed to watch over the servants to ensure they do as told at all times?"

Nico shook his head. "You have a very vivid imagination."

"Tell me that won't work to my advantage here?"

"You don't have an advantage. You are my apprentice." He took a long, lingering look up and down Theodyne's clothes. "You'll need to change into your robes."

"Now? But I'm in my room."

"And we'll need to meet with the others soon."

Theodyne frowned and stepped away from Nico. "Do you need me for that?"

"It is customary for apprentices to attend their masters during all meals and meetings in case there is something that is needed."

Theodyne gave a disbelieving laugh. "Am I to find my way around this massive place like a bloodhound tracking a criminal?"

"You are overstating the matter. I promise if I need anything I'll send one of the lads who live here. I'd not send you on a mission that might see you lost along the halls for eternity." Nico smiled. "It's so hard to find a good apprentice, and despite these trying circumstances we find ourselves in, I do believe you will prove a good one."

"Your friend thinks you're mad to apprentice me."

Nico turned back toward his room. "How would you possibly know something like that? I haven't even discussed the situation with him."

"I saw it in his eyes."

"Rhone looks at everyone like they've one cog short of a clock." He started back through the door to his room. "Change and I'll take you on a tour of the school to get a better feel for it."

Then Nico had to discuss the strategy to help gain Donando's freedom. That was paramount. Too many days had already passed with him in custody. No telling what they'd done to the man. Nico almost hated to know. The *prolates* were known to be cruel when handling members of the school through their courts.

Had a price been set yet? Was it too high to pay from the school's coffers without a little transmutation? It would serve the *prolate* right. A little short-term change on a box of rocks to make them look like precious gems might teach the man a thing or two about dealing with the Gold School.

Nico changed into his adept-level master's robes. A message waited under the door when he finished. He bent over and picked up the stiff piece of parchment. The script was bold and dark, written in a precise hand well versed in the cipher of the masters.

Rhone wanted to meet with him immediately in the arboretum.

Alone.

Theodyne sat on his bed with the primer in his hand. He looked up from his reading as Nico approached.

"Master Rhone wishes to see me at once. I'll have to postpone the tour. Wait for me here and do not leave this room."

"Of course."

Nico wondered how long it would take Theodyne to become bored with his surroundings and leave their suites. It really didn't matter, as he'd not be able to get inside any of the workrooms. The secrets of the school were safely ensconced behind locked doors with wards set to keep out intruders. It wasn't so much that Nico worried for Theodyne as he wanted a chance to explain the things he'd see.

Nico made his way up to the arboretum. It was a lovely place that rested securely between heaven and the world below. Plants grew abundant and full. Flocks of rare birds made their homes high in the branches of exotic trees.

It was Nico's favorite room in the school, so unlike the rest of the institution. This beautiful rooftop wonderland was a constructed paradise where generations of alchemists had come to dream in tranquility.

He found Rhone sitting at a table near the flowering *uta* tree. Soft pink petals the size of pie plates filled the air with soft perfume. A pitcher of a deep-red wine and two glasses sat in front of Rhone, along with various cheeses and fruit.

"I thought we'd share a light repast while we talked."

Nico nodded in thanks and took the seat directly across from Rhone. The under-headmaster poured Nico a drink and slid it across the table to him.

"It's a good vintage, I understand. From some little winery to the west. Name of Valencia," Rhone joked.

Nico lifted his glass in salute. "Then I admire your good taste in selecting what I know is an excellent drink."

He twirled the glass and sniffed the bouquet. It was full-bodied and sharp. Perfect. The lovely surprise was in the fact the taste was soothing and mild, a wonderful complement for the cheese and fruit.

However, Rhone's expression suggested he'd not invited Nico to the arboretum for a bit of wine and cheese.

"What did you wish to discuss?"

Rhone made a face and lowered his wineglass. "I'm worried, Nico."

"Of course you are. We all are. If the *prolates* start taking our headmasters into custody, what's to stop them rounding up the masters and students?"

"You mistake me. That is the greatest burden on my mind, but not the only one." He made a vague gesture toward the door. "How did you come by taking on an apprentice who is of an age to take on his master's robes? And a marked man, no less. It's a stain on the Gold School."

"You can sit there and judge the measure of a man by so short and silent an acquaintance?" Nico shook his head. "You are a better magician than me."

"It isn't that and you know it. The mark. We have problems being trusted by the masses as it is. The *prolates* are watching our every move. Now you throw a convicted felon into our midst."

Nico waved his hand to dismiss the charge. "Theodyne never refuted the charges. On the contrary, he has been quite open and honest about his former profession. He never once professed innocence. He might have been a thief, but he is not a liar."

"Perhaps it would be best if you moved the *Eye of Truth* from your estate."

"That is not necessary."

"I do not understand you." Rhone shook his head. Frustration sat his shoulders like a cloak. "You will see us brought down."

"Is that your true opinion?

Rhone nodded and took another drink. "Yes."

"Then you, my friend, have become very shortsighted. I have no reason to distrust Theodyne, and truly, he pours through the primer of Master Krutarch like wine." Nico picked up a piece of yellow cheese and studied it. He'd not seen the like at the school before. "Is this made here or traded from the town?"

"The town. There is a wonderful cheese maker who has recently brought his trade. He brings supplies to us a few times a month."

Nico raised his eyes. "And have you not thought that perhaps this so-called cheese maker is a spy for the *prolate*?"

Rhone stilled. "What makes you think that?"

"How else would the *prolate* know what happens inside the school in order to level charges against the headmaster? Someone had to bring him the information. If not a simple cheese maker, then who? Is there anyone else who is given leave to come and go as they please?"

Rhone wiped his hand down his face. "We pay all who supply us well for their goods and services. Enough so they might keep their own counsel."

"Not if the *prolate* pays them well to break that silence."

Rhone was quiet for a moment, then said, "The clerics came to a meeting with Headmaster Donando. He offered them peace and openness, and they turned on him like a pack of rabid dogs."

Nico knew there was more to the story and was relieved to hear it finally coming out. "What did he hope to gain by inviting them into the school?"

"I believe it was to show them we were not to be feared."

Nico stood and made an angry circuit around the garden. "I have a healthy respect for the political power of the clerics and have made peace with them myself, but it's quite another thing to allow them into our homes to snoop around. For that alone I should let him rot. My family built this school from the first brick."

"You would turn your back on Donando?"

"By rights I should." A bitter laugh rose from his gut. "No wonder you didn't want me to come."

Rhone let out a sigh. "I never sought to conceal anything from you. The headmaster is in a difficult position. Our *prolate* means to break the school and take the castle as his palace."

"And the headmaster made it all the easier for him to do just that." Nico came back to the table. "Still, I'll not let him suffer."

"Nice to see there is still honor in you."

"Do you doubt it? I'm not so far removed in Lancor that I've become immune to the pains of those who are entrusted to carry on my family's legacy."

Anger he didn't believe he'd ever be capable of feeling surged through Nico's body. Had he given over the running of the school—the very discipline he'd spent his life learning—to those who were unworthy? Though he loved the place and thought of it as home, it was also a prison of sorts. He'd vowed when he'd left, never to return to live here. At his age, he should have learned to never say never.

Chapter Eight

THEODYNE LISTENED from behind the trunk of a large, blooming tree. Sweeping branches concealed his presence. No, he hadn't followed Nico's expressed instruction, but then there was something odd going on at the school that was more than met the eye. Judging from the way Nico became more agitated with the discussion, his estimation wasn't far from the mark.

Theodyne wanted to help. He wished there was something he could do to share the burden. Going up against a gang of clerics and a *prolate* was a monumental task, even for a man as successful and powerful as Count Nicodemus de Valencia.

After hearing how Nico defended him to the under-headmaster, there wasn't anything Theodyne wouldn't do for his master. A fresh flood of emotion warmed his blood. He wanted Nico. There was no denying how much. But as equals. In their current arrangement, Nico had the upper hand. Maybe if Theodyne made a gesture Nico couldn't ignore or brush off as an apprentice doing his duty by his master, it would change the dynamic.

Theodyne glanced up and saw Nico staring directly at him through the foliage. The Count said nothing to alert the other alchemist that there was a witness to their conversation. Instead of further calling attention to himself, Theodyne made a silent yet hasty retreat.

What he needed to do was gather information on the local *prolate*. See what kind of man he appeared to his people. It was possible he might be reasoned with, though Theodyne doubted it very much.

Theodyne made his way back to their rooms by the opposite path he'd taken to follow Nico. This way led him by workrooms and salons, classrooms and offices, then finally the dormitories.

It appeared the school was filled with students and faculty. All in all, there might have been a hundred students. That seemed a high number, if this was only one school. Where were the other institutions and how vast were they? It seemed to Theodyne there were a lot more alchemists in the world than the clerics would have the populace believe. If that was true, then how could the clerics and the *prolates* possibly control so much power? The true power lay with the alchemists. They did the most amazing things, yet never tried to increase their lot. They kept to the background, living in the shadows.

He passed by a room and heard the sounds of vigorous sex. His heart kicked up a notch and his cheeks heated. Theodyne kept walking.

At the end of the corridor, he stopped to get his bearings. The hallways made no practical sense. It was as if the foundations had been poured around the curves in the mountains.

He decided to go right and see where that led him.

"Why are you wandering about?"

Theodyne stopped and turned, then looked up. The man was enormous. His craggy features and streak of white hair in the sea of a jet-black mane gave him a decidedly menacing look. His frown wasn't too pleasant either. Judging from the robes, he was an adept.

Theodyne had also learned a long time ago not to let size or station intimidate him. "I've lost the way to the guest quarters. Can you direct me?"

The master narrowed dark-green eyes. "You are that apprentice of Master Nico's. I've heard about you."

"News travels fast even in a school this size." Theodyne gave a slight incline of his head.

"Insolent." It was said more as an estimation of character than an epithet.

Theodyne curled his mouth into what he knew was a sly half smile. "Truthful."

"And your mark?"

"Earned."

The master began to walk in the opposite direction. "Follow me, young Theodyne."

Theodyne gave a huff in his throat. He wasn't young by any means. What he lacked in chronology he'd made up for in experience.

The master strode down a wide staircase carved from the very foundations of the world. As he walked, Theodyne noticed all the elements were in balance at every turn. Not one held sway over the other.

At the bottom of the stairs, the master turned right and walked in long-legged strides to the end of a glass-encased corridor that showed a full view of the river below.

The master pointed down another corridor that intersected. "Third door on the right."

"I thank you...." He let the words hang, not knowing how to formally address the adept.

"Master Oberon."

Theodyne nodded and made his way to the guest suites. He'd wait until after he spoke with Nico, and then he'd take one of the horses and discover the lay of the land. Delaneux was no different than Lancor. Not in essentials. One city was pretty much the same as another when it came to power and corruption. The rich did as they pleased, no matter where they lived.

Theodyne let himself into the rooms. Pedraus was there, straightening things and emptying a pack into the modest wardrobe.

"What are those?"

"More apprentice robes. You must be outfitted correctly so as not to embarrass the master."

"Old man, I have no intention of embarrassing our master." Theodyne lay across the bed.

Pedraus glanced over his shoulder. "No? Then why were you skulking around the halls after he told you to stay put?"

"You have your work to do, and I have mine." He picked up the primer and opened it to where he'd left off. "Do we not both serve the Count?"

"I've served the Valencias since I was a child, as did my father and his father before him. My loyalty is given because that is my lot. I know no other way. But you, Apprentice Theodyne, know only your own wants and desires."

He looked up over the book. The old man did not condemn with his words, but spoke gently as if to a sleeping child he meant to comfort.

Theodyne contemplated Pedraus's observations. He couldn't take issue with them, nor argue. They were true. More than that, they were his strength.

Pedraus finished his task and left the room.

Alone, Theodyne moved to the tiny square of glass that posed as a window. This one didn't possess quite the view of the glass corridor, but looking out over the east side of the grounds gave him an idea.

Theodyne changed into street clothes and donned one of his robes over it to conceal his appearance. Using the main columns and statuary as cover, he sneaked down to the lower level.

Students in robes of various colors and embroidery crossed his path at several of the major halls. Theodyne hid as they walked by, all headed in the same direction. Scents of roasted meat and baked bread wafted from the room at the end of the hall. No doubt they were headed to the dining hall for midday meal.

This was one meal he'd have to pass on. What he wanted to do was far more important than sitting at a table and listening to a bunch of spoiled magician initiates gossip about him like a clutch of old women.

With most of the school's population at table, there was no one to stop him from taking one of the horses and making his way back down the mountain to the town below. He was sure Nico wouldn't miss him. Not yet. Nico would be tied up with his fellow masters for some time. And even if Nico did notice the absence, it wasn't as if Theodyne would be gone forever.

Theodyne found the stables and the horse he'd rode on the journey. It was unfair to saddle the beast and ride it again after so long on the road, but to take one of the others would brand him a horse thief. That was one particular crime he'd never been guilty of and didn't plan to be any time soon.

He moved into the stall. The horse softly huffed, blowing out air through its nostrils. "I'm sorry, boy, but there is no choice. I can't get down the mountain on foot very fast. And I can't take one of the others."

The animal nodded its head up and down a few times and pawed the ground as if it understood.

Theodyne found the saddle and gently placed it on the animal.

One of the stable lads came into the barn. "What are you doing? We weren't told anyone would be leaving."

"This is an unscheduled leave-taking, but necessary. I can tend to things myself." Theodyne grabbed the pommel and back of the saddle and placed his foot in the stirrup. He levered himself up in one smooth movement. "If anyone asks, tell them I'll return no later than early morning."

The lad looked confused. Theodyne rode out of the stable, taking the horse to a canter. He needed to move quickly, but not tax his mount. He'd leave him on the school property once he got to the wall surrounding the school. Better to not go out around the guarded gate but to find another egress.

If he found a way out, he'd be able to get back inside. After that display in front of the river gates, he doubted he'd ever be allowed entrance alone. Theodyne didn't know the language, and only understood the meanings when he held the primer.

Damn, perhaps he should have tucked it into his robes to see if it worked to translate the words when others spoke them. Ah, well. Better to leave the book behind in case he fell into trouble in Delaneux. If the authorities found the primer on him, he'd be sharing a cell with the headmaster. Prison was no place he wanted to visit twice in a lifetime.

At the bottom of the mountain stood a stone wall that rose high. However, the row of trees ended at least fifty meters from the wall. There was no way to use the branches to climb and get atop the wall. The alchemists had thought that far into their defenses, though they had not thought of some villain bringing a ladder to brace against the wall and climb.

But that wasn't Theodyne's problem to solve. He'd have to take off his shoes and scale the wall the way he did back before he'd perfected his thieving craft. Luckily the stones were imperfect. The alchemists had not made these in their laboratories or smoothed them out before placing them in the wall. Granted, there were few true hand and footholds, but there was enough room for toes and fingertips.

Theodyne tied the horse to a tree with enough lead so it could walk and graze if it wanted. "I'll be back later, friend."

With one last pat to its long neck, he made his way to the wall. He removed his shoes and tied the strings together, then hung them around his neck. After feeling around the wall's face to find the best holds, Theodyne began his ascent.

The climb was hot, sweaty, and arduous. Even in the cool mountain air, Theodyne was soon wet through his clothes. His arms and legs shook from the effort. He'd not climbed anything in such a manner in a very long time and was sorely out of practice.

When he finally reached the top of the wall, he barely had enough strength left to pull himself onto the ledge. That's where his problems really began.

A moat bubbled and boiled past the wall. Steam rose from the surface into the cooler air. Theodyne sat there in disbelief and laughed. What else could he do at this point? He'd spent all that time and energy trying to scale a wall he should have known was not left unattended in some manner.

It occurred to Theodyne as the breeze cooled his wet clothes and his skin began to chill that Menarch was probably right—he should have tried to steal the *Eye of Truth* and make his fortune that way. Instead, he'd gotten caught up in a sexy smile and pair of kind eyes that filled his head with the want to improve—to not have to depend on thievery for his sustenance. But when all was said and done, thieving was all Theodyne knew.

A stronger breeze blew by his face, ruffled his hair.

Air.

A slow smile played across his lips as the answer came to him. Hadn't he spent the last few days reading about the properties of air and the transformative powers of the element? Time to put his book learning to the test.

Theodyne closed his eyes and centered his mind. He visualized the moat before him and the cold breeze against his skin. A marriage of air and water. The cold air staking claim to the heat of the water, tempering it.

Theodyne cracked an eye open to see if his hasty spell worked.

Nothing.

The boiling water below him seemed to mock his failure. Try again. He had to. There was no other option at this point. He'd already spent too much time climbing the damn wall. He'd come too far to turn and go back to the school without anything to offer up to Nico.

"Elements of air, I beseech you, please see fit to turn the water to ice."

Once again the water did not change form.

Was it any wonder alchemists studied their discipline for years? There was a lot more involved in getting elements to bend to human will than it seemed. The spells and mysteries that filled the villa appeared as if they took no more effort than a thought. Perhaps that was what was really meant by the term *master*.

Theodyne took a deep breath in and held it. He centered his mind, concentrating on the temperature of the water. Using the air as an instrument of change, he channeled his thoughts to the water. Slowly the steam began to dissipate. The boil calmed. Ripples softened and the water flowed downstream in a more natural manner.

All around him the air began to grow colder. His breath made puffs of white around his head. He tweaked the image he held in his mind. Liquid to solid.

Same matter, different form. It was only a question of transforming the state, not of changing the material of which it was made.

By degrees the water changed, became thicker, denser, until it ceased flowing. The clear surface turned opaque. Theodyne took his shoes from around his neck and put them back on his feet. The climb down was significantly harder without the benefit of having his toes free, but he didn't want to stand or walk across the ice with bare feet.

Sooner than he'd thought possible, he was there, testing his weight on the icy moat. A few creaks sounded across the expanse. If he ran, he might be able to make it across. At the worst, he'd get wet, but at least he'd not be boiled alive.

With all his force, Theodyne pushed off from the wall and ran over the slippery surface. His feet went out from under him and he came down hard on his backside. The last ten feet of his journey was a pure slide, until he crashed into the far bank.

He rubbed the stiffness out of his rump as he stood. The rest of the stroll down the mountain was done with a limp and a smile.

Theodyne had passed his first test.

Nico glanced around the grand dining hall for Theodyne. Where had the man gone? He was supposed to stay to their suites, and Nico hoped he'd made it back there after eavesdropping on his conversation with Rhone.

He'd sent Pedraus back to check the suites, but as yet the old man had not returned. It was damn frustrating to be kept waiting, especially for one such as himself, who had reached the very pinnacle of his craft. Not once in all his years of taking on apprentices did Nico remember ever having to send people to look for the lad.

But then this was no lad, this was Theodyne. A law unto himself.

What could have set him off enough to make him hide, or had he just become lost in the halls of the giant school? Perhaps he'd stumbled upon the library and become immersed in one of the ancient tomes.

Nico threw his napkin into his plate and stood. "This is ridiculous."

Rhone gave him an admonishing glance.

"Not a word, Rhone. Not *one* word."

He'd started for the door when Pedraus returned, shaking his head. He'd not found Theodyne in the suites.

"I swear to you, sir, I did speak with him earlier. He had taken a spot on the bed and opened his primer. I never heard him leave the rooms again."

Nico clapped the old man on the back. "I believe you. He's just gotten himself lost somewhere and forgotten the time."

No sooner had he started down the main corridor than he saw Oberon heading to the dining area with a stableboy, who was all bloodied and bruised.

Oberon pushed the lad forward. "Tell Master Nico what you told me."

Skinny and scrawny and smelling like refuse, the boy refused to speak. He shook his head a few times, gripping his hat in his hands in white-knuckle fashion.

"Speak, boy." Oberon was intimidating in the best of circumstances and this wasn't one.

The lad mumbled something incoherent.

Nico leaned forward. "What was that?"

He repeated what he'd said, and Nico saw a flash of red. He straightened and met Oberon's curious glance. "He said he'll only tell Master Rhone. Looks like I've been away from my duties here much too long if I have no influence over even the stableboys."

Nico made a motion to Pedraus. "Get Master Rhone out here so we can find out what happened."

Oberon made a face. "It doesn't look good."

Nico glanced up. "What do you mean?"

But Nico already knew it had something to do with Theodyne.

Rhone came out into the hall, along with several other masters and journeymen. "What's this all about? I don't like to have my meals interrupted by trouble that can be handled by others."

Nico crossed his arms over his chest and nodded to the boy. "He has something he wishes to say to you."

"Well, go ahead. I'm waiting."

No longer appearing the timid, scared servant, the boy puffed out his chest. "A thief stole one of the horses and left the school. He beat me up to get it away from me. I held on as hard as I could, but he jumped up into the saddle and kicked me in the head before galloping away."

Rhone narrowed his eyes. "What did this thief look like?"

"Dark-blond hair, golden eyes. He had a thief's badge on his cheek."

"See what you get for bringing men like him into the school? Innocent boys get beaten and our horses stolen."

Nico didn't believe the story for a moment, and judging from the expression on Oberon's face, he didn't either. "What did the horse look like?"

"A big brown one, with a white patch over one eye."

"Then the horse wasn't stolen," Nico said. "That horse belongs to me, and the man you called thief is my apprentice."

Rhone puffed his cheeks in and out as if unable to draw enough air. "That does not give him the right to attack a boy less than half his size."

"Theodyne is unlikely to have attacked anyone."

Nico had no sooner gotten the words out of his mouth than one of the guards from the perimeter came into the hall and said, "Masters, the moat has frozen solid."

There was a moment of suspended silence, then incredulous denials.

"How could this have happened? Are we to be invaded?" Master Jorenson began to shift his gaze right and left, as if the very invading hordes were upon them.

If the situation hadn't been so dire, Nico would have laughed. *Oh, Theodyne, you are a marvel.*

"We also found one of the horses tied to a tree at the bottom of the hill near the wall." The guard stood like he expected punishment for the horse's seemingly errant behavior.

"So the horse never left the grounds?" Master Rhone's eyes narrowed. "How did the boy get over the wall?"

Nico turned. "What does it matter if the horse was never taken off school property? That animal belongs to me. I will lend it to whomever I choose with no interference from anyone. And as for the *boy*, I assure you, he is far from that."

Rhone's face flushed. "I beg forgiveness, my lord. I had not meant to cause offense."

Nico blew out a breath and walked away. It wasn't so much a retreat as a need for some time alone.

The sun cast a blinding light through the glass corridor. As Nico walked by, he glanced out the window. Somewhere out there Theodyne had taken it into his head to either cause a mischief or survey Delaneux. To what end, Nico had no clue.

Worry set in. By rights, it shouldn't have. If anyone stood a chance of getting in and out of Delaneux without being seen, it was Theodyne.

That didn't mean Nico had to like it. As a matter of fact, it angered him immensely. To take a chance like that when anyone seeing the scar on his cheek could turn him over to the local authorities was a risk not worth the price. And yet he had. But why?

Nico paced the halls for hours. His shoes sounded a lonely echo down the corridors after all the school's inhabitants had long gone to bed. He doubted even the mice were still awake. It was a long, lonely vigil.

He retired to the massive library. Rows of books went up as far as the high-domed ceiling. The shelves were built on a spiral, so the students and masters did not have to climb on rickety ladders all the way to the heavens to find a book. The cavernous room was made from cut rock and had the appearance of a hollowed-out mountain. When the light hit the walls in a certain way, tiny bits of precious gems sparkled and winked.

A fire roared in the grate. It was a perpetual flame that required neither log nor spark to keep it lit. It was made from the remains of a fire elemental who gave his immortal life to serve the alchemists who had protected his physical form so faithfully during the dark times—the years of the Great Purge.

"Evening, Anjufer."

The flame grew higher, dancing in delight to have Nico seated before him.

"It's been a long time." The words were more hiss of flame than actual enunciations, but Nico had listened to the peculiar speech patterns of the elemental since he was a small child. Translating the dialect of flames came easy.

Red-gold eyes blinked out at him from the twisting pyre, waiting for an explanation of why he'd come. It had always been so between them. If Nico was unsettled or confused, he'd seek comfort in the wisdom of this most noble and ancient being.

"I am troubled this night, old friend."

"The handsome apprentice with the mark of my kind upon his cheek."

Nico gave a huff that passed for a considering laugh. Yes, he supposed one of Anjufer's kind had kissed Theodyne's cheek—indirectly. The branding iron that burned in the thief's badge had known intimately the loving caress of fire.

And Theodyne had suffered for it.

"Yes. You've seen him?"

"He browsed the shelves for a brief time earlier. I believe his mind was otherwise engaged."

Which translated to: Theodyne hadn't stopped to gaze into Anjufer's ever-dancing form.

"Did he say anything? Were there others present?"

"He stood with his mouth open for a moment, staring up into the stacks." A dry crackle passed for a laugh. "There were only a few journeymen on the upper tiers doing research. I don't believe they even noticed him enter."

Nico rested his elbow on the chair arm and rubbed his chin. "He's remarkable. I've never met another like him. After only a few days with the primer, he's already turned the moat to ice."

Anjufer flared. His red-gold eyes blinked a few times. "Then he hasn't shared his secret."

Nico sat up. "Secret?"

The crackling laugh returned. "Perhaps it's best if you ask your man the means by which he was so successful a thief. I am certain you'll find the answer most enlightening."

Since Theodyne had first walked into the study, Nico knew a feeling the man was holding something back. It was there in the knowing glint of his eyes and the curve of his mysterious smile.

"What is the nature of this secret? Is it something that would bring harm to my house, or this school?"

"You do not need me to answer that for you when it is already there in your heart."

Yes, that was true. A spark, an ignition of spirit when they had first met. He'd trust Theodyne with his life and the safety of the school over others he'd known a lifetime.

"Then what am I to do, dear friend? He's out there on some endeavor he never asked leave to undertake."

"Leave? Would you require the same of Masters Rhone or Oberon? The thief may only hold the rank of apprentice, but he is by birthright your equal."

Nico scoffed. "Are you telling me he is from a titled family now fallen into disfavor?"

Anjufer flared in annoyance. "No. Those are constructs of man."

Higher than the offices bestowed by kings—that only made Nico more curious to hear the nature of Theodyne's secret.

Nico pushed up from the chair and made a circuit around the lower level. He rested his hand on a book here, a trinket there. All the history of the alchemists was held in this room. If this stronghold fell, it would deliver a devastating blow to the discipline.

He glanced around the room and up into the highest point. So many artifacts from centuries of practice were housed here: experiments that went wild and made unexpected but unique treasures, and spells that were so complex even the greatest masters had been unable to unravel their intricacies. A complete world of learning was held within the walls of the Delaneux facility. No other had quite the concentration of materials.

If the school and her contents should fall into the hands of the *prolate* and his clerics, it meant certain damnation for them all. Not by the Grand Matter or any of the Gods who served, but by the human courts. Sometimes that was worse.

"You have to trust in your apprentice. He keeps your best interests close to his heart."

Nico swung back to face Anjufer. If he didn't know better, he'd swear the fire elemental was smiling at him. Probably was—the ancient one had a rather mischievous sense of humor.

"I do trust him. I can't seem to fathom why the others have taken a dislike to him without even knowing him. That makes them as criminally judgmental as the *prolate* and his kind."

"They will come around. Give them time."

Nico rolled his eyes. "Time is something we do not have at present. We must get the headmaster out of his predicament and back to the teachings."

Anjufer roared, shooting his flames high into the chimney. "He brought those men here. Punishment is the only course."

Shocked at Anjufer's angry reaction, Nico made his way back to his old friend. "From what Master Rhone told me, they betrayed the headmaster when he offered a branch of peace."

"They would not have had the chance had he not opened the gates for them. If you and the others are not careful, you will see another Great Purge. It's there, lurking on the horizon like a dark sun."

A shiver swam down Nico's spine. So Anjufer felt the growing menace too. He nodded. "I will consider your words very carefully when I mount my defense."

"There is no defense. He *will* fall. It is assured."

"What have you heard?"

But Anjufer folded into himself, becoming nothing more than glowing embers in the grate. Nico would get no answer now.

Chapter Nine

THEODYNE HID his face from view. It wasn't that difficult given the fact Delaneux was in the throes of what looked to be some kind of night-vigil street fair. Upon entering the gates, all people were issued dark head wraps to drape over their hair. Since Theodyne had scaled the city wall, he'd taken his headwear from a drunk passed out beside a tavern.

Now he slunk around the environs as the revelers raised their cups to the sky and shouted toasts in an unfamiliar dialect. They must have been of foreign extraction, because Theodyne was certain they did not originally hail from inside the borders. He'd never heard that particular tongue before.

The *prolatial* palace was lit up like morning and towered over the other buildings. Even the grand cathedral in the center of town did not boast as high a spire as the residence of the city's governmental head.

As Theodyne neared, the sounds of a party coming from the massive estate sent joyous laughter and cries of delight into the street. People were dressed in colorful costumes, with plumed masks representing exotic birds.

He'd not discover anything of use with those costumes on, but perhaps it was to his advantage. If Theodyne was lucky enough to find another drunk, he might be able to take their costume and present himself as a guest.

He made his way to the front of the estate. Guards with pikes and the new gunpowder weapons stood on sentry. Lances were crossed to keep the uninvited from entering the gates.

One look at the guards and Theodyne knew simply walking through as if he belonged was not going to work. They meant business and took their duties seriously.

He'd have to find his own way onto the grounds. Not a great challenge. After getting off the school's lands, finding a way into the *prolate*'s estate would prove easy.

Theodyne walked around the perimeter, trying to appear as if he was out for a stroll among the festivalgoers. There were plenty of holes where the guards failed to patrol. It was as if they believed the inhabitants of Delaneux were too polite to climb a fence or wiggle through a hole to gain entrance.

After a thorough surveillance, Theodyne decided his best option was in the northwest corner of the property. Not only were there no guards present, but the heavy cover of trees and shrubbery afforded an abundance of natural cover.

The lower branches were the perfect height for swinging up and over the wall. In a few quick, efficient movements, Theodyne was inside the grounds. When he dropped down off the wall, dry leaves rustled under his feet. He stalled his movements for a moment in case someone was close enough to hear.

Theodyne bent a branch down, looking through the foliage to determine if anyone walked the garden paths. Not even the egress from the main house seemed occupied. The guests must have been warned to stay to the front gardens.

Theodyne had been to a lot of parties and there were always those who snuck off to find a quiet corner for a private assignation. It made the fact no one walked in the back gardens all the more suspicious.

He stepped from the bushes and started for the main house, following the rows of decorative fruit trees to use as a hiding place. It was as he came around the corner of the west side of the house that Theodyne saw something through the window that stopped him cold.

He blinked a few times to clear his eyes. No. He was seeing things. Had to be.

He moved just a little closer and rubbed at his eyes. No, he definitely *wasn't* seeing things. Cesare Medovin, Estobán's cousin, stood in a private study, engrossed in conversation with two men Theodyne did not recognize.

One man was dressed in the crimson robes of a *prolate*, while the other appeared in what looked like a burial shroud. Theodyne leaned forward and to the right to get a better look at the oddly dressed man, but saw nothing under the elaborate cowl of his robe. Only darkness.

A cold the likes of which Theodyne had never experienced before entered his body, going straight down to the very marrow of his bones. He crossed his arms and attempted to chafe the feeling away.

He was imagining things. The robes were merely some sort of costume from the celebration. The reason the man continued to wear the cowl to cover his face was simply the fact he didn't want anyone to recognize him, which only heightened Theodyne's curiosity about the stranger's identity.

What did the Medovins have their hands in this time? Were they trying to extend their reach out of Sadonia, to make a grab for city-state of Calabris, the seat of Delaneux, as well? It was no telling with that lot. They overstepped their boundaries at every turn.

Politics was a dirty business, and in some places more than others. Theodyne had no doubt that Cesare was into some underhanded dealings that did not bode well for the Calabrisians or citizens of Delaneux.

Theodyne moved closer, to hear even a small word or phrase of their conversation, but the glass was too thick and allowed no sound to penetrate to the yards. The structure had probably been built that way for that reason.

He dared not get close enough for Cesare to see him. They'd had an ugly falling-out in the weeks before he and Estobán had dissolved their relationship. Cesare had never been in favor of his cousin falling in love with a man so far beneath their station. The Medovins only consorted with those of the ruling classes. Nico would have been more to their taste.

Curiosity fueled Theodyne forward. He really wanted to find out more about what the men were discussing and discover the identity of the hidden one. He crept along the outside wall of the estate, careful to keep low around the windows.

The servants' entrance was probably the best place to get inside. He doubted there were many coming in or out from that direction with a party taking place in the front garden. The door was located down a set of stone steps that most likely led directly into the kitchen. Theodyne tried the handle and was not surprised to find it unlocked.

He entered and made his way down a short, dark hall. A light shone at the end, a soft glow as if from a fire. Voices rang out with the various orders and commands that came with working in a busy kitchen of the affluent.

Theodyne walked toward the sounds. An intersection of two more hallways came right before the area opened up into the kitchen proper. Theodyne ducked down the one to the left.

Instead of landing in a bypassing corridor, he ended up in the pantry.

The door opened behind him. "Hurry and find that butter, boy."

Theodyne mumbled that he was looking. "It must all be gone."

"Don't speak back to me or cook will hear of it."

Theodyne began to open barrels and lift canvases, searching for anything that might contain extra butter.

"Oh, stand out of my way, will you." The man pushed him against a case of cheeses. Theodyne's hand came down in something soft and stinky. He stayed put as the man picked up a large vat and carried it out of the room without looking back.

When the man's footsteps no longer echoed back to the pantry, Theodyne made his way out from the pile of assorted cheeses. As quietly as possible, he walked back to the cross hall and went right. It was the servants' quarters.

At least this way made more sense. Servants had to be able to move quickly and efficiently from one place to another when summoned. There had to be access to the main house from this area. To build such a residence any other way was foolish and impractical.

Theodyne used every tool in his thief's memory to walk silently through the halls. It wasn't as much a skill as an automatic response. The movements of his body and caution in his stride were as much a part of him as breathing. No stint in the prison of Pallonia could ever take away such deeply ingrained behaviors.

With most of those who lived and worked at the estate busy attending to the guests, Theodyne moved through the rooms unchallenged. He found the salon where Cesare and the other men talked. They were still involved in the conversation. Now the words were harsh, forceful. Not surprising, considering Cesare was involved. That man had the ability to make even the most serene of deities want to commit murder. He was self-serving, with little sacrifice to his own skin.

Theodyne entered the room next door and positioned himself against the wall. He leaned his ear against the stucco-roughened surface and listened.

"… they will fold. Trust me."

"I trust no one when it comes to bringing down the alchemists." The voice was scratchy, coarse, as if it hadn't been used in centuries.

"I should be offended by that statement, your most excellent *necromon*. However, I'm willing to let it go for the greater good. If you believe you know a better way to oust them from the mountain, then, by all means enlighten me."

"I assure you, I do." The abrasive voice was filled with as much menace as confidence.

There was a huff and the dull *thump* of something weighty being set down on a wooden surface.

"Ignatius, you've forever taken the world too seriously." Cesare Medovin's voice grew closer, as if he was directly on the other side of the wall from Theodyne. "This is a time to rejoice. The headmaster is in our control. It is only a matter of time until he cracks and all the alchemists' secrets will be revealed."

Theodyne shook his head. Even if they knew all the secrets, they were unlikely to be able to access or utilize them to their benefit. The worse thing was the fact they were trying to take over the school. It sounded more as if they wished to absorb the alchemists into the fold rather than have them killed. If they wanted Donando dead, they'd have done so by now—unless they were waiting for him to crack. Even so, it was no kind of fate for the sorcerers to await.

But why go to all the trouble? If they wanted the alchemists' help for some grand purpose, why did they not ask for their aid? Because it was something they knew the alchemists would never do willingly.

"My sources tell me that the descendant of Mercurian Dante has arrived at the school. Even now he plots to gain the headmaster's freedom." Cesare's tone had taken on a more serious guise when he spoke of Nico. There was bad blood there. The animosity leaked through the wall and threatened to choke Theodyne where he stood.

"He will fail. He must know that by now. When was the last time we let an alchemist go without some form of punishment?" There was a brief pause. "I never liked having that damn stronghold so close to the town. It puts all kinds of thoughts into young people's heads."

"And undermines your authority."

"Yes. They undermine *all* authority and live outside the laws of man."

"Would you live within the prescribed dictates of government if you possessed power to bend the elements to your will?" The scratchy voice slid seamlessly into the conversation. Darkness dripped from every word.

"I am not so disingenuous with myself to believe I'd be even remotely gracious with such gifts." Theodyne had no doubt that for once Cesare spoke the truth.

Theodyne regretted the fact he hadn't arrived in time to hear the entirety of the conversation, but at least it was enough to take back to Nico.

He sat and waited in the dark. Perhaps they'd say something more to incriminate themselves. Problem was that with the conspiracy involving the local vessel of law, there would be no justice for the headmaster, regardless of how good an argument or large a bribe Nico prepared. As they said, the outcome was preordained.

"There are also reports their moat has been frozen."

Theodyne sat up straight. Dearest heavens! If they knew enough to realize the moat had changed forms, then they had someone either patrolling the grounds close to the school, or a conspirator on the inside feeding information to the *prolate* and his cronies.

"Who knows the why and ways of the things they do, Ignatius." Cesare sounded almost dismissive of this new information. "It may have been students practicing their skills. I wouldn't read anything into it."

Theodyne breathed a slight sigh of relief. At least Cesare Medovin didn't believe anything untoward had happened at the school that day, with the exception of Nico's arrival.

No wonder Master Rhone sent a courier to deliver the letter to the villa rather than send it via some other form of communication. Normally, he'd think going overland was more of a risk with any kind of correspondence. But if Master Rhone knew that one of the trusted members of his household had been feeding information to the *prolate*, he might have decided there was more of a chance for interception if he sent the missive through alternate means.

Whatever the situation, Theodyne had enough information to feel his trip down the mountain to Delaneux had been worth the risk. Quietly, he rose and made his way out of the room and back through the residence.

The high, shrill laughter of serving maids floated down the corridor. Theodyne hid in a dark corner, letting his black scarf conceal him as best as possible. He sucked in his breath and held it, as if even that bodily function might see him discovered.

The women drew closer. Their constant chatter and insipid conversation kept them occupied as they turned and went in the opposite direction.

Theodyne waited a few moments, listening for any other company. The only noises he heard were those that filtered in from the party and from the industry of the kitchen staff.

He slipped back down through the servants' quarters and out into the night.

THE DISTINCT click of a door closing woke Nico as if it was a cannon blast. He'd only gone to bed an hour before. He rose and pulled a robe over his sleeping gown.

The sun was an orange glow in the eastern sky, barely making a presence in the window. It was a damnable hour for an apprentice to get in after a night out doing only the elements knew what.

Nico opened the door to Theodyne's room and caught him with his shirt off, bathing at the water pitcher. Arrested by the scene, he watched for a moment before clearing his throat to alert Theodyne to his presence.

Theodyne turned and picked up a cloth. He dabbed at his skin. There were a few scratches on his chest and arms. His fingers looked sore at the tips.

"Where have you been?"

"In Delaneux. At the *prolate*'s estate, to be exact." He threw the towel down beside the water bowl. "He's in league with Cesare Medovin."

Nico came fully into the room and closed the door behind him. "Are you positive?"

"I know Cesare very well. I'd never mistake him for anyone else."

Nico took a chair near the simple desk and turned the seat around so he could see Theodyne. "Why didn't you tell me where you were going? I had to cover for you. A stable lad accused you of horse thievery and beating him bloody."

"The horse?"

"The lad."

Theodyne's eyes grew wide. There was no guile or dissembling in his manner. "I never hit that boy. He never even came close to me."

"I didn't think you did."

"Do your friends believe him?"

"Does it matter?"

Theodyne sat on the bed and pulled his knees up. "Not as such. People are going to believe what they want of me. It's easy to imagine me capable of hurting a child."

"Not for me." Nico captured Theodyne's gaze and held it. "If the other masters think ill of you, that is to their disadvantage."

They lapsed into silence. The only sound in the room was that of Theodyne's breathing. It was a bit labored, harsh.

"Are you feeling ill?" Nico stood and placed his hand against Theodyne's forehead. Theodyne covered Nico's hand with his own and held it flush against his skin.

"Your touch is cool."

"And you have come back with a fever. Into bed with you. We can talk more of what you discovered after you rest a while."

"I need more than a rest. I need some herbs to drive this illness out. I felt fine when I went down the mountain. It was the trek back up that did me in." Theodyne turned and stretched out on the narrow bed. "You should know there might be a traitor in the school. I heard the *prolate* tell Cesare about the frozen moat. Nico, I only did that before going down the mountain. If he didn't hear about it from someone guarding the school, then he's set up regular patrols in hopes of finding a way in."

Nico pulled the blanket over Theodyne's chest. "You've done the school a valuable service tonight, but now it's time to rest."

Theodyne grabbed at Nico's wrist, but his grip was weak. His hand slid back onto the covers. "There is something else... burial shrouds. Darkness. I can't remember now exactly."

No sooner had he said the words than Theodyne's eyes slid closed and soft snores began to rise from his nose.

Nico leaned down and kissed Theodyne's forehead, sending him off into deep slumber with the act.

So there was a traitor in the school. How were they to go about flushing the guilty one out?

He returned to his own room and dressed in his formal robes, then summoned Pedraus.

"You require me, sir?"

"Yes. I want you to inform the Adepts' Council that I wish to meet with them in the council chamber immediately."

"Yes, sir."

Pedraus shuffled from the room. It would take the servant some time to contact the council members and get them assembled. In the meantime, Nico needed to speak with Anjufer.

Nico went to the fireplace and knocked on the flue a few times. It was a primitive way to call the fire elemental, but effective.

The chimneys and flues doubled as a series of conduits that allowed Anjufer to move freely about the school. A subtle roar rumbled through the ducts as Anjufer rolled into Nico's room.

"A summons? You must be in trouble."

"Not me in particular." Nico took a place in front of the fire. "It has come to my attention that we may have a *prolate* infiltrator in our midst."

"If so, it is no one with whom I've had contact. I'll ask the other elementals and see what they say."

"I'll wait to hear from you. And thank you."

Anjufer angled the top of his flame slightly in a nod then bended his form in half and gave what passed for a small bow.

"For now, I wondered if you would care to accompany me to the council room for a meeting with the adepts."

"You do not trust those you've placed in positions of authority?"

Nico gave a shrug. "I have no way of knowing. Many of them came here from other schools, and I've been away for a long time. It's hard to tell when an apple goes bad if the skin is still intact."

"Ah, but it does give signs of turning putrid long before it outwardly shows."

That was true enough spoken.

Anjufer flared for a second. "I will go there now and wait. The masters will not even realize I am in the room."

With that, the fire elemental was gone, leaving Nico alone.

He leaned against the back of the chair and rubbed his chin. There were too many variables in the school at the moment to feel comfortable leaving anything to chance. Not knowing if he should trust men who had devoted years of service to studying the alchemical arts left a bitter taste in his mouth. He hated to imagine one of the masters, students, or servants on the dole with the *prolate*. Accusations such as those changed the entire landscape.

And what about Headmaster Donando? He'd been betrayed by the clerics, yes, but what if the clerics had help?

No matter. Nico would have to play along with the *prolate*'s game until he came up with a way to extricate the school from the web.

Nico made his way to the council room. Students were on their way to classes. Memories swirled around him as he watched the action in a detached manner. It seemed a thousand years since he'd walked the sacred halls in apprentice robes.

He'd known for years that something was off within the order, but he had thought the threat came from outside, not that their enemies had placed someone inside. A wry smile curled his mouth. If Theodyne were here, he'd probably mention they'd been in place for some time. And he'd be right.

Perhaps the spy had been living with them for years. One of the apprentices now turned journeyman or even first-level master. Why not? What better way to learn the secrets of an organization than to place a spy inside as a student? All the teachings would be there for the taking. Every concept, every jewel of wisdom fallen into the hands of men who had no business knowing the crux of alchemy.

Nico entered the council chamber. Some of the masters had already assembled. Masters Gideon, Erhnheart, and Padrig stopped their conversation as Nico made his way to his seat.

All of them looked as if they'd been ripped from their beds and hadn't taken time to consult a mirror before making their way to the meeting. Not that it mattered. Good hair and uncreased faces were not a prerequisite for listening to what he had to tell the other masters.

Nico took the place at the head of the table. All three men stared at him, waiting for him to reveal some small detail of why they'd assembled.

Into the silence, Master Erhnheart cleared his throat. "Has your apprentice returned, Nico?"

"Yes. That is why I've called a meeting of the council."

Master Gideon narrowed his eyes. "I hope you thrashed him soundly for laying hands on that stable lad."

Nico folded his hands in front of him. "I did no such thing, as he assured me he was unjustly accused."

"Pfft." Gideon made a noise. "How likely is that? Do you think the boy beat himself against a tree?"

"I don't know how or who did the deed, but I will get to the bottom of that story."

The door opened and some of the other masters entered. Master Iowain was cross. He pulled out a chair and sat, grumbling the entire time.

Nico raised a brow. "What was that, Iowain?"

"This could have waited until a decent hour."

"And if we wait for a so-called *decent hour,* the school might be overrun by the *prolate*'s men. Are you willing to risk that?" He didn't bother to hide the scorn or tartness from his voice. He was angry, and it seemed as if the entire populace of the school had decided they were above it all. What did they think all their powers were for?

He waited until all the masters were seated. Rhone was the last to arrive, and he did not look at all happy to be summoned from his bed as the sun rose.

Nico glanced slowly around the room, at each of his brothers, and then stood. "I have called this council to discuss new information I've received on the state of our struggle against the *prolate*."

Rhone rolled his eyes skyward. "And this couldn't have waited?"

"No, it could not." Nico rested his palms against the table and leaned forward. "You contacted me to tell me that the headmaster was imprisoned and the school in jeopardy. I expected to arrive and find the place in turmoil. Instead, I have been treated as if my coming here was an imposition at the least."

"Headmaster Donando should never have let those men inside." This came from Master Gervaise.

Across the table from him, Master Iowain sputtered. "Have you lost your mind? It was the only way to negotiate any kind of a peace in this region."

"It was a way for them to get inside and catalog our treasures."

"They already know," Nico said, loud enough to be heard over their escalating argument. "I have it on good authority that the *prolate* may have a man or two of his own working inside these very walls."

The silence that descended after that remark was as absolute as the grave.

Nico let it stretch out until the other masters visibly squirmed in their chairs and stared at one another, as if afraid to break the tableau.

"It is unclear to me who the traitor or spies may be, but I promise I will find them out before I return to the villa." He sat back down. "In the meantime, I will meet today with the headmaster and discover what, if anything, he knows on the subject."

Master Oberon shook his head in a grim manner. "I doubt you'll learn anything useful from him, but I'd like to accompany you on the trip to the prison."

"Thank you. I'd be most grateful for your companionship." He turned to Master Finelli. "If you will ride with us as well, I will appreciate it."

"As you wish, Nicodemus."

Master Finelli was a steady hand. Old and sagacious in the ways of alchemy, he had been a contemporary of Nico's father.

"I also want to point out that there is a connection with *Prolate* Ignatius Agia and the Medovin family." Nico leaned back in his chair. "This makes me extremely nervous."

Rhone made a face. "Why should it? All men of power associate with one another. They might have been meeting about anything from commerce to a marriage between the families."

Nico went very still. "That is true enough. It isn't, however, what was overheard."

"Overheard?" Master Erhnheart leaned forward, looking down the table at Nico. "Do you have a man inside the *prolate*'s palace?"

"My apprentice is a very resourceful individual. He also happens to know the members of the Medovin family on sight. Cesare Medovin is in town, and it does not look good for our school."

"Why should the Medovins even care about the Gold School?" This from Master Atolla.

"Because we are a power to be reckoned with and one they do not control."

At that point it all fell into place for Nico. The Medovins, Agia, the threat to the schools, the spies. All of it had a rhyme, reason, and rationale. There was a larger agenda than merely taking the headmaster into custody. The trouble was getting to the root of what it was the Medovins and Agia wanted.

"Let me make my stance perfectly clear. In no way or at no time will this school or any of the institutions in the Gold tradition cleave to a governmental power. I am firm on this. If any of you oppose me, you may be set free from your obligations here. Is that understood?"

The other masters looked to each other before turning to Nico and nodding.

All save Rhone. He sat at the other end of the table, making his hands into a steeple. He glanced over his fingertips with dark, cunning eyes. "Perhaps there are some things brewing you do not know. I'd reserve such sweeping statements until you have all the facts."

Nico leaned back in his seat. He flipped his hand at Rhone, indicating he had the floor. "By all means, enlighten me as to the *facts*."

Rhone looked as if he had a bad case of dyspepsia. "There are forces out there who wish to unite all the city-states on the peninsula."

Nico waved that statement away. "There have been rumblings of that nature for the last hundred years. There is always one family or another who wishes to consolidate their power base and control the entire country of Dominicál and, in turn, the church. I'm surprised you've given those old rumors credence."

"My sources say this time it might be possible. The *demigoge* is very ill. If he dies, then there will be intrigues, alliances, and deals made to assure his successor. Depending on who takes the holy throne, power lines will shift."

"This is nothing new. Every time the Council of *Cardgrans* meets to elect a new *demigoge*, there are power struggles within the families who control the city-states. It's been that way since the founding," Nico pointed out. "I'm more interested in the new *demigoge* and if he will be friendly to the alchemists or burn us as heretics."

"If we play our cards right, the new *demigoge* will not only be friendly to our plight, but embrace it."

It was a bold statement. Too bold. But Nico was ready to roll with it for the sake of argument. More maneuverings could be illuminated by mere conversation than if he refused to discuss the matter. Besides, how many of the masters felt that way? Perhaps he should put it to the vote once it was discussed.

"And how do you propose we *play* these cards, Rhone? Are you suggesting we place our own candidate up for the post of *demigoge*? I'm afraid none of our brothers of the crucible are qualified for the position."

Rhone gave Nico a sly smile. He knew something, and it made him arrogant. Not once in all their long years of friendship had Nico ever felt he knew Rhone less than at that moment. It was as if the memories crumbled and turned to dust, then blew away on the wind.

"There are those who are more amenable to our plight than others. Some on the short list of clerics who would be gracious to the alchemists are *Cardgran* Faris from Brixton, *Cardgran* Weeks from Trumolo, and *Cardgran* Xaviar from Flurian."

Nico rubbed his jaw in thought. He'd hate to ever owe anything to a *demigoge* or the *cardgrans* who served him. "My concern is what we'd give up in return for their protection. Do they expect us to mint a steady supply of gold and riches for them?"

Rhone had the decency to look away.

"Ah, I thought as much. Having an entire community of alchemists at one's disposal is very attractive if one wishes to raise an army." Nico shook his head. "I have no stomach for wars of any kind."

"But there will be war. The city-states will not stand long against the outside threats of Auger and the Balderic throne unless they band together." Rhone seemed to know more than he should about the situation. He'd turned into quite the politico while Nico had been away.

"There has always been war. It is a matter for kings and princes, not for us."

"And if the city-states fall one by one? Would you rather be forced to swear allegiance to a foreign king than a *prolate* from the city-states?" Rhone challenged.

"If the time comes to choose sides, I'll take it under advisement. Until then we have our own cancer to excise." Nico stood. "That is all for now."

The other masters filed out of the room. The only ones left were Oberon and Finelli.

"When are we leaving for the court?" Oberon asked.

"As soon as we've had a proper meal. I don't wish to go into the *prolate*'s palace on an empty stomach."

They made their way to the dining hall. Students were assembled there, grabbing a meal before the beginning of their next classes.

The only thing Nico really wanted to do was meet with the headmaster and ensure he was being treated well despite the seriousness of the charges. If that included a meeting with Prolate Agia, then so be it.

"First, I want to go check on my apprentice. He returned from Delaneux with a fever."

"Oh no." Finelli covered his mouth with a hand. "First Jolen and now your apprentice. Something happens to our men whenever they leave the school property. I've had my eye on it for a while and can't seem to put my finger on it."

"I believe Jolen's was caused from an infection he contracted riding to Lancor. He'd developed sores from the saddle."

Finelli frowned. "Those aren't the only cases. I sent my journeyman, Madric, down to Delaneux to leave a letter with an herbalist, and the very next day, down with a fever."

"How long ago was that?"

"A few weeks maybe. Before the uproar with the headmaster." Finelli started moving again, watching his feet as he walked, as if that position helped him think. "Before that were two others. Apprentices who went to the village to view a painting that was being moved in from a private collection to the rotunda at the cathedral."

"Were they all able to shake their symptoms?"

"Yes, I believe so. One of the apprentices missed several days' worth of study. He came down worse than his classmate." Finelli tapped his lips. "I really didn't think much of it at the time. We were having odd weather, and there wasn't a reported outbreak of fever coming from Delaneux. It has not escaped my notice, though, that all those infected are of elemental blood."

Nico considered the report. Right now there wasn't much to go on but a few isolated incidents. However, if the boys were of varying blood and exposed to a contagion in town it might mean nothing. But something that affected only the elementals—that was definitely something to take a closer look at.

He clapped Finelli on the back. "I'll be down in a few minutes. Start your meal without me."

Nico nodded to Oberon and turned to leave.

With Theodyne, this was the fifth case, though Nico would hesitate to include Jolen in those numbers. He was almost sure Jolen's fever was secondary to the infection in his leg. However, it never paid to discount anything until further investigation. He'd make it a point to interview Jolen in the afternoon.

Nico made it to their suites and heard a terrible wheeze coming from Theodyne's bedchamber. He hurried inside and found Theodyne with his hand on his chest, trying to draw in air.

"By the Elementals!" Nico threw open the window and rang for a servant.

He took a place next to Theodyne on the bed and pulled him up into his arms. "How long have you been like this?" Nico shook his head. "Never mind. Don't talk now. Concentrate on drawing in air."

Theodyne clawed at Nico's shoulders and back. The wheeze became louder, more desperate.

Pedraus entered the room as fast as his bandy legs could carry him. "Yes, sir?"

"Get me something—anything to help clear his lungs."

Pedraus disappeared again. There was the sound of rummaging and thumps coming from a storage cabinet. Pedraus came back with a vial, stoppered at one end. "Open the top and put some of the liquid underneath his nose."

Nico tried to do as instructed, but Theodyne merely slumped against him, beyond Nico's capacity to help. "Here, hold him so I can see what I'm doing."

Gently, Nico leaned Theodyne away from him. Pedraus gripped Theodyne's shoulders as Nico opened the bottle and rubbed some of the strong, noxious substance under Theodyne's nose. He tried to turn his head away from the fumes.

"No. Hold still. Give it a chance to work."

Theodyne's eyes were wide with panic. His breathing changed, became calmer. He started taking big gulps into his lungs. "Oh Gods. Oh Gods."

At least Theodyne could talk again. He fell back on the bed and put his hand up over his forehead. "I… thought… I… was… dead."

"You're all right now. Take it easy. Slow, deep breaths."

Theodyne grabbed Nico's hand and held tightly. "Don't leave."

"I'll stay for a bit. Then I really must go see the headmaster."

Theodyne nodded. His eyes were closed. There was a faint sheen of sweat that broke out on his face and chest.

Nico picked up the vial again. "What is this?"

"Camphor. Eucalyptus leaves and a few secret ingredients. It's been known to open the airways when people have the breathing sickness." Pedraus tapped the bottle. "My own papa swore by it. I never go anywhere without it."

"Good thing." He set the bottle on the bedside table. "Mind if we leave it here for Theodyne in case he needs it again?"

"No. But he'll not need any more. It's potent stuff, that."

Truly, Theodyne looked to be breathing more comfortably. The wheeze was gone. He still held Nico's hand, but not as tightly. Nico placed his free hand on top of them.

Fear had a way of easing out of a body after the initial panic fled, leaving a person shaken. Thoughts seemed to take chaotic paths. None of them productive.

"Knock on the flue, Pedraus."

"Yes, sir." Pedraus did as told, but without the necessary skill or rhythm used to call Anjufer. However, Nico didn't think that it would matter. Anjufer would know where the sound came from and follow it, no matter how cacophonous.

The fire elemental dropped down as a tiny ember, then came to life. Pedraus jumped back, startled at the sight.

"Keep an eye on Master Rhone while I'm away today. Report back on anything you might discover that is out of place."

Anjufer blinked and went back up the flue.

Nico turned to Pedraus. "And I want you to stay with Theodyne. Do not leave him unless it's to go get food or water. Better yet, I'll assign two of the apprentices to be at your beck and call."

"Yes, sir."

Nico leaned back over Theodyne. He gently pulled the man's arm away from where it covered his face. Two bright patches of color were high on his cheeks. The scar from the thief's badge cut a dramatic contrast with its puckered white flesh.

"Will you be all right?"

"I have to be." His voice was low and gravelly. "I've never had my breath taken before. Not once in all the sicknesses I had in prison."

"I'm leaving you in capable hands. And I promise to come here and check on you straightaway when I return."

Theodyne nodded. "Go. I can manage now."

Nico had no doubt Theodyne could do anything he set his mind to. He'd proven that when he'd frozen a boiling moat with no more than his own will and half a primer behind him.

Chapter Ten

NICO AND the Masters Oberon and Finelli arrived at the palace of the *prolate*. Heavily armed guards held them at spear point until they were cleared by the guard captain to enter the complex.

Judicial proceedings were conducted in one of the smaller outbuildings to the left of the complex proper. There were several rooms where the guilty were imprisoned until their so-called trials could be held and sentences imposed.

Headmaster Donando was one such prisoner. His accommodations were only a step up from squalor. Nico didn't understand how one end of the *prolate*'s palace maintained the latest in furnishings and textiles while the prison section appeared as if it suffered from chronic neglect.

They were led under armed guard to wait in a small cramped room with hardly any light and even less ventilation.

The door closed behind them as one of the guards went to collect the prisoner. The other guard stood inside the door, watching the three alchemists with unconcealed contempt.

Nico sat perfectly still, listening to the sounds filtering in from the common grounds and the street in front of the palace proper. For all that he gave the world his services and made alchemy accessible to the masses if they so wished, Nico had no stomach for government officials. Instead of being in power to help the people, they oftentimes fed off their constituency like parasites. If Nico was against helping to unite the peninsula, it should not have been a surprise to any of the other masters who knew him.

What surprised Nico most was Master Rhone's stance. How could any one man change so materially in so short a time? What did a man who could transmute metals into gold and rocks into precious stones covet from a government body? Immunity? Free rein? He should have been above the want for power and prestige.

There was a knock on the door, and the guard moved to answer the summons. The second guard entered with Donando. The headmaster did not look worse for his incarceration. He appeared well fed and his clothes, though rumpled, only showed the slightest signs of dirt.

"Nico?" Donando blinked as if having trouble adjusting to the dim light of the room. "Oberon? Finelli?"

Nico stood and indicated the vacant chair across the table from him. "Please, be seated. We need to discuss the charges against you."

Donando rolled his eyes heavenward. "There is nothing to discuss. I made a deal with the devil, and he wanted his due."

Those sounded more like the words of a cleric than an alchemist. "I'm told you invited the clerics into the school."

Donando leaned forward as if about to convey a confidence. "War is coming, Nico. It is as certain as the sun and constant as the stars. We need to choose sides or be swept away on a tide of destruction."

Oberon cleared his throat. "And you wish us to align ourselves with the clerics? Whose side do they fight for?"

Donando turned to him. "The clerics hold sway over the city-states. Without them and their support, the individual territories will fall."

Finelli made a churlish sound in the back of his throat. "That may be true, but what do we gain? It seems the Gold School has everything to lose in this proposition."

"We will if we don't choose sides now." Donando spread his hands before him as if the outcome was a foregone conclusion.

Nico leaned back in his chair. The wood creaked under his weight. "I will admit, if I chose any side it would be those families and city-states that have been very kind to our discipline in the past." He held up a finger in caution. "However, I am not inclined to trust any religious or political body that is not accountable to us."

"I did not mean to place the school in jeopardy." Donando's dark eyes were filled with contrition.

"What I fail to understand is why the clerics turned on you? If you invited them there to discuss a possible alliance, then why did they feel the need to charge you with heresy and bring you to the palace?"

"Terms." Donando gave a shrug. "We could not agree on terms."

Red, like crimson rivers of blood, painted Nico's vision. Anger forced him out of his seat. The guards put their hands on their weapons in case Nico charged them. They had nothing to fear from him. Donando, now, he was another story.

Nico made a few circuits of the room, trying to expend the killing rage that swarmed inside him like a thousand bees. He came back around to the side of the table where Donando sat. He braced his arms on either side of the headmaster and leaned in, lowering his voice to a menacing growl. "Who gave you the right to negotiate with anyone on the school's behalf?"

Donando flapped his lips a few times.

"You know my feelings on such matters and yet you tried to go behind my back and take the school and her students into directions that were never intended. Did you sell our secrets to the highest bidder as well?"

"No. Nico."

Nico pushed away from the table and made his way to the door. The scrape of chairs across the floor told him Oberon and Finelli had risen to join him. Once he walked out the door, he would never come back. Anjufer was right; Donando had betrayed the school, the students, and his fellow masters. Whatever punishment the *prolate* decided to inflict on Donando would be more than adequate. From now on, Donando was no longer under the protection or auspices of the Gold School.

THE RIDE back up the mountain was quiet. Oberon and Finelli did not offer advice or condolences. The laws of the alchemists were clear: betrayal met with ostracism. There was nothing other than honor to stop the former headmaster from selling the secrets. But he'd lost that when he'd tried to make a clandestine deal with the clerics.

They rode through the gates of the school and dismounted from their horses as the two young boys came to grab the reins. One of them was the lying little stable lad from the day before.

Nico held the reins of his horse when the boy tried to take them. He looked down with a menacing frown. "You have much to explain, young man."

"Master?"

"I want the name of the person who beat you, and I want no lies or misinformation."

The boy tried to grab the reins again to attempt an escape. "I said who. It was the thief."

Nico shook his head. "No. It was not. My apprentice assures me he had nothing to do with your injuries, and I have no reason to doubt his word."

"Master Rhone will believe me." The boy puffed out his thin chest as if issuing a challenge.

"And Master Rhone, though the under-headmaster, has no authority higher than mine."

The boy looked temporarily confused.

Master Oberon crouched down to be more on a level with the lad. "Tell Master Nico the truth or risk being turned out of the school. It is no place for a lad your size to wander the streets, looking for work and food."

The boy swallowed. His eyes rounded. "I can't tell you. I will be punished if I do. Worse than being turned out."

Nico and Oberon exchanged glances. "Someone threatened you if you did not stick to your story?"

The child realized his mistake and broke out into gales of tears. "I don't want to leave the school. I love the barn and the smell of the horses. They're my friends."

Nico's heart broke for the lad. "Listen, there are people who want to see our school fall. They want to take away everything my ancestors struggled to create. Your silence ensures they win."

"But... but...." The boy's lip trembled. "He said it would fall if I didn't keep my mouth shut."

Nico released the reins. "Put the horse away and make sure Ambrosia here gets an extra good brushing."

The boy nodded. He petted the horse's muzzle and spoke softly to it in a language unfamiliar to Nico. He frowned and turned to Oberon when the boy guided the horse away.

"Where does he hail from?"

"He's a foundling. As a matter of fact, he showed up sleeping in the stables one morning. We aren't really sure how he got in there, or up the mountain and onto the property for that matter." Oberon started toward the front steps. "You don't think he was brought here as the spy, do you?"

"There is a possibility. But who would he report to and when?" One small boy going down the mountain alone and without the aid of a horse or other beast to carry him was going to be noticed by the guards. He doubted the lad had the ability to stop the boiling moat, like Theodyne.

"Keep an eye on him."

Master Finelli was already halfway up the steps to the main hall. The old man walked as if his heart were breaking. His shoulders slumped forward and his feet shuffled hollowly.

"He is very close to Donando," Oberon said, nodding to the elderly master. "I wouldn't be surprised if he'd tried to talk him out of his decision a time or two."

"Did you know about Donando's plans?" Nico wondered if the entire faculty knew about the push to meet with the clerics.

"Not as such. I knew he'd planned a summit with the clerics, but I thought he was to speak with them on behalf of our students."

Nico and Oberon entered the main hall. There was an ominous feeling to the building, as if it now acknowledged the virus that spread through its corridors.

"You need to explain that remark, Oberon. I'm afraid I don't understand what the clerics have to do with our students."

Oberon took a deep breath and let it out. He stopped in the hall, pulling on the sleeve of Nico's robe so he'd stop as well. "There are several boys in Delaneux who have the potential to be educated by the Gold School. The aura reader tested them positive for the capabilities. When their parents were approached by the school, they were delighted. The contracts were signed and enrollment enlisted. Only thing is, they never showed up for classes. When the parents were contacted again, the boys had been taken in by the church instead. Seems they are now training for holy orders."

Nico gave a huff. "So either we side with them, or they are going to see us wiped out by sheer lack of enrollment."

"This is only one town." Oberon leaned in and lowered his voice. "I took the liberty of contacting the other schools when I learned of the problem. They have not reported the same incidents. I'm hoping it is isolated to Delaneux."

"If so, we can thwart their efforts by bringing students in from other towns. We don't have to stock this facility with locals." They started walking again. "There is another matter I need assistance with before you tend to your duties."

"Yes, anything, Nico."

"I need the files on those apprentices and journeymen who came down with the fever after venturing to Delaneux."

"Of course. I'll bring them to your suite."

"Thank you. Now, if you'll excuse me, I want to check on Theodyne. He wasn't breathing well before I left for the prison."

Oberon gave a head bow and left by way of the staircase that led to the offices.

Nico took the opposite stairs to the private suites. Anticipation tempered with worry hummed in his blood the closer he came to the room. If anything had happened to Theodyne, someone would have met him at the front. They'd not have let him go to his suites without first warning him something was amiss.

He entered the suite to a whispered voice. There was no reply to whatever was said, so the speaker had either to be talking to himself or reading out loud.

Quietly, he made his way to Theodyne's chamber and found him on the bed with his arm draped over his face, talking in his sleep. His mouth moved quickly, as if he only had a certain amount of time allotted to get all the words out.

When Nico leaned closer, he noticed the words were taken directly from the primer. Not just any section either, but the encoded chapter.

A smile tweaked the corner of Nico's mouth. He sat down next to Theodyne on the bed. The movement woke him. He turned to Nico and frowned. "You're back early."

"Not much to say to a man who admits he brought the clerics in here and tried to negotiate a deal with them for our support."

Theodyne pushed himself up to a sitting position, leaning against the wall to face Nico. "Why would he do that?"

"I have a feeling the masters are running scared of the forces of government within the borders. They fear a foreign invasion and power struggle if the city-states fall." Nico looked out the small window of Theodyne's room. "I can't say I blame them for worrying, but selling us out to the church is not the way to combat the problem."

"What can you do?"

"As is written in the codex of our laws, I have turned the headmaster out. He is no longer a member of the Gold School."

"Nico," Theodyne breathed. He placed his hand on Nico's shoulder, giving comfort as if he knew the toll such a decision took on the soul. Perhaps he did.

"I have only to discover who else has sold out our brothers, locate the spies inside the school, and then we can return home."

"Do you have to appoint a new headmaster?"

"Yes. I fear my decision is going to anger a few of the masters in residence."

"So you already have a candidate under consideration?"

"I do." Nico rubbed his face. "I want to leave nothing to chance."

"Then don't be too hasty in your decision. It might be one you live to regret." Theodyne scooted off the bed and stood at the washbasin.

Nico watched the play of sleek muscles under Theodyne's skin. There was a series of white scars that laced up and down Theodyne's back. More evidence of his harsh life. "The stableboy would not give me the name of the man who beat him, but he did intimate that if he does tell, he will be punished."

Theodyne splashed water on his face, then turned. His expression was all hard planes and lines. There was little sympathy there. "I am sorry for that, but he cannot be allowed to falsely accuse someone of such a deed, no matter how tempting the target."

"I think it's more a matter of being a convenient one. It wasn't a matter of personal attack on you, but more to take suspicion away from the culprit."

Theodyne turned fully now. He brushed a hand towel over his face. "And you're all right with that?"

Nico gazed into Theodyne's eyes so his words would not be mistaken. "No. I'm most certainly not all right with it, but since I draw the line at flogging a child to get the answers I want, I don't see how I have any choice."

Theodyne looked down at his hands. "Then you're a better man than most."

"I don't feel as though I am. As a matter of fact, I'm suddenly feeling like a ship on a storm-tossed ocean with a broken rudder and fallen mast."

Theodyne crossed the room and pulled a proper apprentice's robe from the wardrobe. He brought it over to the bed and laid it out, smoothing his hands over the wrinkles. The action sent a ripple of awareness down Nico's body to lodge in his belly.

Theodyne's supple hands caressed the fabric as one would a lover. His gaze moved over the garment as if inspecting every inch for a blemish or a stain. Something had changed in Theodyne during his short but potent illness.

"It is only that you are charting uncertain waters. Those who wish to embrace the clergy are only heading for a safe harbor, even if their captain says otherwise."

Nico crossed his arms. "On the seas that is considered mutiny."

"Yes. And it is punishable by death."

"They will inflict their own punishment by trying to make it in the world alone."

"You can't believe that." Theodyne pulled the robe over his head. "As soon as your back is turned, they'll run to the clerics and the Cesare Medovins of the world. A safe harbor, indeed. One that would welcome them like the return of a conquering hero."

"I know that. The problem is they take all our secrets with them."

Theodyne smoothed the robe over his body. He looked up slowly. "Then make it so they forget everything they've learned once they are no longer part of the school."

Nico stared at Theodyne as if he'd never seen him before. A threat of such magnitude had never been made in the history of the Gold School. There had never been such a need. Now, the entire landscape had changed. Was it too late to enact such a punishment on Donando? It would ease Nico's mind about turning his back on the headmaster.

"Such an undertaking needs careful consideration."

"Naturally." Theodyne reached up under his robe and pulled off his pants. "It can also act as a testament to your other masters."

Nico's gaze followed Theodyne back to the wardrobe as he selected a clean pair of breeches. "By asking them to take vows?"

"Of a fashion." Theodyne stepped into the pants and pulled them up his legs. "You let them know what you plan, and if they do not take an oath, they are probably the ones who conspire against the school."

"Or who feel this scheme lacks certain trust."

Theodyne tied the breeches at his waist. "Oh, your masters will feel that all right."

And Nico couldn't rightly blame them if they did. The idea did deserve more thought. These were hard times they lived in. Ever changing. It was enough to make a man question the future. Back in his ancestors' time, the school and her masters had stood firmly and righteously together against outside influences. There was a beautiful purity to the practice of alchemy that had long since gone by the wayside.

"How do I look? Official enough to serve you without embarrassment?"

Nico gave Theodyne a slow appraisal. He'd never seen him looking more serious or solemn. The sadness that had been there before had been replaced by purpose.

He didn't want to pry into what passed between the ancients and a man deep in the throes of fever, but the transformation was so remarkable it made him want to discover the root. Though he supposed, on essentials, the change was not so drastic. There had been a serious streak in Theodyne from the beginning of their association, but then it was more of a hatred for the world. Now, he seemed more determined than ever to confront and change it.

Nico remembered what Master Finelli had intimated about those infected with the fever and frowned. Pair that with what Anjufer suspected, and the air really needed to be cleared.

Theodyne straightened his robe. "It's wrong? It doesn't sit properly?"

Realizing it had been too long a pause after the question about Theodyne's appearance, Nico cleared his throat to explain. "I'm sorry, you caught me deep in my own thoughts. The robe fits you quite well. Dare I say it becomes you?"

Theodyne brushed at nonexistent lint. "I fear your masters already have a low opinion of me."

"No, Theodyne. Not the ones who are loyal to me. They keep an open mind and are as indebted to you as I am."

"You owe me no debt. I did what I thought I must. It was the only thing I knew to do to help."

"And those are the actions that mean the most. They came from the heart, and I appreciate it."

There was a beat or two of silence. Theodyne looked up as if sensing the growing tension. "What is it?"

No sense in concealing the truth, Nico realized. "Master Finelli drew a rather interesting conclusion to a recent rash of fevers going through the school."

Theodyne crossed his arms. "No wonder I came down with something. With all your powers, you should be able to block illnesses as well."

"It doesn't quite work that way."

Theodyne frowned and stepped forward as if the very notion offended him. "And why not? If everything is part of the Grand Matter, then infections and diseases should be within that all-encompassing realm. Why should they stand apart?"

"Perhaps because we still know so little about the human body and the tiny entities that can affect it." Nico studied Theodyne's face and the scar put there by heinous means. "There are some things we can do. For instance, if you so wished, I could mend your face and no one need ever know you had spent time in prison for thievery."

Theodyne touched the spot, trailing his fingers over the puckered skin. "And to remove, alter, or hide it is to commit a crime against the state."

Nico held up his hand. "We're woefully off the subject."

"Then how do Master Finelli's conclusions involve me?"

"All those who have fallen ill are descended in some way from elementals." Nico watched as Theodyne's expression changed from one of anger to confusion and finally went blank as he sat down on the bed.

"I'm not…." Theodyne broke off his rebuttal. The confusion in his eyes was absolute. "I always wondered how it was possible that I knew where every fine gem and precious metal was hidden in a home. It was like they called to me." Giving an uneasy laugh and stood again, and moved to the window. "I thought it was just an instinct for thievery. That I'd studied my profession and the people I stole from so well that they had no secret hiding places from me. And the voices I heard I put down as a strong intuition."

"Theodyne, it is possible you have an ancestor or two who was an earth elemental, a *terrathant*. Given what you've just told me, I'd be willing to bet it isn't that far back in your lineage."

Theodyne let out a sigh, and his shoulders slumped. "There's a lot about my lineage I don't know. My family is so unlike yours. We can't trace our family tree back as far as my grandfather, let alone hundreds of years. I doubt my branch can be traced as far as the trunk."

"Nor do you need to." Nico stood and placed his hand on Theodyne's shoulder. "You have a family now. A rather extensive and loyal one."

Theodyne turned his head and stared at Nico. His gaze dropped to Nico's lips, and heat, raw and hungry, plowed through Nico. "This has been the single most enlightening experience of my life."

"You deserve a little light after the dark." It was hard to talk around the rise of desire in his throat as Nico's vocal cords seemed tight. His voice was low and seductive.

"I wouldn't have been here if not for the dark. As a matter of fact, I don't know as if I'd have changed much in my life if I'd not gotten caught and sentenced."

"In time you might have." Nico slid his hand along Theodyne's shoulder to rest at the back of his neck. "We, all of us, end up in places we were meant to be. The Grand Matter does have a master plan."

"Stop, or you'll start sounding like those blood-sucking clerics."

Nico smiled and ran his thumb along Theodyne's jaw. "It is the truth. Even if the clerics choose to ascribe a different name to the presence, it is all the same."

"So you've said. But it seems to me if that were the case, their holy father would point them in that direction instead of creating a larger rift."

Nico stepped back and moved to the middle of the room. His hand knit into a fist after he'd touched Theodyne. "Ah, see, but that's the theory of religious warfare. Divide and conquer the masses until they believe only in what you say. All outside influences are blasphemous."

"Yes, and we know what happens to blasphemers." Theodyne's mouth thinned. He was silent for a moment, as if contemplating his fate. After a time he blew out a breath. "Does that cavernous library hold any books on *terrathants*?"

"Most assuredly."

"I'd like to see them."

"It's almost mealtime. I'll take you there after and show you the section on elementals." Nico nodded toward the door. "Shall we?"

Theodyne took another big breath, as if steeling himself to confront the alchemists en masse. "Yes."

Chapter Eleven

THEODYNE FOUND the dining hall noisy, chaotic, and too full for his taste. It was every bit as uncomfortable as the prison dining facility. He sat in perfect silence, trying to keep the whispers in his head at bay. Now he knew what they were, he wasn't afraid for his sanity. However, he'd never heard so many of them before. It was as if the knowledge of his background had unlocked a hidden door, and now all the elementals within the school felt obliged to speak with him.

The food was decent. Not as good as what Nico's private cook prepared, but it was a sight better than prison meals. Tree bark and live bugs were better than the slop at Pallonia.

He and Nico sat at a long table with Masters Oberon, Finelli, and Rhone. There was something about the other masters that made Theodyne uneasy. Not collectively—he just didn't know from which one the bad feelings originated. It was hard to tell with all the soup of other sounds in his head.

He speared a piece of meat with a fork and placed it in his mouth. Slowly, methodically, he concentrated on chewing while trying to filter the noise around him. The other conversations were a pesky buzz, like a hundred bees swarming the hall. It was hard to separate them out, to discover what the others discussed around them.

"You are very quiet there, Apprentice Theodyne." Master Rhone had his fingers laced and elbows on the table, looking over his hands. He had a very thoughtful expression on his face.

Theodyne glanced at Nico, who gave a small, imperceptible nod.

He kept it simple and straightforward. "Absorbing the atmosphere."

"And how do you find... *the atmosphere?*" It was a question loaded with double meaning and innuendo. Well, two could play that little game.

"Dense." Theodyne tucked back into his food.

He heard a snort that turned into a cough and caught Master Oberon with a red face. At least he'd amused one of his dinner companions. Master Rhone did not look happy with the comment.

"I would think you'd be used to crowded spaces and the gaggle of conversations. Though I'm sure the places you're used to aren't as fine as the school."

Such a direct insult was not to be taken lightly, but that didn't mean he had to show offense. "On the contrary, Master Rhone, I have been entertained by the Medovins themselves. By foreign princes and dignitaries. By the wealthiest of the world's merchants. In palaces that would make this school look like a poorly furnished hovel."

Master Rhone narrowed his eyes. "And stole from them all."

"An exaggeration. Can you imagine how I might walk out of a residence with silver clanking and jewels bulging from every pocket? Even the actions of a thief must be tempered with judgment and reason. Nothing is served to procure items in such an opportunistic fashion."

Master Rhone directed his attention to Nico. "If you are looking for a spy in our midst, you should look no further than your own apprentice."

No matter how ill-advised, Theodyne could not help but give Master Rhone a dark look. The man had a heart as hard as stone and twice as cunning as any thief. If he wished to *act* the stone, let him *be* the stone.

The way Master Rhone sat, as if he were the master of the world rather than just of alchemy, disgusted and annoyed Theodyne. Master Rhone looked over the arch of his fingers as if pronouncing such judgments were his given right.

A crack in the dike emerged, and Theodyne struggled to hold back his anger. Surely there was no harm in exercising just a sample of his newfound elemental powers. Theodyne concentrated his will on the master's hands. First the nails—already hard and small, like pebbles in a pond. Different sizes and shapes. Bumpy, lumpy, and jagged.

Then the fingers, palms and backs, chunky and crude as if hacked out of granite by a monkey with a chisel. There were no fluid lines or motion to show the gentle hand of a sculptor. That would be too good for the master. He was as heavy-handed as if he carried anvils at the ends of his arms.

Surprised gasps went up around the table.

Master Rhone's eyes rounded. He tried without success to pull his hands apart. "Ahhhhh."

Nico glared at Theodyne. "Cease your actions," he said between clenched teeth and so low the others could not hear.

Theodyne placed his fork in his bowl and stood. "If you'll excuse me, masters."

He started out of the dining hall, noticing the noise level had diminished significantly. A hundred sets of eyes watched him as he headed toward the door. With shoulders back and head up, he kept walking, refusing to let the combined weight of their stares slow his stride.

Let them see he was no man to be taken lightly, or baited with barbed comments. That he was destined to be their equal in every way.

He'd almost made a clean exit when Nico pulled his arm and swung him around.

"What were you thinking?" Anger and disbelief shot from Nico's eyes, and for the first time Theodyne felt the lash of real power. It was an awesome and fear-invoking moment.

"That I am not going to let anyone, no matter how high above my station, determine my worth." Theodyne jerked his arm from Nico's hold. "Were you not going to defend me? Or is it common for masters to accuse apprentices of certain crimes? If that is the case, I'll go back and apologize most humbly. If not, then I'll keep walking until I reach a place where I *do* belong, because it's obviously not here."

Nico looked as if he'd been hit. His head physically jerked back from the score of the words. "Theo." Then he pulled Theodyne fiercely into his arms. "Don't you dare leave."

Theodyne held himself stiffly. There was too much emotion swirling through him at the moment. Too much heat as he pressed against Nico's body. Too much want and need, and he was about to be overwhelmed by it all.

There had been many lovers in Theodyne's life. Some had commanded him to stay or risk the consequences of leaving. Others had let him go without reservation. But none of them had ever issued a threat in so raw a manner that the words sounded as if they were ripped from a heart on the verge of breaking.

Theodyne turned his head, sliding his lips along the textured, stubble-roughened surface of Nico's jaw. His eyes slid closed, and he found the lips he sought without error. The kiss raised powers Theodyne had no wish to control; he let them burn hot and bright, igniting the air around them.

Nico's hands found Theodyne's face, cradling it in a tender grasp. At length he ended the contact and pulled away from Theodyne. "You are the single most important person in my life at the moment, and for the life of me I can't explain how you came to take such a place so soon."

Theodyne widened the space between them. He gave an incredulous laugh. "And here I thought I was alone in my confusion."

Nico gave a solemn shake of his head. He placed his hand on Theodyne's shoulder. "Please return Master Rhone's hands to normal."

"You mean he can't do it himself? The high-and-mighty Master Rhone is beholden to nothing more than a common thief to set him back to rights?" Theodyne glanced over his shoulder. So far no one had tried to follow them out into the hall. He liked to think it was because they feared him a bit now. Perhaps the rumors and whispers would stop if they had even the slightest bit of fear for his untapped potential.

"I'm sure he could, but he should not have to expend the energy. Especially when he was not the one to do the deed."

"Very well, but the next time he decides to place blame on me where there is none, I'm turning him into a rather lifelike sculpture, and nothing you say or do will make me change him back."

Nico sighed. "Remind me to lecture you on the ethics of our order."

A lecture on ethics, how ironic. Theodyne nodded in the direction of the dining hall. "Should you go back and tell the other masters I've been summarily disciplined?"

"No. You need to go back and apologize in person."

Stubborn pride reared its unforgiving head. "I won't."

"Theodyne, you must. It isn't a question of who is right and who is wrong. This is about the fabric of our order. The very foundation of the

Gold School. What would happen if suddenly all the apprentices were allowed to rise up and abuse their masters because they took offense to something their masters had said? We'd be a school of chaos and anarchy. There would be no stopping those on the lower rungs of the alchemical ladder from thinking they ran the place. We simply can't have that. Respect for your superiors is part of the creed."

"And what about showing respect for those you teach? The right to not be trampled on by those who are in a place of authority just because they can. Abuse of power is every bit as much of a crime as disrespecting your betters." Theodyne had been down that route too many times to want to go back there.

"I'll deal with Master Rhone in good time. You just do what you're supposed to and let me handle the rest."

Theodyne was deeply sorry for putting Nico in a bad position. Truly he didn't want the other masters to believe Nico had lost control of his apprentice, but there had to be some recompense for the unfair charges.

Nico squeezed his shoulder, getting his attention. He stared deeply into Theodyne's eyes. "Do you trust me?"

Theodyne's heart gave a hard thump or two. "Yes. Of course."

"Then prove it. Go in there and apologize to Master Rhone in front of the entire student assemblage, and I will take care of him later."

Theodyne swallowed down the humiliation. He'd thought those days were over for him. That his new life in the protection of Master Nico had seen an end to the humbling experiences he'd learned in Pallonia.

Nico lifted Theodyne's chin, forcing him to lift his gaze from where it had slipped to the floor. "Does it help to know I think your powers far outpace your studies? I believe, with a little more discipline and a care for our codex of laws, you will advance very quickly to master?"

Theodyne sucked in a deep breath. "It just might give me the strength I need to get through it." He gave Nico a quick, impulsive kiss.

There was nothing to stop the knot of anger and hatred for Master Rhone burning him from the inside out. There were few people in his life he'd loathed from first meeting, but in all areas the under-headmaster qualified for that dubious honor.

As he entered the dining hall, the chatter of conversations quieted once again. Theodyne lifted his head and gazed straight ahead. With a demeanor to rival the finest soldiers, Theodyne walked with his shoulders back and spine straight.

Master Rhone sat in the same spot with a glass of wine in front of him. He continued to open and close his hands as if working the feeling back into them. When Theodyne approached the table, Master Atolla got Master Rhone's attention.

Theodyne did not take a humble posture. That was one consideration Theodyne was not about to afford Master Rhone. He nodded with a slow incline of his head. "Masters and Master Rhone in particular, forgive me for my transgression in using my talent against you. Master Nico has instructed and chastised me. It shall not happen again."

The masters turned to Master Rhone to await his pronouncement.

Theodyne did not flinch or let his inner turmoil show. This was more about honoring Nico and presenting a façade of strength than displaying any of the emotions he felt. Nico deserved a strong apprentice—a better one on any count.

Master Rhone linked his hands over his stomach and leaned back in his chair, regarding Theodyne with a haughty expression. "Pretty words, but said without an ounce of remorse."

Theodyne acknowledged the accusation with a nod. "It's a promise made in the utmost sincerity."

"A very fine line."

"But no less true."

Theodyne felt the weight of the other masters' stares. He longed to turn his gaze to them and see what was in their eyes. Did they find him a hopeless hellion who deserved what the city-state of Lancor had given him, or did they admire him for standing up to Master Rhone's attempts to humiliate?

"I need to consider this matter carefully before I accept or reject your apology. You will come to my office in the morning to learn your fate."

Theodyne bowed his head in understanding and left the dining hall.

So, that was the way it was to be? The master was going to make him wait all night to find out if he was to be forgiven or his name sullied in the records of the Gold School forever. Did it really matter to him which way the master decided? No matter how the dice fell, it was only Nico's opinion that truly mattered. *His* reputation that was at stake.

However, Theodyne had no qualms that Nico's esteem in the eyes of his brothers would not falter.

He made his way out of the dining hall and took the back way to the library, letting the earthy call of paper and ink lead him on.

If he had to wait for the ax to fall, he might as well pass the time learning about earth elementals. It was hard to believe that some long-gone ancestor of his was a being that sprang from dirt, rocks, or hidden volcanic pocket. How did one have sexual congress with a hill in order to breed a human? It didn't make sense to him. As a matter of fact, it sounded like a parable from one of the ancient religions where life sprang spontaneously from a crack in the earth.

The library was empty. Students were still in the dining hall. The masters had not moved from their conclave around Master Rhone. He'd have the place to himself. It was the only way he wanted it at the moment. No other thoughts but his.

He briefly wondered where Nico had gone. There was no way Theodyne would be able to find the books he sought without assistance. He didn't even see a place where a catalog or ledger was kept with entries of the books. Unless he wasn't looking in the right place.

Theodyne made another circuit around the room, searching unlikely crevices and shelves stuffed to overflow. Were the volumes divided into category, then author name, or in chronological order?

There were infinite ways to catalog the many tomes in a library this size. No matter what method was used, it had to be in some logical order.

Then Theodyne noticed them, the symbols on the walls. Pictures and sigils indicated individual sections and division of categories. No wonder he hadn't recognized it; he'd been looking for something more overt.

Books and scrolls on earth elementals were located under a painting of a tree whose branches spread out to encompass a disk meant to serve as a symbol of the earth. He pulled one book off the shelf, titled *Bound to Earth*. It was of the same vein as the primer. No words appeared on the page. Another book that needed some kind of secret key to unlock its mysteries.

Before Theodyne even attempted such a feat, he randomly pulled the other books in the section off the shelves and opened them. All were keyed in some fashion. Some had the same blank pages, others were written in the language of the ancients. None of the volumes were going to be easily read.

Theodyne took the first book he'd selected to a chair and sat down. He opened the cover with a creak of leather bindings. Now to find the method of the locking mechanism.

AFTER WATCHING Theodyne make his solitary walk, Nico retired to the workroom. There was a memory-wipe experiment he wanted to try. Ideas had germinated since Theodyne had proposed the unusual punishment. Such an endeavor needed care and patience to accomplish.

The question was what form the spell should take. Possibilities were limitless. He thought of the little spheres he'd made to capture storms. Perhaps there was some way to extricate the memories of all alchemical knowledge and store them in a globe? If it worked for storms, it stood to reason it might work for things not quite as potent as weather.

Once, Nico had even used one to capture an especially beautiful dream. It had not been a difficult process, merely a lengthy one.

The sphere used the practice of spagyrics to purify the components of the dreamstate in order to pull out specific memories. Certain herbs had different harmonic frequencies and therefore resonated in different parts of the body.

It was only a matter of finding the correct combination with which to draw out the knowledge of alchemy and put it into a sphere. Risks came when trying to perfect or purify the human mind. Herbs and metals were more amenable to the process of spagyrics than human tissue and soul.

"Your concentration is to be commended, Nico."

Nico glanced up from where he was drawing schematics on a piece of bleached parchment. Master Oberon stood in the doorway with a knowing smile on his face. "And why is that?"

"You haven't spoken to your apprentice, I take it." Oberon stepped into the room and made his way to the opposite side of the worktable.

"Not since I sent him back inside the dining hall to apologize to Master Rhone."

Oberon pulled a stool to the table and sat. He linked his hands on the desktop. "Rhone *requested* to meet with Theodyne in the morning to reveal whether he will accept the apology or not."

"Damn the man!" Nico threw down his pen and pushed up from his seat.

Oberon raised his hand to stall Nico's coming tirade. "You should have seen your apprentice. He was simply magnificent in his disdain."

Nico rolled his eyes. "Theodyne's arrogance is both his gift and his curse."

"I believe he shows surprising strength, given the circumstances."

"With a desperate need to learn the rules." Nico came back to the desk and sat. The schematics would not draw themselves. More was the pity.

"He's a remarkable talent for a novice. A man such as Theodyne in master's robes will be very powerful." It was spoken like a portent.

"My thoughts exactly."

They were silent for a moment before Oberon glanced down at the drawings and tapped the paper. "What are you building?"

Nico blew out a long breath. He wondered how best to explain what he intended. "Actually, it is an experiment."

"It looks somewhat like your weather spheres." Oberon turned the paper so he could study it. "Why revisit an experiment you've already proven successful, unless you wish to change the scope."

Nico gave his friend a grave smile. "You were always too clever by half."

Oberon's eyes lit as if he'd figured out the implications of the newer experiment. "You insane bastard." The epithet wasn't given as a curse but with awe. "You mean to extract the alchemists' secrets from Headmaster Donando."

"Or any alchemist who decides to betray us. I'll not have our secrets out there for public consumption once a brother is ousted from the order."

Oberon rubbed his brow. "Not that I don't think your experiment has merit, but what's to stop the accused from passing the information via written missive or using the ether before the punishment is meted out?"

Nico had to agree that made perfect sense. Only honor lay between alchemists and sharing their secrets with others. In a world where political turmoil and threats of war crowded in on the very air they breathed, honor was sometimes a hard commodity to obtain.

Nico would like to believe his men were trustworthy, but Donando had shattered that illusion, thus the drastic step.

"If I can employ a working model, it must be done in secret. Only the headmaster will know the spheres exist. It will be passed down upon his installation to the seat."

Oberon frowned. "Then you mean to use one on me to see if it works? To take this conversation away so I never realize we've had it?"

Nico shook his head. "No, Oberon. I mean for you to become the new headmaster."

Shock stilled Oberon. The only thing he did was blink a few times.

"Well?" Nico chuckled. "Are you inclined to accept the position or not?"

Another moment or two passed before Oberon cleared his throat. "I don't know what to say. I never suspected your thoughts lay in that direction."

"And this is why you'll make the perfect one. You have no expectations of accolades. You practice the discipline as you live your life: with joy and honor. I can think of no better member of the Adepts' Council to elevate than you."

"What about Master Rhone?"

"He'll feel slighted, I'm sure." That was putting it mildly. Nico had no doubt Rhone would take the elevation of Oberon straight to headmaster as a humiliating insult.

"He'll have a rupture of some sort," Oberon predicted.

"Not if he knows what's good for him. I'm already disposed to believing he was in league with Donando."

Oberon shook his head. "There was someone who sided with the former headmaster, but I can assure you, it wasn't Rhone. No matter how guilty he appears."

"How do you know?"

"He might have agreed with the need to align our lot with the *prolate* and clerics, but he did try to talk Donando out of meeting with them here."

"Would he have been for a meeting with them elsewhere, then?"

"Not as such." Oberon stood. "For what it's worth, I don't know who his conspirator is, but it's definitely not Rhone."

Nico watched the master walk out of the laboratory. His footsteps echoed down the hallway.

The drawing in front of him seemed to blur in the candlelight. He let out a breath he didn't know he'd been holding. He hadn't realized how desperately he wanted to be wrong about Rhone until that moment.

But if it wasn't him, who was it? Which of the masters stood to gain from an alliance with the Agia? None of them, as far as Nico was concerned. The *prolate*'s gain was the alchemists' loss.

He turned his attention back to the schematics. He had bigger problems to solve at the moment than who had conspired against the school. That information would remain within these walls as long as all the other masters remained in place.

Chapter Twelve

FULL NIGHT had fallen when Theodyne looked up from the book. He blinked several times to clear his eyes. Alchemical equations and symbols danced before his closed lids, imprinted there from his long hours of study.

It was worth every moment. What he'd learned in the past few hours counted for more than he'd ever learned in the whole of his life. So many of the questions he'd held in his heart for a lifetime were answered. The knowledge ushered in a new era of enlightenment. One where he knew his place in the world.

Energy surged through his veins, a gift from the elementals whose blood nourished him. It was a shame he'd never know the identity of the ancestor who'd risen from the very fabric of the earth. He still wasn't sure of the mechanism that made it possible for elementals to breed with humans. That aspect still bothered him somewhat. But did it matter? If, as he was fast learning, all things sprang from the Grand Matter, then there was no difference between the two races once broken down to their essential materials.

The feeling of being watched lifted the hairs along his collar. He turned to look behind him, but saw no one. Not that there weren't any hiding places in the library. The cavernous room was full of dark corners in which to conceal one's self, but he'd think anyone watching him would grow tired of observing nothing more than him reading a text. Not very exciting news to report back to their master.

Anyhow, it was late and he needed to return to his room if he was to rest and renew before his meeting with Master Rhone in the morning.

He set the books back onto the shelf where he'd found them, ignoring the way his gut tightened at the thought the meeting brought. Nico would not be proud.

The fact Master Rhone had chosen to forgo accepting the apology at the time it was given was nothing more than a show of power. Theodyne could live with that, but it was the knowledge that, as an extension, Nico might be embarrassed or shamed in front of the other masters that hurt more than Theodyne cared to admit.

He'd promised Nico he'd give him no reason to doubt bringing Theodyne to the school, and so far all he had shown was insubordination and spectacle. It was enough to make his face burn with humiliation and self-loathing.

He'd returned the last of the books to the stacks and turned to leave when he caught movement out of the corner of his eye. "Who's there?"

Journeyman Jolen stepped out from behind a stack of books under the symbol for Air. "I didn't mean to disturb your studies."

Theodyne glanced back at the reading area he'd left. "I'm headed to my room now. I have an early day, it seems."

Jolen had a disturbed look in his eyes. The haughty disdain he'd displayed on the journey to the school had been replaced by some deeper emotion. "Do not let Master Rhone expel you from the order. We need you."

A cold fear moved down Theodyne's spine. "Is expulsion a possibility?"

"You attacked the under-headmaster. It is the least of the punishments you face."

Theodyne relaxed. "Ah, punishments. I'm well acquainted with those."

Jolen bit his lower lip. "Not the ones imposed by an angry alchemist. There are books aplenty in the private stacks that go into great detail about the punishments doled out to unruly apprentices in the past. We are all taught the histories in our first years as a deterrent to disobedience."

Nico had warned him as much when they'd arrived. Theodyne's palms grew cold and damp. "I thank you for the warning, but I'm afraid my fate is set. It's too late to call back what I did, but I can't feel remorse for the action either. Only for Master Nico's sake. Not for my own."

Jolen gazed at him. "You are an odd one, Apprentice Theodyne. I cannot seem to figure you out."

"That's no surprise. I find it hard to do that myself sometimes." Theodyne gave him a gentle smile and squeezed his shoulder. "I take it from your presence here you are feeling better."

"Remarkably so." Jolen frowned. "I heard you had taken ill after venturing down into Delaneux."

"I had trouble breathing. Pedraus gave me an herbal that helped." He brushed away the experience as one would a pesky bug.

"He's doing something to us. Those of us with elemental blood, but I haven't been able to prove it yet."

Theodyne leaned in. "Who?"

"The *prolate*."

"I never put anything past a man of power. They are not above committing heinous acts to get what they want."

"But why go after the elementals specifically?"

Theodyne shrugged. "Perhaps the Agia has found in us a vulnerability to exploit that isn't present in those without elemental blood."

"But how? It would take an alchemist of immense knowledge and skill to accomplish such an act." Jolen paced away from Theodyne, then returned. "I don't wish to think of my masters and fellow journeymen as culpable for such cruelty."

"How many schools of alchemy are there?"

"Seven in the city-states. Why?"

"Because the guilty could be from any one of them. He didn't necessarily have to originate from this particular institution." And that material point made the entire situation so much more frightening.

How many of the masters at the other schools had turned to an alliance with the *prolates* and clergy? Which ones had decided to make war against their own order for a chance to unite the city-states?

Weariness settled on Theodyne's shoulders like an iron robe. "We need to be ready for whatever the future brings. Be that internal strife or those outside the gates. If we fail to prepare for either eventuality, we've failed the order."

"I've misjudged you, Apprentice. For that I am sorry." Jolen gave Theodyne a shy smile. "I'm not ashamed to admit I fear your power, but I fear your beauty even more."

Theodyne stood mute. He'd never heard a confession more honestly given in his life. He gave a careless wave of his hand. "Think nothing of either. They are of no moment."

Theodyne turned to leave. He'd stayed long enough in the library and had learned all he cared to for one day. The hour must have been late, for there was no one about the halls. He returned to his room without encountering even a single soul. It was a small miracle. His head was so full of elemental knowledge he had no room for much else. Greedy to hang on to the feeling, Theodyne hurried past Nico's room to his small quarters.

A lamp burned low, giving off just enough light to ensure he didn't stub a toe. The bed was cold, the fireplace empty. Theodyne took off his robe and spread it over the back of a chair to preserve it for the morning.

He climbed under the covers and pulled them up to his chin. Even without the benefit of a fire, the room remained a vast improvement over what he'd endured at the prison.

Theodyne lay on his back with his hands under his head. In this position he made a catalog of every rock and stone used in the school's construction. They called to him, answered him by giving their names. So many of them.

A castle this size used millions to build hallways and classrooms, kitchens and bedrooms. They spoke of their pride to be part of such a beautiful piece of architecture. Through them he learned the entire history of the alchemists who had inhabited the school from the very first day.

The earth elementals whispered it in Theodyne's ears as he drifted off to sleep.

"WAKE NOW."

The words brought him out of his slumber as abruptly as a cannon blast. Theodyne sat up and looked around, disoriented in the predawn light.

Strange dreams faded from his mind's eye.

He looked around for the person who had awakened him, but he remained alone. Perhaps his earthly brethren had ensured he did not sleep past his appointment.

He slid out of bed and went over to the washbasin. The water was freezing cold, but perfect to help revive him.

Theodyne needed to think clearly for his interview. Nico's future might depend upon it.

Quickly, he donned his robe and left the room. Nico's door was closed. Theodyne paused for a moment to listen if any sound came from inside. There were no telltale snores or movement to indicate the master was present.

Theodyne placed his hand on the doorknob with the intent to see if Nico was there, but drew back. What would he do if Nico wasn't there? He'd much rather not know and wonder, than to know and speculate where Nico had spent the night.

Guilt festered in his soul. Nico had not sought him out at all after they parted in the corridor outside the dining hall. Not after that impulsive kiss.

He rolled his eyes heavenward. Navigating the world of the alchemists had not been easy. He'd made too many missteps to ever correct them all. The impressions he'd left on those who called the school home were probably all bad.

Well, at least he had an unwitting ally in Journeyman Jolen. Though he'd not call the man a friend, he might count on him as a supporter.

As the night before, the halls were empty of students or faculty. He doubted the dining hall served breakfast this early. Not that Theodyne would be of a mind to eat. As it was, he had to keep swallowing in order not to gag on his nerves.

It wasn't like him.

Some strange being must have inhabited his body while he slept. Where he was once immune to such humiliations, he now felt it most acutely.

The under-headmaster's office was located in the uppermost turret of the east-facing tower. More punishment than prestige seemed to be at the heart of its placement. An awful lot of stairs separated the guilty party from meeting his fate. The climb made for some deep soul-searching.

Master Rhone's door was locked and no one answered Theodyne's knock. Had he shown up too late or too early? No. Surely the elementals had not let him oversleep.

He crossed the great circular anteroom to sit on the windowsill. If Master Rhone thought to increase his anxiety by making him wait, it wasn't going to work. He'd not let the extra knife to the ribs draw any blood. It was the act one might expect from a petulant child, not a grown man in master's robes.

It was also no way to try and bring Theodyne to heel. As a tactic, it was as transparent as water.

Theodyne drew his knees up and rested his back against the window frame. Whispers from the elementals were ever present in the background. They mumbled and murmured to one another like old gossipy women at the local fountain. It was a comforting sound, but somewhat invasive as he tried to prepare for whatever punishment Master Rhone might impose.

No matter how bad, he'd suffer it in order for Nico to save face. It was the only thing that mattered. For once in his life, Theodyne meant to set aside his pride and think of someone else... of the greater good.

Lisette had always accused him of selfishness. Theodyne had never wanted to see it or believe it was possible. He'd tried hard to provide for them and take the place of their parents. No matter what he'd done, it had never seemed enough. Upon reflection, he had to admit that perhaps it was the method he'd chosen as much as the reputation he'd garnered that had finally driven a wedge between them.

All because he hadn't wanted to listen to her concerns. It was arrogance that made him believe his needs and motives were above those of others. It was an attitude he meant to change. It took more than one brick to build a castle, and more than one alchemist to further a discipline. Now, more than ever, they needed to stand together.

The shuffle of footsteps shod in soft-soled shoes ascended the stairs. Theodyne jumped from the window ledge and stood with his hands folded in front of him in a reasonable show of humility.

A head and shoulders appeared as the person came into view. It was not Master Rhone. This person Theodyne did not remember meeting the day before, and he wore the robes of a journeyman alchemist.

He spotted Theodyne and his eyes widened slightly. "I see you are prompt for your meeting."

Theodyne thought not to answer, but then found his new humble beginning break away under the stress of misconception. "I may have faults aplenty, but punctuality was never one of them."

The journeyman gave a wry smile and stood on the landing. He held out a great key ring and stuck one of the largest ones into the lock. "I am Journeyman Bontello."

At least the young man was friendly—or seemed to be.

"Theodyne."

The door came open and Bontello held it. "Yes. I know. I don't think there is anyone present at the school who doesn't know who you are."

"Or why I'm here this morning."

Bontello nodded. He had eyes the color of the brightest peridot. Light-brown hair fell over his forehead in shiny disarray. There was a badge sewn onto the left shoulder of his uniform that he'd not seen on the other students.

Theodyne pointed to the elaborate patch of gold-and-silver threads. "What does that signify?"

Bontello looked down at his robe as if only now discovering the symbol there. "It's so everyone knows I'm assigned to the under-headmaster. If they did not know it by virtue of the fact that I see them every day and live in the same community."

Theodyne followed Bontello through the office and into an antechamber. The journeyman pointed to a wooden chair. "Please be seated. Master Rhone will be with you soon."

Soon was a relative concept. As it was, Theodyne waited for a good part of the morning before Master Rhone decided to grace the office with his presence. When he did finally sweep through the antechamber, he did so without acknowledging Theodyne's presence.

Bontello followed him into the inner chamber and closed the door behind them. Voices carried to where Theodyne sat, though the words were indistinguishable. Something must have happened to cause Master Rhone an upset.

At length, Bontello came out of the office and stood at the door. His face had gone ashen. A white line appeared around his mouth. "Master Rhone apologizes for the delay, but he cannot see you this morning. He asks that you return at first light."

An entire morning wasted when he could have been in the library reading more books on the elementals or going through the next volume of the primer series. Anger started to rise, only to be dashed by the look of abject misery on Bontello's face. Whatever had upset Master Rhone had affected the journeyman as well.

"Is everything all right?"

Bontello shook his head. "Go find Master Nico. He will tell you."

Theodyne had no idea where to find Nico. He went to their rooms, but no one was in residence. Not even Pedraus.

A quick trip to the dining hall revealed it had been empty for some time as well. His stomach let out a loud rumble to remind him he'd missed breakfast. He rubbed a hand over the area and kept looking.

Nico was not at the sky garden, nor was he in the library.

"Where is he?"

The whispery voices of the castle stones grew louder in his head. The word laboratory was the only one he heard with any clarity. Damn, if he'd known he could have asked the elementals, he would have done so at the start of his search. Of course they would know the location of every living being within the school.

The laboratories were located on the midlevel between the classrooms and the dorms. He finally found Nico in the last one near the western wall.

The master looked tired. His eyes were bloodshot and dark circled. His hair was mussed and finger-combed to where it stuck up in places. He had soot and some unidentifiable substance on his gown and cheeks.

Concern tightened Theodyne's gut. He stepped forward with a hurried gait. "Have you been here all night?"

Nico looked out of the window. "I must have been."

"So you don't know what it is that has Master Rhone upset this morning?"

Nico frowned. "No. I haven't heard. Did you see him?"

"No. I waited for him to arrive, then waited some more to see him. He never did admit me to his office. Journeyman Bontello informed me I was to return in the morning. They both looked as if they'd had a shock."

Suddenly Nico was in motion, striding to the door with purpose. "I must find Oberon."

Theodyne trailed behind, trying to keep up. For a man who looked fatigued, Nico had found a well of energy.

By the time they caught up with Master Oberon, Nico was practically in a dead run.

"Have we some news?"

Oberon nodded and hung his head. There was pain in his eyes as he took Nico by the arm and guided him into an empty classroom. He closed the door.

"I suggest you have a seat. This isn't going to be pleasant to hear."

Nico felt for a chair and sat, staring up at Oberon with a fierce expression. "Well, tell me."

"Headmaster Donando is dead."

Nico let out a moan.

"Killed by his own hand, so we're told. The guards did not think to limit the implements allowed into his cell. He transformed a spoon into a blade and struck himself through the ribs and into the heart. The guards found him this morning as they made their morning rounds."

Nico covered his face with his hand. Even from where he stood, Theodyne could see Nico's hand shaking. Though he made no sound, Nico's grief filled the room.

Theodyne placed his hand on Nico's shoulder. "There is nothing you could have done to stop him. He was in an untenable situation, caught between the clerics and the alchemists."

"I turned my back on him."

"He turned his on the school." Theodyne squeezed as if the action made the words penetrate deeper into Nico's pain. "You did what you had to do. There is no guilt in that."

Nico ran his hand down his face. "No matter his crime, he didn't deserve death."

"Perhaps he felt he did."

Oberon leaned against a lectern. "I have my doubts about the story given us by the guards."

"You believe he was murdered?" Nico seemed to latch onto that explanation with a bit too much enthusiasm.

Theodyne hated the hope he saw in Nico's eyes. If Donando had died by the hand of the guards, absolution might be found. Otherwise, Theodyne feared the depth of despair Nico might succumb to.

On the other hand, Master Oberon did not strike Theodyne as the type of man to make accusations of murder lightly.

"Forgive me, Master Oberon, but is there any solid evidence to support the guards' involvement?" Even knowing intimately the corruption rife within the judicial system in the city-states, Theodyne did not want to give Nico false hope or send him on a crusade to find the guilty party if Headmaster Donando had died by his own hand.

"Several reasons. The first of which is their refusal to let us have Headmaster Donando's remains."

Nico looked up sharply. "Why? Without benefit of next of kin, we have legal right to see he receives a proper burial."

"The *prolate* maintains Donando's body is his property since the death occurred on the palace grounds."

Nico made an outraged sound.

Theodyne laughed bitterly. "They mean to have their physicians open him up and see what's on the inside."

Both masters turned to Theodyne as if he'd denounced the Grand Matter as a tool of evil.

"Trust me. Prolate Agia wants nothing more than to discover what makes an alchemist of Donando's stature different from other men." Theodyne leaned forward as if his posture might give his words more weight. "If I were him, that's exactly what I'd do. The alchemists are the last bastion of power he has yet to breach."

Oberon took a defensive stance. "We are not different from other men. We've only studied the principles hard enough to alter matter. It is true we do seek in our students the potential to weave matter, but that just makes the task of teaching easier."

"And those of us who are born from the elementals? We've already been targeted by the *prolate*." Theodyne gave a shrug. "If you believe the rumors."

Nico finally glanced up with more than abject grief. "Words *are* power. Rumors as much as any other spell or incantation, for they take on lives of their own, growing and spreading like a vile cancer."

"Not all rumors are lies or half truths," Theodyne reminded him.

"No. Perhaps not, but very few of them are repeated without a certain amount of embellishment."

Theodyne couldn't rightly disagree with the observation.

Oberon crossed his arms over his wide chest. "What do we do, then? Allow the *prolate* to defile the body of our brother to satisfy his curiosity, or demand our rights are honored?"

Nico managed to rise from the chair. He didn't look all too steady, but he made his way over to the window and looked out over the mountain vista. "The real Donando is gone. His soul has crossed the great divide. Let them have his body."

Oberon frowned. "Are you sure, Nico?"

"Positive." He turned from the window. Strength was once again evident in his eyes. "I'll not give those bastards reason to provoke us."

"This might not be the best time to declare war," Oberon warned.

"It's never a good time to declare war." Theodyne hopped up on top of a long credenza that housed a multitude of implements and took a seat. It looked as if it was going to be a long conversation if the masters were going to discuss a possible war. Still, there was a kernel of doubt that niggled at Theodyne's brain. Leaving Donado's remains with the *prolate* was not a sound course of action, but at the moment he just couldn't remember the reason why.

Nico made a circuit of the room. "I want to know why it is only this particular school that is under attack. Why is this place a lodestone to the local *prolate*? What advantage does he see in taking us over?"

"For the *prolate,* the Agia, there is no disadvantage." Oberon walked over to a bookcase and pulled out a thick volume. He flipped through the pages until settling on one midway through. He brought the book back to the table.

Theodyne read the page title upside down: *Invoking the Veil.*

He had no idea what that meant.

Oberon slid the book closer to Nico. "I think it's time we disappear for a while."

Chapter Thirteen

MASTERS AND journeymen were stationed at key locations around the school. Each had a specific duty to perform to weave the fabric of the veil around the entire structure. It was a huge task. Nico did not remember having to perform an act of transformation on so large a scale before, but Oberon had been correct. They needed to disappear for a while.

Unfortunately, the move would seal them in with the Agia's conspirator, though Nico saw that as a slight advantage. It gave them more of a chance to discover the alchemist's identity. As far as Nico was concerned, the conspirator was as culpable for Donando's suicide as he.

Theodyne stood to his left, his face drawn into a worried frown. So far the outspoken apprentice had not given an opinion on the invocation. He'd quietly read the spell, then awaited instructions.

"There is no need to worry. Invoking a veil is a long-trusted work, though never on so grand a structure."

Theodyne made a face of disapproval. "I'm sure it is, but it seems too much like hiding to me. I think you'll fare better confronting the *prolate* head on. You need to get control of the headmaster's remains."

Nico sighed. They'd gone over that before. It was what the *prolate* wanted, Nico was sure of it. Ignatius Agia was using Donando's remains as bait, and Nico would not play so twisted a game. "I have no doubt that such a meeting will be inevitable. However, this grants us some much-needed time to better prepare."

Oberon stood on one of the upper balconies and signaled to Nico.

"Let us begin."

As with any rite of transmutation or other spellwork, a great deal of energy was required to power the illusion. Under the guise of the veil, to anyone traveling the mountains, the property where the school stood would be empty of anything save nature. No longer would pilgrims see the towers reach high into the air, seeming to touch the heavens.

From now on, the only people able to visualize the school would be those who lived within her protective walls. Those with a clear conscience and enlightened heart.

That was the key.

Nico worked in silence, concentrating to tweak the fabric of the veil just enough to give a sign should one without motives true to the alchemists pass through the perimeter.

He'd alert Oberon to the changes, but no one else. Not even Theodyne. As much as he hated to do it, that was the way it had to be.

They finished folding the mesh of energy over the structure as the sun began to set. Exhausted, Nico's legs shook as he made his way into the school and to the dining hall. Those who were not involved in creating the protections were busy setting out food for the masters and journeymen who had participated.

One type of energy had been exchanged for another.

And yet Nico had no appetite. He picked up a piece of apple and put it in his mouth. The fruit tasted dry, with a lingering metallic flavor.

He didn't reach for another one. Instead he tried a slice of bread with honey butter. That went down smoother, but again there was something odd in the taste. Not that the butter seemed rancid, but just not as fresh as it should be.

If he didn't know better, Nico would think he was being poisoned.

The very idea made him set the bread aside and glance around the room at his brothers. Paranoia was not generally in his nature and yet he had a hard time shaking the feeling he was a target of some sort.

Theodyne leaned close. "What is it?"

He hesitated mentioning anything to Theodyne. Knowing the apprentice's passionate nature, he'd challenge every person living at the school if he thought for one moment the food was tainted.

"Lost my appetite."

"You need to eat anyways. Anyone looking at you can tell you're past the point of exhaustion. Refuel and then lie down."

The tone of the command made Nico smile. "Yes, Theodyne."

The apprentice lowered his face. His hair obscured most of his expression from Nico, but what he saw of Theodyne's face had gone red.

"I'm only trying to care for you, since you are far too stubborn to care for yourself at the moment."

Nico leaned closer. There was a scent of wild cinnamon coming from Theodyne's skin. "I know, and I appreciate it."

Theodyne was quiet. He concentrated on his meal as if it were the last one he was allowed. After a time he put his utensil down and turned to Nico. "When are we to leave for the villa?"

"In the morning. Master Oberon can take care of any other problems that come their way."

The knowledge that Nico had spoken louder than intended was written over the shocked expressions of his brothers. He had not made the announcement of Oberon's elevation to headmaster yet. This was not the time or place.

"I would think you of all people would know the value of every one of us who live here," Master Atolla said.

"I don't remember questioning the value. I merely mentioned Master Oberon will know what to do in a crisis." Nico kept his attention on Atolla. It was hard to determine what the others thought without making eye contact, but judging from their unmasked attention, it was not in his favor.

"Does this mean you've filled Headmaster Donando's vacancy?" Master Finelli pushed his plate away and folded his arms in front of him. "Without a vote from the council?"

"Did the council vote to allow the clerics into the school?" Nico scanned the assembled masters, looking for guilt. All he found was defiance. "Because I do not recall ever receiving notification of that nature."

When exactly had he lost control of those he'd placed in charge of his family's legacy? When had they decided as a collective to violate philosophies held dear for generations? Nico was honest enough to realize there were aspects of his existence he was not proud to claim. He'd taken money for services in order to strengthen the bonds of trust with the locals in Lancor. He'd spent the coin he'd earned to build cathedrals where the people could worship. All to keep the peace. If the people wanted their Gods and Heaven, he'd given it to them.

And for this, his own brothers had turned against him?

He stood and pushed in his chair. His meager appetite had deteriorated to nonexistent. It was better to return to the laboratory and finish working on the globes than sit in the dining hall and defend a decision it was within his right to make as head of the Gold School.

Theodyne glanced up from his plate. After a moment's hesitation, he wiped his mouth, then set the napkin in the plate. Without saying a word, he, too, stood and followed Nico out of the dining hall.

They didn't speak until they were ensconced in the lab. Nico returned to the pages he'd abandoned that morning. Looking over them with fresh eyes, he noticed the flaws his fevered mind had not seen clearly.

Theodyne stood on the other side of the workbench, staring at the plans. "Are you going to be able to finish one of those before we leave?"

"I'll be able to complete more than one. Alchemists do not need to create glass in the traditional way. I can simply take a bowl of sand and other minerals and form it to my specifications. Doing so ensures it is less flawed than using fire and a glassblower."

"May I watch you work?"

Nico let the side of his mouth curl into a sly smile. "Of course you can. It will do you good to watch the process."

THEODYNE HAD never seen anything so remarkable in his life—and he prided himself on having been witness to quite a bit in his twenty-five years.

Nico waved his hands over a bowl of various powdered granules. Sand, ground shells, silt, and granite swirled faster and faster until they coalesced into a rotating ball. The faster the globe spun, the more translucent it became.

A slight, high-pitched whistle issued from the sphere. As it changed in tone, the object began to vibrate. Theodyne blocked his eyes in case it shattered and sent glass flying through the room.

Nico gave a silky laugh. "Have no fear, Theodyne. I've never lost control of a sphere yet."

"Well, I'd hate to lose my eyesight to the first time."

"You have so little faith in my abilities."

"On the contrary, I've put all my faith in your hands."

Nico's smile grew. Theodyne's heart pounded. There was a connection, an invisible wire that pulled and tugged on Theodyne's soul every time he was in the adept's presence. He tried to hide his reaction to the knowledge by turning his face away. Heat rose to his cheeks.

"Is there something wrong?"

Theodyne cleared his throat. "No. It's the spinning. It's making me dizzy."

Not a very convincing lie. He decided to sit down to improve his credibility.

"Do not get too comfortable. I'm going to have you attempt to construct one."

Theodyne couldn't hide his surprise. "I don't believe I have acquired the skills to do something quite so involved."

Nico set the completed globe aside and filled the bowl with more of the mixture. "Your skills are beyond those of a normal apprentice. You've already proven your gift for transmutation. You only need to pass the written examination of principles."

"You never mentioned a written test."

Nico straightened. "Does that worry you?"

"Not really." There were not that many instances in his life where he'd had to prove his intelligence or learning by regurgitating knowledge back onto paper. The little tutelage he'd had growing up had been as informal as it had been irregular.

"That wasn't convincing."

Theodyne gave a small shrug. "I didn't realize I needed to be."

"In all things, you—we—need to be convincing. No matter if our hearts tell us we're bitterly wrong. No matter if our backs are to the wall.

We must be strong. Before this is over, I fear we'll have lost a great number of our brothers."

Theodyne frowned. He might understand feeling disappointment over losing people he once depended on, but he saw no reason to mourn those who wished harm to the order.

He stood and stepped up to the credenza where Nico worked. "What do I do first?"

"Take one of the bowls and place one part of each powder inside."

Theodyne did as told, though his bowl didn't seem as full as Nico's. "Should I add more?"

Nico leaned over and inspected the contents. "Not necessary. It will result in a smaller globe, but for this first one, size is immaterial."

Theodyne watched closely as Nico moved his hand in a circle. Granules lifted from the bowl and began to swirl.

"Concentrate on the end product. How do you want it to look? What physical properties or characteristics do you wish the globe to contain?"

With a firm picture in his mind, Theodyne lifted his hand and moved it in a circle. First there were only a few grains of sand that lifted to trail his hand like a comet tail. It might not be an impressive show of his power, but he took heart that he'd managed to raise at least some of the particles.

Focus. It was hard to do with Nico only two feet away. The soft, spicy scent of his skin filled the space between them. More particles lifted and swirled. They didn't, however, form quite the sphere he had intended. Instead, it looked like some crystalline phallic symbol rising from the depths of the bowl.

"Sweet mercy." The entire structure disintegrated.

"You will create what you think. Make sure you keep your mind on what you wish to achieve."

He had been. That was the problem.

Starting from scratch, Theodyne cleared his mind and closed his eyes. It was easier to work without the distraction of Nico in front of him. After a deep breath to relax, Theodyne centered all his thoughts on the particles, connecting with them on the elemental level. Through the connection, he could monitor the speed and spin of the granules without having to open his eyes. They knew and understood what he wanted and were eager to comply.

Theodyne opened his eyes in time for the crystal sphere to drop into his hand. It was perfectly formed and completely clear. There were no blemishes or bubbles in the composition. The surface was entirely smooth.

Theodyne held it in the palm of his hand, offering it to Nico for inspection.

"Remarkable." Nico took it and hefted the petite globe in his hand. "Very lightweight."

"I had help," Theodyne confessed. "My elemental blood puts me at an advantage when dealing with earthy substances."

"It's good to have such, but remember to never take them for granted. It is proper to thank the elements for the assistance." Nico returned the sphere to Theodyne. "Ready to make more?"

With the prospect of working beside Nico, how could Theodyne refuse?

NICO DROPPED one of the globes into Oberon's palm. "There are six in total. Use them only if you have unimpeachable proof of guilt."

Oberon turned it over, inspecting it closely. "How does it work?"

"You must make a connection between the globe and the person you wish to empty." Nico demonstrated by placing his hand on top of the sphere. "A simple touch like this is all that's required. It will not take more than that."

Oberon's brow furrowed. A concerned expression crossed his face. "You know the other masters came to me after the meal and had a lot of questions about your unofficial announcement."

Nico was sorry for their anger, but it was inevitable. "I would not have wished to install you as headmaster in such a fashion, but I'm not going to change my mind about your appointment because they did not get a say in the matter. My family started this school and has run it for over five hundred years. I'll not lose control now because a few of the masters have their noses out of joint or feel slighted because I've decided to exercise authority that is rightfully mine."

Oberon set the globe gently on his desk. "You don't have to convince me. For too long we've been sailing in treacherous waters. It's time we got safely back to the open ocean of reason."

"Unfortunately, we live in times where that is not always possible. We've long been an island unto ourselves, with good reason. I will not, however, bow down to the clerics. I will work with the people to help them on whatever spiritual path they decide, but I'll not cleave to an institution that has labeled us daemons and heretics." Nico made a fist. The hypocrisy alone was enough to put him into a raging fury. He took a few breaths to calm himself, and then continued. "When all is said and done, we will be judged on our character and good deeds. Not by the fact we sold our souls to the highest bidder or aided the city-states in a continental war."

Oberon gave an incredulous laugh and crossed his thick arms over his chest. "More like we will be accused of allowing our country to fall by *not* taking sides."

"And when the time comes to fight, we will, but not under the banner of any city-state or *prolatial* house colors. We will fight as the Gold School. United. As an aid to our countrymen, but not a tool to be directed by them or thrown away at their whim."

Understanding lit Oberon's face. "You've seen where this is headed, haven't you?"

"I don't have to scry into dark waters to know this will not turn out well if we align ourselves with the Medovins, Karnackis, Jezdels, DiCarnis, Rinnis, Agias or any of the other *prolatic* family dynasties. I have only to look at history to know once you are sided with any of the great families, they seize all control until you choke on their bureaucracy."

"When will you convene the council?"

"For the evening meal. We'll gather in the council chamber. Arrange to have our food sent up there. I want the gathering to be informal. The other masters need to be at ease when they hear my proposal."

Oberon raised a brow. "Dictate, you mean."

"I will let them decide."

"And if they decide against you?"

"They are free to form their own institution, but without the knowledge of the Gold School."

With that, Nico gave a nod to Oberon and left the office. He had much to prepare before the meeting. He made his way back down to the library. He'd not spent much time there on this trip. Normally it was one of his favorite places in the school—that and the laboratory.

He needed to read the codex in the *Eye of Truth*.

If the other masters were going to challenge him—and Nico had no reason to believe they wouldn't—he wanted the laws on his side and readily available. Just because they used a vote to conduct business now did not mean they *had* to. Voting had never been written into the body of the rules that dictated governance.

To Nico's knowledge, there had never been an amendment of such on the books. In times of crisis, it had always fallen to the family member in control of the school to take measures into their own hands. The vote was a courtesy, not a right.

And yet, he was torn.

Should he exercise his rights as the direct descendant of Mercurian Dante and risk alienating the entire council? With Nico being so far away in Lancor, he might not have time to return should they decide in his absence to align with the *prolate*.

Wearily he sat in the chair before the fire. Eyes blinked back at him from the flames.

"What am I going to do, Anjufer?"

The fire elemental turned what passed for his head, contemplating the question. "Do as you always do. Lead with strength and integrity. Leave room for negotiation."

Nico smiled. "You should have been a diplomat."

"I might have been. If things were not as volatile in my time as they were."

"No, back then there were clear divisions between men of state and men of science." Perhaps that was one of the problems. Lines were blurring with greater frequency. Other than loathing violence, what was to stop the mystics and alchemists from positioning themselves to inherit one of the offices of *prolate?* As a matter of argument, what was to stop them from taking a step to secure the *demigoge's* seat at the head of the church?

Nico stood and made his way to the section designated for law. There were several textbooks of the alchemists' codex in the library. None was as vast and complete as the *Eye of Truth,* but they would do in a pinch. Nico picked up one and leafed through it. There were notes in the margins and additions to some of the articles. He recognized the handwriting. The sharp sting of nostalgia pierced his heart.

Nico ran his thumb over the script. It had been years since he'd even thought about Hazrael. Odd how the memories flooded his system after a brief glimpse of Hazrael's perfect penmanship. It was as if he reached out from beyond the grave to comfort Nico in his time of need.

"Thank you, old friend," he whispered to the ghost of Hazrael that still clung to the pages. He closed the book and tucked it under his arm. This was one treasure he'd not leave behind.

He turned once more to Anjufer. "Will you attend the master's council tonight? I'd like for you to weigh in on my decision should the others pose opposition."

Anjufer nodded. "You may count on the support of the elementals."

Chapter Fourteen

THE PLATES of food remained untouched. The masters sat around the table glaring at Nico with mutinous expressions following the announcement that he had elevated Oberon to headmaster. Only Masters Finelli and Oberon showed him a friendly face. Rhone had turned away from him, refusing to even look Nico's way.

"Can any of you think of a better candidate for the position? If you can, then write it on the piece of paper provided and slide it to me. I'll take your suggestions under advisement."

Master Atolla leaned forward and folded his arms. His eyes were so squinted in disapproval they disappeared into his wrinkled face. "You expect us to believe that after your high-handed, single-vote elevation of Master Oberon, you will listen to our recommendations? You have turned this school into an absolute monarchy, with you as king."

"By the blood that runs through my veins and the written codex of our laws, I am within my rights to do just that, with any of the schools that teach the Gold standard." Nico held up the book in question. He'd not brought Hazrael's copy of the codex, but the *Eye of Truth*. The most valued and cherished book of the alchemists' collection. "I dare any of you to find even one line in our rules where it says the elevation of masters to headmasters shall be run in a democratic fashion."

Master Atolla leaned back in his seat. His lip stuck out like an insolent child who did not get his way. He grumbled something unintelligible.

Nico turned his attention to Rhone. "This was not meant to slight you. As a matter of fact, Master Oberon came to your defense when I spoke with him about the elevation. I, however, need more convincing. Your blatant contempt for my apprentice has cast you in an unfavorable light with me. I would not wish the students of this institution to be treated thus by one they should strive to emulate. It sets a very poor example for future practitioners of our sacred arts."

Rhone closed his eyes. Pain etched lines on his face. His jaw tightened as if he barely kept the words of a rebuttal in check by the barest of threads.

Nico lifted his hand to indicate Master Rhone. "If you wish to speak, please do. I will hold nothing you say in your defense against you."

The under-headmaster shook his head.

"And before you and the other masters accuse me of showing favoritism to Apprentice Theodyne as the only reason for my refusal to elevate you, know I do have other concerns. For instance, you failed to relay in any of your missives to me that there were problems with the local clerics. This omission is most disturbing. Nor was I notified of the fevers infecting the students with elemental blood, or the fact the church has conscripted our potential students into holy orders."

Rhone continued to sit in silence. The failure to defend his actions was very damning.

"I have no plans to ask you to step down from your post. You will continue in the capacity you now fulfill."

There was still no response from the under-headmaster.

Nico glanced around the room at the other masters. Only Atolla had been bold enough to speak. It was not at all like these men to remain silent. It boded very ill for what Master Oberon faced once Nico left, but he had no doubt his choice for headmaster would prevail and flourish in the post.

"Such a silent and bewildered bunch you are this evening." He picked up a piece of cheese and bit down on it. The tangy, ripe flavor filled his mouth. It tasted much better than the food earlier in the day. Whatever had been wrong with his sense of taste had since corrected. "Go ahead and use the papers before you and write your choice for a candidate. I will open them and read them here in front of you."

When the men did not do as told, the fire roared in the hearth.

"*Do it!*" Anjufer's voice filled the room like an explosion. The flames of his body flared high, coming out of the fireplace to rise above the table and hang there. "How dare you sit there and lick your wounds when you have only yourselves to blame for the injuries. Do not think the elementals are blind to the selfish desires that are so beneath you. We see. We hear. And we remember."

The men scrambled to pick up papers and pens and began scribbling.

Nico glanced over at Anjufer with a nod of thanks.

The flame stayed high, but not as bright as before. Papers were passed to Nico. He made it a point of mixing them around so no one knew who the other men had suggested.

One by one he opened the slips and read the contents out loud. "One vote for Master Cenzo. One vote for Atolla. One vote for Finelli." Nico glanced at the old man and raised a brow. That one surprised him, but Master Finelli looked stunned. Perhaps he did not enter his own name after all. The remaining four votes were for Master Oberon. Not one vote for Rhone, which meant he didn't even write himself into the position.

"It seems that after your outcry and claims of unfairness, you have voted a consensus for my original choice. We shall let it stand. Master Oberon, congratulations."

Oberon stood and cleared his throat. "I want every man in this room to know I did not seek this post. I was deeply shocked when Master Nico told me of his plans. I will strive to be a good headmaster. To make this institution one that generations of alchemists will be proud to join.

"We are heading into some very difficult times. I will not pretend to have all the answers we'll need to get us through them intact, but I call on those seated at this table to join with me to keep our visions for the future alive."

The masters banged the table in support. Master Oberon took his seat.

"Thank you, Master Oberon. I'm sure you will not let down even the lowliest of stable boys during your tenure." Nico indicated the food before them. "If you are quite settled with the decision, please take this light repast with me. Enjoy the wine from my vineyard, for I leave in the morning and do not know when I will return. I would like for our last meeting together to end in the spirit of fellowship."

Reluctantly, the other masters filled their plates and goblets—all but Rhone. Before long they were talking of other matters. The balance was tentatively restored.

THEODYNE SAT with a book of elemental alchemy in his lap. The theories and practices of the ancients were so much more streamlined and comprehensible to him than those written by Mercurian Dante or Master Krutarch. It was as if he'd opened the tome and found the missing piece of his soul.

A throat clearing tore his attention away from the explanation of infusing crystal energy into a transmutation spell. Nico stood at the door with his arms crossed. Lines bracketed his mouth and his jaw was dark from the shadow of stubble.

Theodyne closed the book and placed it on the bed beside him. "You don't look as if it went well."

"Not entirely." Nico pushed away from the wall and came to sit on the bed. He picked up the book and read the cover. A brief smile flashed across his face.

"Are we set to leave in the morning?"

"Yes, and I for one will be glad to see the road before us."

Theodyne knew the feeling. "I never thought I'd ever be happy to see Lancor again, but even I'll be glad to return."

"When we do reach the villa, I am going to have to revise your studies. You've not been the typical apprentice from the start. It would be a shame to make you stay at that level when you've proven capable of doing so much more."

An uncomfortable feeling of humility stole through Theodyne's blood. It was an emotion he was unfamiliar with, having never experienced an ounce of regret or remorse for any of his actions in the past. "I don't want advanced until I've rightfully earned it. It's not fair to the other apprentices."

Nico turned a troubled gaze to him. His dark brows were knit into a frown. "I would never give you a promotion you didn't rightfully earn. To do so is to invite danger into the ranks. I can, however, amend the lesson structure to accommodate what you've already learned and incorporate your elemental status."

His gaze moved to the forgotten volume of earth-bound spells. "You seem to already have an affinity for delving into the study on your own."

"It has opened an entire world I never knew existed."

"But you've worked in concert with your entire life."

"It appears so." Theodyne didn't want to talk about the years he had spent as a thief. The memories were unproductive. He'd already dwelled on them too much since his release from prison. It was past time to move on.

As if reading his mind, Nico reached up and gently traced the path of the brand. Theodyne's eyes closed against the pain of knowing he'd let down so many people in his life.

"I can take this away, you know." The words were said so low, Theodyne hardly heard them.

He opened his eyes and stalled Nico's hand as he started to trace the bar of the T. "You've offered that once before. Does it offend you to see it on my face? To know I'm at my core untrustworthy?"

"No. It gives me pain to know you had to endure such torture."

Everything inside Theodyne went tight and hot. He'd never wanted anyone as much as he did Nico, and it was all wrong. The promises he'd made to himself about not getting involved with a man who had power over him seemed silly and selfish in the face of what he and Nico might have together.

The silence grew, filling the space. Tension knotted Theodyne's gut. He'd not be the one to make the first move this time. He'd wait Nico out. It was a matter of pride.

Nico traced his thumb down the side of Theodyne's face and across his bottom lip. Then he leaned in and took his mouth, hot and passionate.

Theodyne melted into Nico's embrace. Everything right in the world could be found in his strong arms.

Nico ran his tongue along the seam of Theodyne's lips, seeking permission for a deeper connection. Who was Theodyne to refuse such a sensuous offer? The kiss became a slow, methodical seduction.

Nico's taste filled Theodyne's head and heart, the flavor of his mouth unlike any of his other lovers. No, this was different in every way. More. Significant.

Nico lowered Theodyne to the soft mattress and lay on top of him. The rigid outline of Nico's cock pressed against Theodyne's thigh. Theodyne rose up and turned slightly, offering proof of his own arousal.

Nico moaned into his mouth.

Theodyne took the sound as consent and moved his questing hands down the front of Nico's robes, gathering the length of fabric in his fists. With the robe bunched around Nico's waist, Theodyne ran his hand over the top of his lover's breeches.

Nico tore his mouth away and rested his forehead against Theodyne's. "Yes. Theodyne, by the Gods, touch me."

He wasted no more time. The tie that held Nico's pants together came undone as if by arcane magic. Theodyne slid his hand down the flat plane of Nico's firm stomach to the hot, velvet smoothness of his cock.

Nico moaned and bit Theodyne's chin. In response, Theodyne wrapped his hand around Nico's length and began a slow, firm stroke.

Nico shuddered against Theodyne. His breath came fast and warm along Theodyne's neck. Soft words of endearment and promises of fidelity peppered the air as Nico began to make love to him in earnest.

Theodyne closed his eyes tightly against the emotions running riot through his body. Physical love was one thing—he'd enjoyed that with many lovers in many different circumstances. But letting down his guard to give his heart away went against everything he knew.

Yet, the sensual pleasure of Nico's touch could not be denied. It ran through him like quicksilver, chilling and burning at the same time.

Before too long they were lying face to face, devoid of clothes and inhibitions. Hands, lips, legs all moved in a slow, seductive dance of perfect union.

Nico trailed his hand down Theodyne's cock, then turned to cup his balls in a gentle squeeze. "You feel so alive. So vital. Like all the elements transformed into flesh and blood."

Praise unlike any he'd ever heard rang out as a musical language in his soul. The words changed him, altered his very essence from its former course. Tears he tried desperately to conceal leaked from his eyes.

Nico moved away. "Theo?"

Theodyne shook his head. The mood shattered. He extricated himself from Nico's embrace and sat up on the edge of the bed.

"Did I do something wrong?" Nico laid a gentle hand on Theodyne's shoulder.

"No." The word came out strangled, tight. He cleared his throat and tried again. "No."

"Then what? It's been a long time since I've taken a lover. If I've done something to offend you, please tell me."

Theodyne could not suppress the sadness that welled in him. "You've done nothing wrong, Nico."

"Then what? Tell me."

Theodyne turned enough to lock gazes with Nico. "No one has ever spoken to me like that before—said such tender words. I don't dare trust them."

Nico pulled Theodyne flush against his chest. "I find that impossible to believe. You are the most miraculous individual I've ever met. How could you not be used to praise from a lover?"

"Pretty words only. They meant nothing and were only hollow sentiments."

"Then your other lovers were fools." Nico placed his hand under Theodyne's chin and turned his face enough so their lips met. "And I am no fool."

Chapter Fifteen

THE SUN poured through the window, blinding in its intensity. It was the beginning of a new era in Theodyne's life, and he didn't want to miss a moment of it. He'd been up since before the sunrise, watching as the sky gradually grew to lighter shades.

Nico was still asleep, snoring softly with his face buried in the pillow. Theodyne could hear him from the annex room. At one point during the night they'd moved to the bigger bed. Now he sought refuge in the smaller chamber, if only to hide from the memories of the night before. Not that he wanted to forget. By the Gods, he didn't think he had the strength to remember and perhaps be wrong about the intense connection he felt.

It was power and light and the very core of what the alchemists taught.

And fragile.

In the Medovin house there was a collection of porcelain eggs, decorated with gold leaf and precious gems. Though the constructs looked sturdy on the outside, they were terribly delicate.

His heart felt as brittle as those damned eggs.

A loud shout came from the other chamber. "Why didn't you wake me?" A thud sounded right before the slap of feet over the floor.

Theodyne reluctantly turned from the window. "Because you needed your sleep. I didn't think it mattered what time we left. The trip is the same distance regardless."

Nico stuck his head around the corner. A sensual smile curved his mouth and his hair stuck up at odd angles. "I appreciate the extra time in bed, but I wanted to be down the mountain and through town before midsun."

"The wagon is already packed and the horses in harness. We were waiting for you."

Nico canted his head. "You were busy while I slept."

Theodyne gave a shrug. "I woke early and couldn't get back to sleep."

"You aren't dressed yet." There was a slow up-and-down appraisal.

"Neither are you."

"Yes, but I have an excuse." He moved away from the door and back into the larger chamber. "A bit of breakfast would be nice before we leave."

"I'll ring for Pedraus."

Was it just Theodyne, or did the morning feel uneasy? He'd never been uncomfortable the morning after the start of an affair. But then he usually left the bed while the sheen of sex still glistened on his lover's skin.

He grabbed his robe and stuck it over his head, only realizing then he had it on backward. Once he got the garment corrected, he headed out of the rooms.

Nico's voice echoed down the hallway, calling him back.

He didn't go. He needed a few minutes to settle his unease. It was then, as he wandered the halls, that he realized it wasn't his night spent with Nico that troubled him, but rather something in the air at the school.

The elementals were on edge, readying as if for battle.

He stopped in the center of the great hall and turned slowly around, lifting his gaze to take in all the paintings of past masters of the craft. Their eyes seemed to implore him to some greater purpose, warning him to tell the others to prepare for the coming danger.

But it wasn't real danger he felt, more a sense of terrible unease. As if the elementals held their collective breaths.

"You are out of your rooms early."

Theodyne recognized the voice but wished he'd run into anyone but Master Rhone. "I am going to the dining hall to arrange for Master Nico's breakfast to be brought up to him."

"Such a dutiful apprentice. I wonder if you realize quite what you enlisted for when you agreed to serve such a mercurial master."

Theodyne raised a brow. "Mercurial is one word I'd never use to describe Count Nicodemus de Valencia."

"Then what word would you use?"

It was an odd question, but Theodyne saw no harm in playing along. "Loyal."

"May you always find it so." With that cryptic remark, Master Rhone bowed his head and moved on down the hall toward the stairs.

Theodyne continued on to the dining hall. There were a few people seated and enjoying an early meal. Theodyne filled a plate and placed it on a serving tray. He'd really meant to send Pedraus to do the task, but it did give him something to do besides wander the halls.

He put a small carafe of wine on the tray and turned to make his way from the dining hall. Nico walked in at a fast clip, his brow drawn into a frown.

Theodyne stopped and waited for Nico to reach him. "You coming down for a meal kind of negates me bringing one up to you."

Nico's gaze skimmed lovingly over Theodyne's face. "I was worried about you."

"Me? Why?" He knew damn good and well the why of it, but thought to at least feign ignorance.

Nico leaned closer. "I don't have reason to worry, do I?"

The words were a warm brush of breath along Theodyne's neck. He held the tray so tightly, to keep from dropping it. The wood protested under his grip. "No."

Nico let out a deep breath. He put his hand on Theodyne's arm and turned him toward a table. "We can sit and eat in here if you want."

He glanced down at the tray. "I'd as soon go back to the room where we can speak without censure."

"All right."

They spoke no more as they made their way back up to the rooms. In the master's suite was a small table and chairs. It wasn't a banquet table by any stretch of the imagination, but it was large enough for two.

Theodyne set the tray down and handed Nico utensils. They took places across from each other and remained quiet until Nico stood up and paced the room.

"Tell me what is wrong. I don't like this not knowing if I've done something to offend or if you have regrets you aren't willing to admit."

Theodyne leaned back in his chair and crossed his arms. "I regret nothing. I spent the night doing exactly what I've wanted to since the moment I met you. How is that for an admission?"

Nico took two large strides and held Theodyne's face between his palms as he rendered him speechless with a savage kiss.

When he pulled away, he held his forehead to Theodyne's. "Then don't by Gods shut me out like that again."

"I didn't mean to." Theodyne closed his eyes against the tenderness. If anything brought him to his knees, it would be that unapologetic wave of tenderness. "The elementals are so unsettled this morning. I can feel it and it unnerves me."

Nico moved back a bit, running his thumb down Theodyne's cheek. "I'm sorry. I hadn't even considered that possibility. I've never taken an elemental for a lover."

Theodyne shook his head and raised a hand. He moved out of Nico's hold. "If it is any consolation, this is the first time I've taken one since discovering my elemental blood."

Nico gave him a crooked smile.

Suddenly the outside lit up like a green flash from an explosive. Tingles moved along every inch of Theodyne's skin. "What in all the blazing hells was that?"

"My net has caught a rather suspicious fish."

Theodyne frowned. "I don't understand."

"Come on." Nico left the room, running for the stairs.

Others had started out of their rooms, filling the hallway. Some were still in their nightclothes. Their lack of proper attire didn't stop them from following along to discover what had happened.

Frantic whispers from students and faculty speculated whether it was an attack by the clerics or the *prolate*'s forces. It didn't halt their progression down the stairs or stall their curiosity any.

Master Oberon met them in the great hall. "Are we under siege?"

Nico shook his head. His lips were compressed into a tight line. "Only from within."

The rolling river of alchemists made their way from the school and down to the cobbled drive. Where gate met river, a large black heap lay on the ground, unmoving save for the gentle ripple of fabric in the slight breeze.

As Theodyne moved closer, he realized what he looked at was a man lying injured. It was difficult to see if he still breathed or had died in the blast. Unbelievably, nothing in the area appeared burned.

Master Oberon urged people to stay back as he moved closer to the body. He leaned over and rolled the prone form to better see the face.

Journeyman Jolen.

Master Oberon and Nico exchanged glances but said nothing as the former picked up the lad and put him over his shoulder, then started back up to the school.

Nico lagged behind, falling into line with Theodyne as he neared.

"What was that all about?" Theodyne whispered.

"I tweaked the protections to give warning when the *prolate*'s mole neared the gates." He pointed to the unconscious form of Jolen. "That is the result."

"I don't think that's possible." Gods above knew he had no reason to defend Jolen, but he'd not thought him capable of betraying the school.

"Why?"

"Because he came to me in the library with concerns over what the *prolate* might be doing to harm elementals."

"What does that have to do with if he's the inside man or not? More reason for him to believe he was soon to be not only the betrayer but the betrayed."

Theodyne wrestled with the answer, but it was elusive. He supposed it didn't matter. He'd known more than one spy to have a change of heart when the depth of evil was uncovered, knowing they'd picked the losing side.

"What will happen to him now?"

Nico shook his head. "It is in Master Oberon's hands."

Theodyne wished he had studied the codex, but he was afraid he already knew what the sentence would be: banishment after having a close liaison with one of Nico's spheres.

A mix of emotions filtered through his soul. He didn't know what he'd do if someone decided to take away his memories. Most of the experiences might not be good ones, but they had brought him to this place in his life, and he could not condemn or deny the impact.

Theodyne leaned in and lowered his voice. "This is wrong, Nico."

Nico frowned. "What is wrong?"

"Taking his memories."

"It was your idea. By turning against us, he's become the enemy. We can't afford to let him keep the memories of all he knows about the order."

"As long as that's all you take." The enormity of what he'd suggested did not sit well with Theodyne. Matter of fact, it opened a pit in his belly that made the gorge forged by the river seem a tiny stream. "He deserves to not be left an idiot, unable to care for himself."

Nico's expression grew troubled. "Oh, Theodyne, do you think me capable of such a thing?"

"Not intentionally, no. But what if it's a byproduct of taking away the memories of his time at the Gold School?"

"Then Master Oberon will have to be very specific when he performs the extrication."

They entered the school once again and followed behind Master Oberon as he carried his unconscious burden to the stairs. Master Rhone was fast on their heels, muttering incoherent thoughts to no one.

Nico stopped and turned. "What are you mumbling about, Rhone?"

"Unprecedented." Master Rhone shook his head as if unable to comprehend it all. "What is the world coming to?"

"It's not coming to anything more than it was yesterday or the day before, or need I say when you failed to inform me that Master Donando was entertaining an overture to the clerics." Nico's voice was taut with anger and recrimination.

Theodyne wished he were anywhere but walking with the masters. The way they sniped at each other was uncomfortable. It had become evident that there were two factions within the school. Master Rhone had shown more sides of his personality than a stage player. There was nothing stable about the alchemist. It wouldn't surprise Theodyne if they discovered the master was the nexus for all the strife within the institution—not that the man would ever admit it.

They reached a room on the second level. Master Oberon placed Jolen on a long settee and then splashed water in his face.

The journeyman woke up sputtering and coughing. He held one hand to his chest and covered his mouth with the other. "What… happened?"

The spasms continued. He moaned and put his hands to his head. "Ow."

Master Oberon glanced at Nico. "Will he be all right?"

"No worse a headache than a nasty hangover."

Master Oberon gave a nod to an apprentice standing nearby. "Give him something for the pain. I want to be able to question him."

The apprentice bowed and left the room at a run. In the quiet that followed his departure, no one seemed eager to speak. It was maddening.

Theodyne felt the unease move through all the elementals. From the foundations to the battlements, there wasn't a stone in the school that didn't cry for vengeance. There was a surfeit of things going on here of which Nico was not aware, of that Theodyne was most certain. There were times he had the feeling the elementals knew a lot more than they unveiled to the alchemists—as if they toiled under a separate agenda.

The apprentice returned and handed a small vial to Master Oberon. The master uncorked the bottle and placed it under Jolen's nose. "Drink."

The journeyman shook his head. "I don't want anything."

"Take it or I'll force it down your throat."

Jolen looked up. His eyes were red-rimmed and confusion clouded. "Why are you treating me like this? I haven't done anything wrong."

Master Oberon pulled a chair over and set it in front of Jolen. "Then tell me what you were trying to do by leaving the school grounds this morning?"

Jolen's brow drew into a frown. "I never left my bed. I swear to you."

Master Rhone leaned in and put a comforting hand on Jolen's shoulder. "You were found unconscious down by the gate."

"I swear, Master, I don't remember going outside."

Theodyne watched the faces around him. Expressions varied from skepticism to consternation.

Nico merely looked deep in contemplation. He took the vial from Master Oberon. "You need to take at least a swallow to get rid of your pain."

Jolen's gaze moved to Nico. "Why don't I remember?"

"I don't know, but drink up and we'll get to the bottom of this."

Jolen finally took the vial and tipped it up, only taking a very small dose. If it was anything like the medicinal Pedraus had given Theodyne for his lung ailment, it was strong. Jolen made a face and stuck his tongue out.

"Give it a minute to work." Nico sat on the arm of a chair facing Jolen. "When you feel better, I want you to try and remember if there have been any other incidents where you've woken someplace strange without a memory of how you've gotten there."

Jolen rubbed a hand over his forehead. A light sheen of sweat broke out on his brow. He was hiding something. "It started about a month ago. I would be in one of the workrooms, and then suddenly I would be standing in the stables. Once I was in the washroom and ended up in the library. I have no idea how I'd gotten to these places or what I did on the way."

"Why didn't you tell Master Oberon or Master Rhone about these problems?"

"I don't know." He shook his head. "I meant to, but then I seemed to forget that too."

Master Oberon crossed his arms. "Did you go down the mountain before your trip to Lancor?"

Jolen frowned. "About six months ago. I went to see a group of traveling players. A carnival of fools they called themselves."

"Did anyone go with you?"

"Journeyman Celsi, Apprentices Lothan and Dauss."

Nico turned to Master Finelli. "I want the others in question brought here, along with those who became ill after going into town."

The master gave a nod and hurried from the room.

Nico did not look pleased with the turn of events. Theodyne didn't know what to make of the tension in the air. Nico suspected something, but he wasn't saying anything out loud. Whatever the situation, Theodyne didn't think they'd leave the school anytime soon.

Guilt began as a slow simmer in Theodyne's heart. What did he have to feel guilty over? He'd done nothing wrong. He'd not tried to escape from the school.

He slipped from the room and back down to the front drive. There he directed a few of the servants to unload the wagon and get the horses back into the stable.

Pedraus hobbled down the steps. "What are you doing?"

"I don't think Master Nico will want to leave today. We should probably stay another day or so."

"Let me see to the unpacking." Pedraus took one of the cases from Theodyne's hand.

Reluctantly, he relinquished his hold. There was little else left for him to do. He made his way back to the library. It was the only place in the school he felt of use—or that he might learn something to be of use.

There was no one there. Most of the students and faculty were still milling about, trying to figure out what had gone wrong and how Jolen had come to be down by the fence, hurt by a force they couldn't see or hear.

He didn't know what he was searching for, but it was there somewhere, tucked between the volumes composed from over five hundred years of arcane study.

"Show me," he called to the elementals. "Show me where it is."

Low mumblings began whispers from those forces that guided him. He followed the sounds, listening intently as they grew louder.

Finally he was drawn to an alcove.

"Pull the lever."

The voice was more a brush of wind against his ear, but he heard it clearly enough to look around him for a handle or pulley. There was nothing but a sconce on the wall. He grabbed it and pulled it toward him. The wall of books shifted to reveal a hidden room cut into the stone. Crystals glittered like jewels in the surface of the stones.

Theodyne ran his hand along the wall, feeling the energy infused in the natural structure. Shelves of books were lined up in the hidden alcove. Flames came to life in the sconces. He swore he saw eyes in the flickering depths.

A wind blew through the room from an unknown source. One of the books fell off the shelf and landed at his feet. *Supplanting an Existing Consciousness.*

"Is this what you wanted me to find?"

The flames grew higher, flickering in the breeze. The stone beneath his feet groaned. All the whispers of the elementals floated around him in disembodied voices.

"Thank you. I'm sure it will help."

He picked up the slim volume and headed back out of the room. The door closed behind him, shutting out the secret section from the rest of the library.

As he hurried back through the corridors to the room where the masters were interrogating Jolen, Theodyne thumbed through the book, trying to do a quick deciphering of the ancient text. The pages were as thin as an onion skin and almost as transparent. The ink was a dull brown. Odd. There was a resonance to it like the kind felt with living tissue.

His halted when he realized why—the volume was written in human blood.

Instant revulsion made his own run like a river of ice through his veins. He nearly dropped the book on the floor. Only determination and a need to find a solution before they wiped Jolen's memory kept him going.

He'd never truly understood the consequences of his actions before—or the repercussions of his words. Not until he realized taking someone's memories was not just an abstract idea, but a punishment that could be used against anyone the masters deemed unworthy.

There were more people in the room than had been there before. Everyone was talking at once and the noise and emotions ran too high to stay inside. Theodyne backed out, shaking his head to clear it of the confusion.

Nico turned his head, as if sensing Theodyne's presence. He beckoned to the master. Nico excused himself and came out into the hallway.

"What is it?"

"A few things. I've had the wagon unloaded and the horses unharnessed." He handed the book to Nico. "And I found this in the library."

Nico took the book. He turned it over a few times and then ran his hand over the cover. "This was locked away for a reason. How did you gain access?"

"The elementals."

Nico gave him a roguish smile that instantly heated Theodyne's blood. "You seem to be the favorite son."

"I don't know about that, but they do seem eager to assist me when it's needed."

"This now makes sense." Nico flattened his hand on the cover and patted it a few times. "As a matter of fact…."

He hurried back into the room and showed the book to Master Oberon. Enlightenment spread across his face, and he nodded as if he understood the significance without having any words spoken.

Master Oberon left the room. His retreating footsteps were unheard in the din of the room. Theodyne went to sit next to Jolen. The journeyman was not so arrogant now. He was the very portrait of a broken man.

Theodyne leaned in and lowered his voice so the others could not overhear. "The elementals want to help you. They showed me a book, and I gave it to Master Nico. There might be an answer to your problems in it."

"I hope so. I don't like feeling as if I've lost time."

Theodyne stared at the journeyman. "What I don't understand is why you didn't tell someone sooner. The masters could have already found a solution before it got this far."

"I've been asked that question, and I have no answer." Jolen rubbed his hands together. "The masters will turn me out for this. I feel it."

"Maybe not." The comfort was hollow, and they both knew it. Jolen glanced at Theodyne before turning his attention back to the masters as they moved to another room. "They are leaving to discuss my punishment."

"Perhaps it is your course of treatment." It hadn't escaped Theodyne's notice that Nico was the one to pull the masters from the room. "You have to trust they will figure out a solution."

Chapter Sixteen

NICO KNEW the book by reputation only. Over a hundred years had passed since the elementals had taken all texts judged too dangerous for mere mortals to possess and hidden them away in the secret library, only to be released when they deemed someone worthy or the need great. This time satisfied both qualifications.

The masters retired to a larger meeting room not far from where Journeyman Jolen struggled to regain his lost memory. Nico placed the book in the middle of the table so they could all take in the significance.

Master Atolla glanced up with wide eyes. "Where did you get that?"

"Apprentice Theodyne was invited into the secret library."

Murmurings and whispers began among the assembled masters. Nico lifted his hands to quiet them. "I think we all know the implications of this book, if not what it means to Jolen and the others. The spies we've been looking for have been here all along, not working of their own volition, but under the direction of a mind infecting theirs like a malignancy."

"Only another alchemist can perform such a spell. I don't believe anyone here has the knowledge."

Nico shook his head. "No. This evolution is beyond where my ancestors wished to go—a direction they cared not to follow. There is, however, one group that can perform such spellcasting, but they were banished from the city-states centuries ago."

Master Oberon gave an incredulous look. His head seemed to go back a bit, as if he'd suffered a blow. "Not the necromancers?"

"I'm afraid so. It is a most disastrous turn in an already tenuous situation." Nico wished he had better news to share. At least now there was a way to build a fortification against future attacks. "We have to reverse the effects of the spell on our students. No telling how many of our secrets were gained over the course of their mind enslavement."

"What do you propose we do to cure them?" Master Rhone had an air of complete and utter bewilderment about him.

Nico raised his brow and regarded the new Headmaster of the Gold School. "Master Oberon knows what to do."

The other masters turned to Oberon.

Master Oberon bowed most humbly. "I believe I do. If you will excuse me, I will go prepare for the extrication."

At his departure, Master Finelli turned to Nico. "Extrication? That sounds dangerous for both parties."

"I assure you it is only dangerous for the subject. Master Oberon will feel no ill effects."

Master Rhone made a shocked sound. "You would risk Jolen?"

Nico leaned over the table and pointed to the book. "He is already *at risk*, Master Rhone. As long as there is another consciousness inside his mind, able to control him at will, he is a risk to himself and everyone around him."

He waited for the words to hit their mark. It wasn't long in coming. With a necromancer in the area, they had to take all precautions. What unsettled Nico most about the situation was the silence from the elementals—especially Anjufer—on the subject. They should have alerted someone the moment they felt the presence in the school. There were enough elementals housed at the school to have been sensitive to the violation when it occurred, and that included both students and environment.

Nico took in the masters before him. "While I am assisting Master Oberon in the extrication, I would like for you to decide how we are going to go about discovering the identity of the necromancer, and more importantly, why the *prolate* needs our secrets if he's thought to bring a forbidden sect back into the city-states. Also, it is now paramount that we secure Donando's remains."

There was a moment of stunned silence while the significance of that statement sank in. All the assembled masters looked as if they were on the verge of getting ill. To a man, they paled.

"We need to formulate a plan." Master Finelli stood. "I will preside over the discussions. I don't want this to get lost on unimportant tangents."

Nico gave a curt nod. "Very well. Carry on."

He left the room and returned to where Theodyne still sat, trying to comfort Jolen. A distinct stab of unfamiliar jealousy coursed through his veins when he saw how close the two men sat, their heads bent together in what appeared an intimate conversation.

Theodyne glanced up and tapped Jolen. "Master Nico is here."

Jolen looked young and scared. There was nothing for it—this was a terrifying place to be. Words of comfort would only spread so far.

Jolen swallowed, then said, "What is my punishment to be?"

The other students—who were in the same predicament as Jolen— quieted down their conversations to hear the news.

"There is not going to be a punishment. Not the kind you believe you'll get." Nico regarded the other students. "If you will please wait out in the hall, you will be called in one at a time."

They shuffled from the room. The soft leather of their shoes made whispery sounds on the marble floor. Master Oberon braved the tide of students to come inside. He held a series of black velvet bags tied with gold strings in his hands. "This is what you intended?"

"It is." Nico walked to the door. "Theodyne, if you will excuse us."

Theodyne stood stiffly. He squeezed Jolen's shoulder and left the room without ever giving Nico so much as a glance. Nico closed his eyes briefly. He'd have to explain it all later—though if Theodyne had been any other apprentice, there would never have been an expectation of being allowed to stay and watch the proceedings.

But then Theodyne had proven time and again, even with a little bit of training, he was more advanced than any apprentice had a right to be. Maybe when they returned to the villa he'd give Theodyne some time to read and study the codex, then test him on the material. If he passed, he'd be advanced to journeyman.

Nico let the thoughts dissipate as he turned his attention back to Master Oberon and Jolen. Master Oberon had just removed one of the spheres from a black velvet bag.

Jolen backed up in fear. "What is that for?"

"There is another essence inside you—a part of one. Separate from that which connects you to your human and elemental core. This is other. Darker. Not of alchemy."

Tears filled Jolen's eyes. He nodded slowly. "Then I've not been imagining it."

"It doesn't appear so." Master Oberon held up the sphere. "I want you to focus on all the times you felt as if your memory had deserted you."

He moved the sphere to place it in the middle of a table. Next he lit a candle and placed it behind the sphere. Smart thinking. Use the flickering flame as a focal point and Jolen would relax while staring into the depths.

Nico watched with growing interest as Jolen's eyes grew soft and unfocused. Master Oberon held his hand over the orb, drawing forth the lost memories, and placed his other hand on Jolen's shoulder. A tiny tendril of silvery thread came from the center of Jolen's forehead. As it moved through the air toward the sphere, it churned and twisted into ghostly images. Some of the faces were wholly recognizable to Nico, others strangers. None of the apparitions were given voice, though phantom mouths moved on silent words.

Analysis of the memories would come after the extrication—once the extra presence inside Jolen was gone. It would take time to get to the point where it was safe to lift the necromancer's influence. All the instances of overt mind control had to be lifted out first in order to take away the foundation. Once that was complete, Master Oberon could go to work on finding the anchor that had attached the evil consciousness to Jolen's.

Watching the process, seeing the strain and tension bead up as perspiration on Oberon's brow made it clear he would require rest before attempting another extrication. Nico would have to perform the next one. If they were both spent for the day, they would have to sequester the other students for the night and start afresh in the morning.

At least he was here to assist.

A cold dread swept over Nico. *Theodyne!* He'd come down with the same illness the rest of the elementals had. He'd even admitted there was something he could not remember but knew it had been important.

Nico now had no doubt Theodyne had been in contact with the one responsible for casting the spell on the elementals. Why else would he not send up an alarm? Infect the person watching so they in turn became another spy—another unwilling minion in the bid to take over the Gold School.

Too bad the alchemists had no way to reverse the spell—to gain an unwitting spy among the *prolate*'s household. Alas, such sneaky and underhanded means were not on the path to enlightenment. The soul would not ascend with such strings tethering them to the ground. Not that they meant to send Jolen to his ascension. This was more about saving his life than ending it.

According to the *Eye of Truth*, the mindtouch of a necromancer often proved fatal if allowed to remain imprinted on the soul of a living host.

The color of the thread pouring from Jolen's mind began to change color, grow darker, more sinister. Stench from rotted flesh wafted through the room. Master Oberon made a face, but held steady as he drew the soul-crushing toxins from Jolen's essence.

This last anchor of the spell did not go quietly. Jolen's face contorted. Sweat beaded on his forehead and ran down into his eyes. His mouth opened and horrible sounds issued forth. The words were unrecognizable and the moans inhuman.

It was enough to make Nico clench his teeth to keep from ordering Master Oberon to stop. There was nothing for it—the extrication must continue.

Jolen's breath sputtered, caught. His face turned first red, then purple, and finally blue. The necromancer held on to his subject with deadly force.

Master Oberon's body shook as he pulled harder at the entity, trying to disentangle the tenacious claws from the heart of its prey. Nico lifted his hands, easing them into the dark river of rotten thoughts and twisted desires. It was like submerging his body into pure evil. Bile rose to the back of his throat. His head pounded with the forces knocking against the iron control of his will. The necromancer would not breach his defenses.

He was descended from Mercurian Dante. His blood ran with five hundred years of alchemists, and he used his connection with every last one of his ancestors to drive the beast back from the consciousness of Jolen.

Jolen slid to the floor, an unmoving heap of flesh and bone. The connection to the sphere shattered, sending the trail of the necromancer's control spinning wildly through the room. Nico reached for it and tugged.

He felt the claws rip free. Jolen jolted up from the floor. His mouth opened on a silent scream. Eyes wide and staring into a terrifying abyss only he saw.

Nico struggled with the entity. It was like capturing a sea creature whose only ambition was to sink all its tentacles into flesh. He'd give the death dancer credit—the hold was stronger than any he'd ever seen.

Nico slung the slimy essence at the sphere and watched as the glass ball sucked it up greedily despite violent resistance. The sphere expanded and contracted a few times, trying to hold together under the internal force of dark magics. Nico didn't know if the construct might splinter and release the energies.

A storm brewed within the glass depths, worse than any he'd captured during his experiments. It was like looking into a hurricane in hell. Motion inside made the globe spin, faster and faster, until it was in danger of falling off the table. Nico grabbed for the sphere, but it was too hot to touch—not from flame, but from cold. Frost formed on the outside, making it harder to see the rage and anger that continued to try and fight its way out. If the glass cooled too much, the risk of the globe shattering increased.

Nico looked around the room for anything he might use to contain the spell. There, on the top shelf of a curio, was a small metal cask. Quickly, he grabbed the box and emptied the contents onto the credenza. Scattered bits of leaves and stems from some long-forgotten spell fell dry upon the table.

Nico snatched up the sphere and winced in pain. The surface of the glass was now hot, as if it had been set over flame. *Damn*, sudden temperature fluctuations were even worse. He shoved it inside the box and closed the lid. It was well known that iron did not conduct magic, but rendered the power null.

There was a tiny lock on the box, but Nico had no idea if the whereabouts of the key was still known. It didn't really matter much. He ran his thumb along the seam, changing the shape of the metal to seal the container—anything to keep prying eyes out and the necromancer's essence in. Later he'd have it resealed at the foundry. But first, there were other things to attend.

Nico set the cask aside and went to Jolen. The young man's hair was in his face, obscuring the view. Nico gently brushed it back. Not surprisingly, Jolen's skin was cool to the touch, his complexion waxy, nearly deathlike.

"Come on. Breathe. I will not let you die." He covered the journeyman's mouth with his and blew out a big lungful of air. Jolen's chest rose with the effort, but he did not take up the breath on his own.

"Damn it. Do not let the evil win!"

Master Oberon dragged himself over, his gait slow and unsteady. He dropped to his knees on the other side of Jolen's lifeless body. "Does he live?"

Nico stopped to feel for a pulse. It was there, but weak and thready. "Yes, but barely. He's slipping from this world."

"We've done something wrong. I was too ham-fisted in my extrication."

"Do not blame yourself. It's a mechanism to prevent Jolen from speaking should someone try to pry the memories from him." He leaned over and pumped another breath into the journeyman's lungs.

Anger creased Master Oberon's face. "No matter the method of discovery."

"He'd not take that chance. Not and let the vessel live." Another breath. This time Jolen began to cough and wheeze.

He helped Jolen to sit up, to get in a better position to breathe. "Open the window, Oberon."

Jolen took in gulps of air, as if he could not get enough. Slowly his color returned, though he remained pale around the lips. His hands shook as he rested them between his bent knees. He didn't speak, but regarded both masters in wary silence.

Nico put a comforting hand on Jolen's shoulder. "I am not going to press you to speak, but a simple one-word answer will suffice. How are you feeling?"

Jolen swallowed and bent his head onto his hands. "Terrible." It came out as a shuddery croak.

"That is probably to be expected."

Master Oberon returned to them, but did not sit on the floor. "Let's get you up and onto the settee near the window. More fresh air will be good for you."

Jolen allowed Master Oberon to assist him to stand. He sagged against the master as if his legs were still too unready to support his weight. Neither of them looked all that steady.

Nico gave Oberon a speculative glance. "I don't suggest we attempt any more extrications today. I am fairly certain neither of us has adequate energy to sustain another bout like that one."

"And yet the thought of leaving the others with such vileness inside makes me want to press on even at the risk of my own mortality." Oberon rubbed his chin. "I suppose we can lock them in their rooms for the night. Make sure they have plenty to eat and drink and are comfortable. It is the only way to ensure they or the school does not come to harm in the meantime."

"We also need to obtain more iron casks. The spheres, once filled, must be secured. They were not constructed for such a purpose. I fear I underestimated their viability in such a venture." There might be time to construct more. What if iron shavings were poured into the sand mixture before constructing the sphere, would that work to contain the presence better?

"You've got an odd gleam in your eye, Nico." Oberon regarded him with a narrow expression.

"Speculating on how to solve two problems at once." If he added iron to the mixture, would the presence of the iron make it impossible to create the sphere in the first place, or did it depend on the ratio of other components to iron?

It was something he'd have to work on.

Perhaps he'd spend more time in the laboratory or go to the foundry and… yes, that might work even better.

He needed to consult the *Eye*.

THEODYNE DIDN'T bother to congregate by the door of the workroom or to sit waiting with the other injured parties. There was no need. What he wanted to do was return to the town proper. There was something he wasn't quite remembering about his time at the *prolate*'s palace. Something that had faded more and more with each hour he was away.

What had he lost?

It was right there, so close he could almost grab onto it, but too far to slip his hands around. The memory stayed slightly out of reach and fuzzy no matter how far he stretched his mind.

He turned down a corridor and forgot where he was going. It was as if he ran into a brick wall both mentally and physically. The hit knocked him back three feet onto his behind. He lay there for a few moments, staring up at the ceiling.

What had happened?

Oh, he didn't feel right at all. It was as if someone had picked through his brain, siphoning off memories one by one. Was that how it felt when the spheres were used? If so, he didn't wish it on anyone. Not even the guards at Pallonia or Estobán Medovin. Just as the names moved through his mind, their significance was gone.

He curled into a fetal position, hands to head.

"Theodyne?"

Warm hands capped his shoulders. A soft, masculine voice came from what sounded like very far away. He knew that voice—it was important to him, but he didn't know how or why.

"What's wrong?" One of the hands moved to his forehead. "You're burning with fever again."

"Can't remember." He tried to roll over but was too weak to move.

"All right. Let me get you to your room and we can figure out what happened." The man tried to move him, but his legs didn't want to support the deadweight of his body.

"Theodyne, love, you have to help me." There was a desperate plea in the man's voice—almost like his heart was about to break.

"No strength. Sorry." His eyes fluttered a bit before he closed them. The pat of a hand on his cheeks failed to get a response. His body was too tired to move even that much.

He slid to the floor, but landed on the warm nest of the man's chest, cradled in a pair of strong arms. A rocking motion started, threatening to raise bile to the back of his throat, and yet he had no way to warn his caretaker.

"Nico! What's happened?"

Heavy footsteps followed the deep, booming voice.

"I don't know. I found him on the floor. Help me get him up to his room."

Theodyne knew that voice as well, but the memory was elusive. A whisper of smoke on the wind. He felt himself being lifted and carried. Each movement jarred his body in a painful manner. It would be a miracle if they arrived at his room without him being ripped apart.

In time, he was laid on a comfortable bed. He sank down into the layers of quilting and feathers and slept for he knew not how long.

When he woke, he found a man sitting next to his bed with his head bent forward. The man had fallen asleep in the chair with a thick book in his lap.

Theodyne smacked his lips together. His mouth was as dry as a dust bowl. He rested up on his elbows to look for a pitcher of water, but a wave of dizziness spread over him like a wool blanket. He lay back against the pillows.

"Excuse me, sir." The words were a croak of sound and not without a good deal of pain.

The man startled awake. "Theodyne?" He came over and rested his warm hand on Theodyne's forehead. "How do you feel?"

"Thirsty."

The man moved around the room and came back with a goblet of water. Theodyne drank deeply with the man's help. When he'd had his fill, he lay back again, staring into eyes that were so familiar he should have remembered them.

"Do I know you?"

A glimmer of panic filled those eyes. The man cleared his throat. "I'm Count Nicodemus de Valencia, Adept Alchemist at the Gold School. You call me Nico. Do you remember your name?"

"You keep calling me Theodyne, so I have to assume that's correct."

"But you don't recall?"

"Not as such, no."

Nico took Theodyne's hand in his and squeezed it. "Rest for a while, I'll return after I've consulted with the others."

He wanted to ask what others, but right about then a face appeared in his mind's eye. A horrible visage, as if it had been pulled from the grave and left to finish rotting in the sun. Theodyne shuddered. The clarity of the vision was as if the death mask was in the room with him, staring down onto the bed, but when he blinked in rapid succession, the image faded from sight. No, it hadn't been real, but some leftover scene from a nightmare.

He rolled over onto his side and hugged the pillow, bringing his knees up to his chest. For some reason the position brought him comfort and eased his troubled mind. In no time, he slid back into the arms of sleep.

Chapter Seventeen

NICO HAD never been so scared in all his life. Not even as a child had the shades of fear fallen so far over him as to infect everything he touched. This was a complete nightmare. Necromancers had been gone so long from the city-states the alchemists had stopped training their brethren on how to combat that particular ability.

"All the others who were affected by the fever have lost their memories. It's as if they were all mentally linked during the extrication." Oberon ran a hand through his hair, making the locks stick up in places. "I have no idea how to reverse this without giving the memories back to Jolen."

"This necromancer is powerful. He's infected them with a thread that runs through all the lads." Nico rubbed his chin and stared out the window of the laboratory. "I fear there may only be one way to stop the spell."

Oberon nodded. "But who will you get to do the deed? If an alchemist is involved and it is discovered, we will all suffer."

"I don't even know if such a thing is possible. Someone who dances with death will know best how to avoid it."

"Then what other solutions do we have?"

Nico shook his head. The *Eye of Truth* had not given any insight into the use of iron to hold in the magic, so he doubted it would give indications of how to neutralize a necromancer. "I'm not sure."

"We cannot let this go unanswered. It was a trap built into the spell, of that I'm sure." Oberon crossed his arms over his chest. "Anyone who tried to counteract the control would strip the lads' memories of all they held dear."

"I do not plan to let it go unanswered. I need more time to consult the texts and the *Eye of Truth*. Perhaps even Mercurian Dante wrote something about this sort of wrinkle. He did live in a time when the necromancers were the alchemists' greatest foes."

"True." Oberon stood. "While you're searching through books, I am going to gather the men together in one room so we can better attend them."

"Good idea." Nico started out of the door, then stalled. "Do me a favor and leave Theodyne where he is. I'll tend to him myself after I pull a few books from the archives."

"Very well."

Nico left, feeling the press of a question coming from Oberon. What would he do when the other master finally asked? Answer it truthfully, demur and defer, or simply tell him it was none of his business? He'd not worry about it today. Possibly not even tomorrow. What he did in his personal life and with whom was not open for question or debate. He'd fallen hard and fast for Theodyne, no matter his past—maybe in spite of it.

Nico made his way to the archives, determined to save Theodyne and the others. As the head of the Gold School, it fell on him to protect their students from such noxious attacks, and he'd failed on the most basic level.

Anjufer waited for him in the fireplace grate. "The elementals are watching over him. Do not fret."

"I'm more worried about how I'm going to purge the necromancer from the minds of our students while giving them back their memories." He sat down in the chair in front of the fire. "Theodyne doesn't even know me."

"Fundamentally, he does." Anjufer's golden flame eyes blinked. "He was going to leave the school and find the necromancer when he was stricken."

"The elementals knew this?"

"Yes. He knows what the death dancer looks like. Saw him with the *prolate*. He just doesn't remember that is what he saw." Anjufer grew larger, brighter. "He wanted to make it right."

Nico rubbed his forehead. No matter what the rest of the world or the judicial system thought of Theodyne, Nico knew his lover's heart was in the right place. It probably always had been. How different would things have been for Theodyne if he'd been discovered by the alchemists as a child?

Nico burned with fear and worry that none of the spells or incantations—none of the formulations or elevations—would bring Theodyne's memory back. Would it matter? He could learn all over again and lose all those memories that had caused so much pain in the past.

But no. This was what Theodyne meant when he said taking the memories away was wrong. The change of heart had been real and forged by compassion.

"The answers you seek can be found in the book Theodyne gave you earlier and in the *Eye of Truth*." Anjufer blinked a few times. The flames that made up his body wavered in the wind from an open window. "That and in your own heart. You know what you must do and how to do it."

The book, along with the *Eye of Truth*, remained upstairs in Theodyne's room. Nico thanked Anjufer and started back to the suite. He'd not made it even halfway when Master Finelli and the others intercepted him.

Finelli's face was ashen, his expression grave. "We must take an attack party into the town."

Surreal as it sounded, Nico had to ask himself if he'd heard Master Finelli correctly. The man was as gentle and passive a creature as Nico had ever known. Hearing him speak of an attack waged by the alchemists turned the world upon its axis.

"Why should we do that?" Even as he asked the question, something in the depths of Master Finelli's eyes told the tale. "You saw something."

Master Finelli closed his eyes briefly and nodded. "In the scrying bowl."

This did not bode well. "Tell me."

Master Finelli swallowed. "Headmaster Donando has been… reanimated."

They had run out of time. "See that the students infected by the necromancers are secured in their rooms and unable to get out. Find Master Oberon and have him meet me in the adepts' workroom."

"Yes, Nico."

Nico changed direction and headed for the closest stairwell. With every step, a plan formed in his head. Forget the *Eye of Truth,* or any other volume from the time of the necromancers' reign, he was going on pure instinct and nerve. And why not? Over the course of his studies he'd read the *Eye of Truth* from cover to cover. The teachings were locked somewhere deep in his memories. It was up to his subconscious to regurgitate them now in his time of need.

At this time of night the workroom was empty. Bottles clinked together and metal twanged as Nico pulled ingredients and implements from the shelves. The containers he needed to construct were of a particular variety. Air vents were required on one end of the sphere to allow passage into the glass globe.

With his hands full, he used his elbow to rap on the fireplace conduit.

Anjufer was there before the resonance quieted. "The necromancers have moved."

"And are using Donando's body to gain our secrets. How would you care for a bit of vengeance?"

Anjufer flared. His lot had battled the necromancers centuries before and lost. Many of his kin of the flame had perished, reduced to spent ash. "How do you propose such a thing?"

"Give me a moment." Nico set the materials on the table. "I'm going to transport you to Delaneux in one of my glass spheres."

Anjufer's laughter popped and cracked like dry wood under intense heat. "I will accompany you."

The workroom door opened and Master Oberon entered, slightly out of breath. "Is it true?"

"I have not confirmed the news, but it was given to me by Master Finelli and his face told the truth."

Master Oberon glanced at the assembled materials. "You work on those, and I'll verify the information."

Anjufer's flames rose upward and outward, coming a good six feet out of the hearth. "It is true. I've already consulted with the others."

Master Oberon held up his hand. "Calm down, my friend, or you'll turn us all to cinders before we leave the school."

Nico blocked out the conversation that continued between Master Oberon and the fire elemental. His concentration centered absolutely on crafting a vessel in which to transport Anjufer. As far as Nico knew, the task had not been attempted since Anjufer took the vow to devote his eternity to the school.

In less time than it took for the alchemist and elemental to debate Anjufer's bloodlust, Nico had the spheres finished. He held one up in front of the flames. "Can you squeeze inside?"

"Yes."

"Nico. Here." Master Oberon tossed something at him. He couldn't very well catch it while he held the globe. He tossed the glass ball into the air and let it hang suspended for a moment. Ah, it was gloves to protect his hands from the heat of the globe.

Nico put them on, then let the sphere drop into his covered palm. "Anjufer, if you please."

The fire elemental diminished into a thin thread of flame no thicker than spider silk. He poured into the opening at the top of the globe, filling the interior in a swirling mass of color and light.

When he was completely contained, Nico held up the sphere and saw two small eyes staring out at him. "Are you all right in there?"

"I do not like it in here, Master Nico, but I shall endure."

"Very well." Nico took a leather pouch hanging on the wall and dumped the contents out into a bowl. He placed the spheres inside for protection. "Come, Oberon. Let's bring Donando home."

ALL THE way down the mountain, Nico felt they were being drawn into a trap. It did not stop or slow his descent. On the contrary, it made him push faster to meet their enemy.

The streets of Delaneux were deserted. Silent. Not even the night watch made regular patrols. This did not bode well. It was as if the entire town had fallen into their beds and been there for some time. If he checked in on them, would they be covered in cobwebs and dust straight from a child's tale?

The wind changed and a stink like the rot of a recent battlefield filtered between buildings and down streets.

Master Oberon turned to him. "I don't like this."

Neither did Nico, but they'd come this far—for his part, they were committed. If they left Donando's body in the hands of the necromancer, the secrets of the alchemists were forfeit. No telling what the necromancer would be able to get out of the deceased former headmaster.

"Should we try the *prolate*'s palace?" Master Oberon leaned over his horse's neck and glanced into the night-shrouded distance.

Nico lifted the flap on the leather pouch. "Can you tell where the necromancer has Donando?"

There was a pause. The sphere glowed brighter, casting a light around Nico. "To the west of town, near the entrance to the Agia family crypt."

Nico motioned for his horse to move as he pulled the reins to turn westward. He'd grown up in this region, knew every rock and tree of Delaneux like an old friend. The ornate, iron fence that surrounded the Agia cemetery appeared in the night like crooked skeletons holding lances pointed skyward. Each guardian had a skull for a face, mouth open on a terrifying scream.

Nico remembered the first time his father had walked him past the structure. He'd clung to his sire's hand in fear, watching the twisted metal with distrustful eyes.

He knew no such fear now—only the righteousness of his quest.

The Agia buried their dead in a mausoleum far under the ground. Calling the area catacombs was stretching the truth, since they were packed into a single large chamber like old, dried wood in a shed. Every so many decades, the servants came and took the older remains to a grinding mill, where the bones were crushed into fine powder and returned to the earth. Though the practice sounded grim, Nico could not find fault with it, since the bodies replenished the soil long after the soul had departed.

As they neared, a whisper reminiscent of dry leaves moved on the wind. Pale lights swirled in the air—they were neither comforting nor illuminating. A chill of warning moved down Nico's spine. The necromancer was near. Those were no fireflies or embers from a fire—it was the recalling of a spirit that had already found release.

Nico brought Anjufer's globe from the bag and held it aloft, using the glow like a torch. He didn't dare ask Anjufer to grow brighter. As it was, they had not yet been detected.

They rode closer but were still outside the gates. Nico pulled in the reins and dismounted. Getting inside the enclosure was not the hard part— it was getting inside without either the necromancer or his accomplices finding out.

The mechanism was sealed and refused to turn by either brute force or alchemical manipulation. Nico held the sphere to his mouth and whispered instructions to Anjufer. The fire elemental sent a tendril of flame into the lock and turned the apparatus so hot it liquefied.

A distinct scent of burnt metal filled the air. That would surely not go unnoticed by those near the crypt. Nico slipped inside, holding the gate for Oberon to follow him through.

Nico crouched low, moving as silently as possible over the leaf-strewn ground. The Agias had let the place go in recent years. Neglect was present everywhere he stepped.

He followed the pattern of dancing lights to the mouth of the tomb. As he neared, he could make out a body on the floor and someone standing over it, arms raised and moving through the air as if mixing the particles. It appeared as if the reanimation had not yet taken hold. Or the necromancer was having a more difficult time with the headmaster. From what Nico had read, infusing life into a corpse was a pretty instantaneous process if death occurred soon before the act.

Headmaster Donando's body seemed resistant to the measure.

Nico tapped the side of the globe and Anjufer shot from the container like a cannonball. He wound his flaming body around the necromancer. Robes as thin and brittle as ancient burial shrouds ignited.

A horrific scream rent the night. The death dancer spun in a circle, casting light and shadows along the tomb walls. Nico hid his face from the heat but continued to watch the spectacle, unable to look away even if he wanted to.

The odd lights that twirled over Donando blinked out of existence— extinguished stars no longer able to give life. Nico crawled closer, Oberon on his heels. They grabbed Donando's lifeless form and dragged it to safety. No telling what kind of power might be unleashed if Anjufer destroyed the creature.

Suddenly, there was an explosion of sound, and sparks shot off in every direction. Anjufer flickered in the middle of the tomb, alone.

"What happened?" Nico rose, brushing off his pants. There were crawling, slithery things on the floor. Bones of long-gone Agia ancestors and random animals littered the shelves. Some of the skulls had fallen off and rolled to land in corners, staring up with sightless sockets.

Anjufer returned to the sphere. "He disappeared. Transmuted into another dimension. Beyond our grasp."

Nico and Master Oberon exchanged glances.

"With power like that, how can we know when and where he will reappear?" There was anger and frustration in Master Oberon's voice, and Nico didn't rightly blame him for either emotion.

"Ward the school and keep it so. Allow no one onto the grounds. All deliveries must be left at the gate and inspected before being brought inside." Nico studied Donando's remains. "I think we need to cremate him. Leave nothing behind that could be of use to the necromancers."

Master Oberon nodded. "Agreed."

They stood back and allowed Anjufer to perform the honors. It took no time for the body of the former headmaster to reduce to ash. With the act complete, Nico stooped down and scooped the remains into the second sphere. Any straggling fragments he lifted with a thought to join the others in the globe. He rubbed his thumb over the hole at the top, sealing it forever.

Chapter Eighteen

NICO AND Oberon returned to the school tired, frustrated, and planning their next move. How were they to fight an enemy they could not see—or who had the ability to disappear on a whim? Not even the adepts connected to the Gold School had mastered that skill. The elementals had the power to bend natural substances more readily to their needs, but as far as Nico knew, not one of them could fold or bend distance.

Nico said good night to Oberon and headed to the suites. He'd worried about Theodyne in his absence, but knew Pedraus would care for him better than anyone in residence.

He entered the rooms and quietly set the leather bag down.

A candle burned in the small annex room. Nico moved to the door and watched Theodyne as he flipped pages of the *Eye of Truth*, as if looking for something he couldn't seem to locate. Frustration bled off the apprentice and filled the room with an odd, tangy odor.

Panic set Nico's nerves on edge. He'd hidden the book away before he'd left so just such a thing would not happen. Yet, he didn't want to startle or admonish Theodyne directly. No telling how deep the necromanical influence went. Would Theodyne attack or protect if threatened? Best to play it off and see how things went.

"What are you searching for, Theodyne?"

Despite Nico's soft voice Theodyne looked up startled at the interruption. He looked back down at the book as if he had no idea how the tome had gotten into his hands. "I don't know. I thought I remembered something, but it's gone now."

He closed the book and set it aside as if it was of no importance.

"It's all right. If you want to look through it, you are more than welcome to, though I'd much prefer you to wait until you are well." Especially since there was still the chance the necromancer could see through Theodyne's eyes and gather information on the alchemists. Until they knew where or what had become of the death dancer, the alchemists were not safe.

The *Eye of Truth* was like no other book in their possession. Inside its yellowed pages were both codex and canon of alchemical law. It brought together chemical and spiritual reactions, and married souls and molecules as the Gods themselves had done at the beginning of creation. The last quarter of the book was made up of rubbings taken from the very surface of the Emerald Tablet.

"Do you understand the writing?" Nico took a place on the bed next to Theodyne. The book was handwritten by Mercurian Dante, so Theodyne might have recognized the script from another text.

"Yes. It's like the notes of a song I have stuck in my head long after the musicians ceased to play." He ran his long, elegant fingers over the cover of the book. "The words echo in my head and heart, but when I try to grasp the meaning, they flee."

"It will come back to you."

Theodyne stared at him. His golden eyes had softened. It was a look Nico had never seen in Theodyne before. "I love you, don't I?"

Nico smiled, feeling his throat close with emotions. His eyes burned with the onslaught of tears. He'd never been so tired in all his life. "We've never said the words to each other. I will not presume to put them in your mouth now when you can't remember if it is that emotion or something else."

Theodyne gave him a soft smile—almost shy. "I think maybe I do."

Nico made a fist with the hand facing away from Theodyne. He didn't wish for him to see how the words struck. The pain the words inflicted were akin to stone striking flesh. Hard. Forceful. The loss of such basic knowledge was a painful reminder of how much more work he and the other masters had yet to do.

"How are you going to help me?"

"Have you ever seen a tapestry fray and begin to unravel? Can you imagine that?"

Theodyne nodded.

"That is how we'll do it: one thread at a time."

THEODYNE SAT in a hard chair, facing the rest of the affected souls. Some of their faces looked familiar, but he didn't have names to put with them. The man beside him he felt he knew fairly well. A name floated through his head but never stayed long enough to recognize.

By appearances, the man was in worse shape than Theodyne. He was strapped to the chair with a couple of belts and a length of rope. The knots were not made with malice, as one would tie a prisoner to a chair during a torture session, but with care and tenderness. How Theodyne knew torture methods, he couldn't rightly say.

Had he ever been to prison? As if his hand was working from some ancient ritual, Theodyne raised it to touch his face. He let his fingers trace along the edges of the puckered flesh. It was the shape of a *T*. What was the significance of the mark? He wanted to ask Nico, but the adept stood in the middle of the circle, dressed in the finest robes Theodyne had ever seen. A quick survey of the others did not reveal a brand on their faces.

The mark set him apart, made him different.

A funny feeling crept up his spine—as if he'd always been apart from everything. Never truly belonging to anyone or anything. If getting his memory back meant he'd remember being alone, maybe he didn't want to know. If he refused to undergo the treatment, he could start again from this point and move forward as a new man.

His gaze fell on Nico and he knew. No matter how deep the pain or vast the loneliness, he didn't want to forget if he loved Nico or not. That was worth everything.

Nico moved in a circle. His eyes were closed and his lips moved as if reciting a poem of great emotion.

Though Theodyne couldn't hear the words, he felt them, and it made him extremely uncomfortable. He twitched in his seat.

The feeling of a single thread being dragged across his body began at his forehead and ran down across his face, then over his arms. No matter how hard he wiped his skin, the sensation remained. Then there was the slightest tugging from between his eyes. The phenomenon ran straight through his brain and pulled at the back of his skull. It wasn't a wide path of pain, only about the width of a hair, but it dug in tenacious claws as if afraid of being taken out of his brain.

He leaned down, putting his head in his hands. Immediately a sense of disorientation turned the world upside down. This healing might go much better if he voluntarily moved to the floor rather than fell to the stones.

It was not a graceful move. He more crumpled than slid. Around him, he became aware that the others followed suit. Soon only the poor soul who was tied to his seat remained upright.

Still the chant continued.

Images out of time and place passed through Theodyne's mind like a trip through a gallery where the paintings were animated. All through it, a pair of intense eyes was watching him as if by the sheer power of their stare they could compel Theodyne to do something heinous to his friends.

Inside, a core of self-knowledge bloomed like a flower that opens its petals under the sun's influence. Theodyne knew he'd never betray his friends. That was as engrained on his being as breathing.

A loud pop sounded in his ear, followed by an ooze of matter from the center of his mind.

If he looked down, Theodyne was sure he'd be melted like a candle left unattended, his body nothing more than wax on the floor.

Nico bent down and dipped a cloth into the wax that used to be Theodyne and then lit it on fire. He danced around the circle, spouting gibberish.

Theodyne blinked a few times, trying to clear the fog from his vision. Nico stood before him again—he wasn't moving around the room. That was all illusion.

It made him wonder what was true and what was fabricated from his splintered mind.

NICO DID not like the way Theodyne looked. His skin was ashen, his lips pale. His breathing was erratic. There was nothing for it but to push on.

The *Eye of Truth* warned that death might be a result of dragging the presence of a necromancer from those under his influence. The spell took root and grew thorns that anchored the influence into the deepest areas of the mind.

He had to take care with the extraction, but he meant to get all the pieces out of the students' minds. Even one thorn left behind might fester and grow, giving the necromancer a hold in which to retain his grip.

That particular rite would come later, when he and Oberon split the group in two, and each began the arduous task of ridding the affected of any splinters.

Now he concentrated on gathering all the threads of consciousness that contained the necromancer's signature. It wasn't hard to find—dark and cold like a starless night spent inside a crypt with the restless souls of the dead.

Nico looked for the next collective thread and pulled. It took finesse and a little persuasion to get it to move even a bit. The thorns had a tendency to catch on the other threads, making the strands snag. Though he'd wanted to work clean, there was nothing to do for some of the residue left behind at this juncture. He'd have to go back in and sweep away the remains later. It was more important to get the largest pieces out now and save the tiny details for later. Gently, Nico turned the thread a bit, then gave it a little slack. He turned it again and was able to ease it along. Finally it came free. He deposited it with the first one in the iron sphere. The inside of the globe was infused with a spell meant to nullify the intentions. As each thread went into the bowl, it burned and disintegrated. When all the pieces were removed and burned, they would then be encased in the iron sphere and buried where the elementals would protect them from falling into the wrong hands. In this case, from the necromancer reacquiring them.

Anger filled Nico every time he thought of how it had not been one agent but many who had infiltrated the school—their own students used against them. It was as devious as it was ingenious.

The work was intricate and dangerous. If he didn't pull the correct thread at the correct time, the strings of memory might become tangled and lost forever.

Theodyne moaned and rolled to his side, curling up into a ball. Some of the others lay there like corpses. He'd be surprised if they didn't lose one or two of the students. Although their loss would break his heart, it did not negate the risk he had to take to clear the necromancer from their minds.

Nico worked on the next thread. When he pulled the strand, it did not move even a fraction. He tried another one and the same thing happened.

What was that? This was more than a snag, tougher than any thorn. Nico concentrated hard, moving his consciousness along the thread and into the heart of the problem. There, just beyond his reach, was a knot about the size of a man's fist.

Surprised by the size of the tangle, he paused for a moment, trying to determine the best course of action. If he approached the problem the wrong way, he'd end up tightening the threads and the students would never be free. This was one more way in which the necromancer sought to make it impossible to sever his hold on his victims.

Since the necromancer knew the students' superiors in the study of alchemy might be able to transmute the threads, there were blocks placed around the body of the knot to keep an adept's influence at bay. Nico might be able to grasp the strings and tug, but he'd have a significantly harder time doing much else. Not even turning the filaments to dust would help. Each attempt to change the property of the bound threads only made the knot stronger, denser.

Nico was fast running out of ideas. For each solution he came up with, he found only more problems. It seemed the necromancer knew the ins and outs of alchemy well enough to anticipate all possible scenarios.

Damn and blast! They should not have been caught so off guard. The *prolates* he'd made allowances for, the clerics he'd tried to appease, but a death dancer?

If only he had recognized the signs on the wind for what they were. Why had teaching to spot the changes of atmosphere and protection against the necromancers been allowed to drop from the curriculum? He was as guilty as any of the custodians of the craft who came before him.

No more. From this day forward, they would teach every novice, every apprentice, journeyman, and first-level master the art of identifying, confronting, and defeating the necromancers.

More determined than ever to set the students free, Nico considered the problem before him. There was no other choice but to work the knot as a tailor might remove one while making a suit. Often such a step required cutting away the tangled ends and picking up the seam where the thread left off. It was hard to tell by looking at the garment where the splice occurred. Only a trained eye might look at a sleeve or collar and notice. However, this was a mind—more intricate and delicate a design than any tailor ever thought to fabricate. If Nico made even the slightest miscalculation, the victims might never regain their memories, or worse, live in a catatonic state for the rest of their lives.

This required careful study. There was no margin for error.

Master Oberon quietly approached. It was not so much a physical presence, but a blending of consciousnesses. Nico did not hear Oberon's voice in the material world, but knew it in the ethereal.

Nico sensed Oberon next to him. If they were in material form, the master no doubt would have his hands settled on his hips. *"It is all chaos in here."*

"Worse than I ever imagined." Nico led Oberon to the source of their current problems. *"Look there."*

"By the ghost of Mercurian Dante! What has that corpsemonger done?"

Nico made his essence smaller, diminished until he stood beside the massive ball of memories. *"He's thwarted us again, it seems."*

"Can't we cut it loose? We were going to rid them of these strands anyways."

"That is my hope. Though how to go about it without causing injury, I do not know."

The bundle appeared as a hideous tumor in the midst of beauty. One had only to look inside another's mind to see swirling spirals of colorful lights. White points that appeared like starbursts shot off from the central body. It was what alchemists called the seat of inspiration. That was the true soul, not the heart, as the clerics preached. The heart was a more fickle tool, while the mind had the ability to reason and weigh decisions.

It was one of the few tenets of alchemy that students either understood and accepted or rejected and fled. Most of the students were easily persuaded of the truth when the proof was so clearly in front of them. How could they not be?

But this abomination the necromancer had placed in the collective minds of the students was not to be borne. He'd never seen anything quite as heinous or damaging.

Nico reduced even more, made his consciousness smaller. He had to get under the tangled mass in order to see how to cut it free.

The underside was even denser than the top. It was hard to determine exactly where the threads were moored.

"Oberon, go to the other side and see if you can find a tether keeping it in place."

Minutes passed when there was nothing but the sound of the pain leaching from each of the students.

"Nico, it's like nothing I've ever seen. Come around here."

He hurried to comply. It wasn't easy. Strands floated down from the central core like spider webs. One wrapped around his essence, holding him in place. Others began to disperse and wrap around him as if he were the prey they sought.

And then he felt it.

There was a life force there. A living entity that was apart from the students. The necromancer had not only given his victims the order to spy, he'd placed himself inside each of them. The mangled mess of thought-strings was held dead center of the connection the necromancer had with all the unfortunates.

Nico finally broke free enough to make his way to Oberon. Nico let out a mental sigh of frustration. The thorns were like huge, curved talons, digging into the foundation.

"How are we going to set it free?"

Nico studied the formation. Where the claws gripped the students' minds, there appeared to be some compression of the area. No wonder the memories had been stripped away when Oberon had attempted the extrication. It wasn't so much that the stripping caused the memory loss, but that the memories were being choked off by a tenacious hold.

"We need to work these free. Once we do, the students might regain some control of their faculties, as well as aid us in ridding them of the rest of the necromancer's essence."

The necromancer had effectively cut the alchemists off from changing the substance of the growth, but he had not placed blocks on changing the shape of things.

"Oberon, concentrate on flattening out the talons. Once it lets loose, we'll push it out as one unit."

The two masters worked in concert, opening the clawed anchors as if forcing fingers on a hand to relax. Finally, they were out straight, and with a harsh thought, Nico and Oberon began to push the growth of tangled thoughts away from the students.

Suddenly, bright lights began to flick on—consciousnesses returned to the affected minds one at a time. They were groggy and disoriented; perhaps it wasn't wise to ask their assistance at this juncture, but Nico did not wish for the necromancer to use that as an advantage to gain another foothold.

"Listen, pupils. You must help your masters free you from this burden. Take control of your thoughts and expel the darkness that infects you."

Nico's mind began to spin a bit as he, too, became disoriented at the onslaught of returning memories. He held fast to his mission and continued to push. It was akin to rolling a boulder the size of a house uphill.

Slowly more minds joined with his—familiar ones—and even those of the elementals assisted, brought in by the now-lucid essence of Theodyne.

If Nico had been in his physical body, he would have cried for joy. Theodyne's presence glowed brighter and hotter than any of the others. He was a sun against a sea of planets.

Together the alchemists pushed the interloper out of their minds and into the material world, depositing the spell into the iron sphere.

Nico blinked a few times to clear his vision. The spell glowed a sickening green and pulsed with unholy light. He dropped the lid on the cask and sealed the lock. The only thing left to do was to send it to the forge to have molten iron placed around the seam, shutting the contents away for eternity.

He turned around and surveyed the journeymen and apprentices, who were now moving, though slowly, and let out a breath of relief.

Nico handed the sphere to Oberon. "Take care of this."

"With pleasure."

Nico wiped a hand across his brow. The sleeve of his robe came away wet. He'd worked harder than he thought, but it was worth it.

Theodyne rose up on an elbow from his place on the floor and gave Nico a weak smile. "I feel like I've been thrown from a large, angry horse."

"Other than that, how do you feel?"

"Like I've been asleep for a very long time and have only now woken up and am slightly confused. It's all coming back slowly."

Nico leaned down and gave Theodyne a hand up. After making sure Theodyne was comfortable, Nico turned to Jolen, who had begun to struggle against his bonds.

"Easy. Easy." It was like trying to talk down a fractious horse. "Let me untie you before you do yourself harm."

Jolen looked up with big, teary eyes. "I didn't do anything wrong. I promise."

"We know. It wasn't your fault. As it wasn't the others' faults either."

"What is going to happen to us? Are you going to turn us out, Master Nico?" Tears ran down his face. The young man was misery personified.

"No. We are turning none of you out. As we've both observed, it was *not* your fault. You were used most ill by another presence—and for that, it is I who must apologize to you." When Jolen looked confused or as if he'd argue, Nico patted his shoulder, offering comfort. "Besides, I believe there is an important lesson we all can learn from your experience. If the *prolates* are now using necromancers to try and obtain the secrets of the alchemists, then we need to learn how to combat them. You are a valuable piece of information in that equation."

Jolen nodded. "I'll do whatever I can."

"I know you will."

With the last restraint free, Jolen rubbed at his arms to get feeling back. There were marks on his wrists where he'd fought against his bonds at some point.

Nico motioned to another one of the students who looked to be in better physical condition after the ordeal. "Please help Jolen to his room."

"Yes, master."

Nico took a seat next to Theodyne as the rest of the students shuffled out for some much-needed rest or refreshments. Nico took his lover's hand in his and brought it to his lips, placing a gentle kiss on the hard knuckles.

"You had me worried."

"It wasn't my intent. Believe me." Theodyne wiped his hand across his scar and surprise lit his eyes. "It's odd to know you've forgotten something and still have the feeling of remembering you'd forgotten it. If that makes any sense."

"It does." Nico wanted to pull Theodyne into his arms and kiss him hard, but refrained. He doubted such a display would make the apprentice feel better at the moment. If anything, it might make him skittish.

Then there was the even more frightening thought that perhaps Theodyne's body had been used as a sexual puppet for the necromancer, without consent. Theodyne might not want Nico in that way, now he had been freed.

Theodyne's hand fell away from pursuing his scar. "What are your next plans? You can't let this go unchallenged. I heard what you said to Jolen, and you're right. If they infiltrated our ranks so easily, who is to say they haven't unleashed undue influence on the *prolates?* Not that I have a reason to trust the Medovins, but they might not even know they're being manipulated."

"I suppose that possibility does exist." And it troubled Nico in no small measure.

"What do you want to do, Nico? Do we stay here longer and help clean up the mess, or turn it over to Master Oberon and head back to Lancor and inspect that region?"

"We return home. There may be necromantic influences there as well. My estate might very well be in jeopardy as we speak."

"Yes, and if it is?" Theodyne raised a brow as he pushed himself up from the chair. "You'll need to tread softly as not to bring yourself under suspicion."

"I won't let all I built become forfeit to Medovin ambition. I don't care about the face of their minions." Nico moved to the window and stared out at the mountains. Snowcapped and pristine, it didn't appear as if anything could ever touch the peaks. Long after man stopped infecting the world with his presence, the mountains would still be there, standing in judgment.

"It might not have reached that far yet." From the look on Theodyne's face, he didn't believe what he said either.

"You are a good man to try and give me comfort, but we both know if Cesare Medovin has access to a necromancer, he's taken that knowledge back to his cousin in Lancor."

At the mention of Estobán, Theodyne looked down at his hands. "If it comes down to it, let me handle Estobán. I might have an easier time of it than you."

"We'll see, when and if that becomes necessary." Nico crossed the room and ran his hand down Theodyne's cheek. "You should get some rest."

Theodyne turned his face so his lips pressed against Nico's palm. "I'd rather say a very private thank-you."

Heat shot to Nico's groin. His cock hardened. Those beautiful golden eyes of Theodyne's captured Nico's and held them prisoner. Perhaps that part of Theodyne's consciousness had been under his own control.

"Are you sure it's not too much too soon?" Nico wanted no part of hurting Theodyne, even if it was in the course of making love—especially then.

Theodyne dipped a shoulder in a casual way as if to say *so what*. "If it becomes too much, we'll take it slow. We do have all night, and have lost time to make up for."

They left the room and closed the door.

Chapter Nineteen

IT TOOK very little time or encouragement to get them out of their clothes and rolling across Nico's bed. Theodyne had never been so starved for love. There was an empty well in his soul that needed a constant fill. He worried it was not going to heal and that the necromancer had left a permanent scar on his heart. The Gods knew he had enough of those for a lifetime.

Nico pulled away and glanced down into Theodyne's face. He was already breathing hard and his cheeks were flushed with color. Desire darkened his eyes. "I missed you."

Theodyne grabbed Nico by the back of the neck. There were so many words tripping over his tongue and yet none of them seemed adequate to express what he felt for this master of alchemy.

He owed Nico gratitude for sure, but there was so much more he could never repay. Love, Theodyne had in abundance to give. It was the only true thing he possessed. The only attribute he had to offer that was not owned by someone else.

Theodyne nudged Nico over so Theodyne was on top. It wasn't so much a position of dominance as it was a driving need to show Nico how he felt. To prove that, no matter what had transpired while Theodyne had been under the influence of the necromancer, what happened in this bed at *this* time was real and purposeful. It meant the world to Theodyne.

He brushed his lips over Nico's mouth, but did not linger there for any length of time. For what he wanted to express, for how he chose to show his love, he needed to move much farther down Nico's body.

Suddenly, the room grew hot as an inferno. This was no simple act for the sake of pleasure—it was more. Deeper. Significant. Perhaps it was the single most important act he'd ever perform in his life. Not that he'd never taken Nico into his mouth before, but because of the emotion behind it. That changed everything.

Theodyne's fingers trembled as he slid them down Nico's muscled abdomen. Soft dark hair tickled his palm. The skin underneath was warm and alive. Vibrant. Energy swirled in patterns above Nico's body in a bright aura.

Nico sucked in his stomach and let out a low moan. His cock was hard and pressed close to his body. Theodyne wrapped his hand around the base and moved up and down in a slow, torturous rhythm. Nico wound his hand in Theodyne's hair, a pleading look in his dark eyes.

Theodyne caught Nico's gaze and held it as he took Nico into his mouth. The room filled with the sounds of Nico's pleasure. Some of the words Theodyne didn't understand, not out of the context of the primers. Hearing them now as Nico fought back an orgasm, Theodyne smiled.

It was like sweet music.

Nico's hands wound into Theodyne's hair more, cupping his head and pushing down as Nico brought his hips up to meet Theodyne's ministrations. Theodyne palmed Nico's balls, squeezing in a steady cadence with his mouth.

"Theo. By the Gods, Theo."

Before Theodyne knew what had happened, he was on his back with Nico looming over him.

Nico's dark features were stark, his eyes hot. "Put your legs around me."

Theodyne was almost afraid not to. There was a hungry power to Nico Theodyne had not seen before. The aura had changed colors, muted to a deep crimson.

If Theodyne didn't know better, he'd swear there was more than a bit of fire elemental about Nico. Or was it because his blood was so full of alchemy from the first drop that the powers could not be contained inside a corporeal vessel?

Nico leaned over and took a vial from the nightstand. The scent of sandalwood filled the air, teasing Theodyne's senses with its sensual fragrance. Nico tipped the bottle up and coated his fingers. Theodyne's gut tightened. He knew what came next and welcomed it—welcomed Nico with open arms.

Then Nico was there, pushing inside Theodyne's body, joining them as they were meant to be. It was as if the lost piece of Theodyne's soul had found its way home after a long journey. He bit his lips back to keep from saying the words that bubbled up his throat.

How he longed to tell Nico how much he loved him.

Between the brush of Nico's body hair over Theodyne's cock and the fact Nico began a slow steady stroke of it with each thrust, Theodyne was soon panting and holding on to his lover like a lifeline.

None of his other lovers had ever prepared him for such a tidal wave of emotion or powerful passions. There were words whispered on the air, but Theodyne no longer knew or cared if they came from him, Nico, or the elementals. Then it no longer mattered as the stars exploded and constellations realigned. At least, that's how it felt to Theodyne as they both fell into orgasm with each other's names on their lips.

NICO LAY there for a while. He didn't know how long, only that the quiet between them seemed to stretch out into infinity.

He rose from the bed and wet a towel, then handed it to Theodyne. "Here. You'll leave a mess on the linens."

Color painted Theodyne's cheeks, and he took the cloth and began to clean himself.

The silence stretched out again. A quiet lover was a thoughtful one, but sometimes those thoughts turned to regrets. Theodyne had assured Nico the last time they were together he'd had no regrets and was with him because he wanted to be—but that was before he'd known about the necromancer's influence.

Theodyne looked up. "What's wrong?"

"You've grown very quiet." Nico sat down on the bed, facing away from Theodyne. Maybe Theodyne would be more inclined to open up if he didn't have to look Nico in the eyes.

"So have you." Theodyne rolled over and threw the cloth at the bathing pitcher, landing it perfectly on the side of the bowl. "What were you saying before? I couldn't translate fast enough."

It was Nico's turn for his cheeks to catch flame. He hadn't realized he'd spoken. "When?"

Theodyne pulled on that cloak of arrogance as if it were his favorite robe. "When we were making love. Or were you speaking in the language of the ancients because you *didn't* want me to know?"

Nico turned. "I don't recall." He ran his hand up Theodyne's thigh and over his belly. "I only remember that having your mouth on me felt like the most acute form of perfection."

Theodyne's golden eyes widened a bit. "Oh. Then I guess the words don't matter so much."

Oh, they mattered all right. They mattered so deeply they ached. However, that didn't mean Nico wanted to share them. Not yet. Not until Theodyne was well again. Not until Nico could be sure it was really Theodyne he made love with and not the residual of the infestation.

Instead of saying those words to Theodyne, Nico changed the subject. It was better this way. "We are leaving for the villa in the morning. Perhaps we should get some sleep."

Theodyne started to get up as if to go into his room, but Nico quickly stayed him of that hasty retreat. "No. Lie by me."

Theodyne nodded and crawled under the covers. "All right. I'll stay."

Now why did that sound like a concession?

Chapter Twenty

THEY WERE finally leaving the school behind. For a while, Theodyne didn't think they'd ever make it off the grounds or down the mountain. He'd sincerely doubted they'd ever see Lancor again—but now that the horses and wagon were rolling for home, it did seem real.

He glanced over at Nico, who sat tall and proud in the saddle. A memory, like the brush of a dragonfly's wing, moved over Theodyne's skin. While under the influence of the necromancer, he'd asked Nico if they were in love—Nico had demurred to answer.

What was it, then?

Not that Theodyne wanted to probe the feelings or make more out of an affair than what it might be, but there were emotions roiling under the surface he did not remember ever feeling before. From the first moment he'd walked into Nico's study and saw him behind that desk, it was as if he'd taken the first good breath of his life. The first true beat of his heart had begun that moment when their eyes first met and Nico welcomed him into his villa.

Perhaps Nico did not feel the same way. Theodyne had to prepare himself for that eventuality. It might come to pass, but that didn't mean it would for a certainty. In love, anything was possible. Or in lust. The fact Nico had brought Theodyne and the other students through a dangerous time made Theodyne not question the man's commitment to safety and protection. It was the matters of the heart that were often harder to untangle than the call of duty.

Then last night, Theodyne had given Nico the perfect opportunity to state his feelings, and Nico had deferred again. Perhaps it wasn't anything more than an affair for Nico. Theodyne had to steel himself against the possibility and know that, one day, he might be turned out of Nico's bed.

The thought alone paralyzed him.

Was this how Estobán had felt when Theodyne had left?

"You are deep in thought." Nico brought his horse in closer so they rode side by side.

"Nothing to worry over. I'm not having a relapse or hearing anything from the elementals to suggest we're in trouble. No need for alarm."

"Is there anything else you wish to discuss?"

Color and heat rose to Theodyne's cheeks. He'd never wished to discuss the boundaries or future of a relationship before. For one of his former profession, love was a fleeting thing. A concept best cultivated only long enough to gain information about the family vault or obtain a secret treasure. It had been a part of his skill as surely as picking a lock or scaling a garden wall. Until Estobán Medovin had turned things around and shown Theodyne the poisonous side of love. After that, he wanted nothing more to do with the emotion. Now… now all things seemed different. Possible. Fear kept him quiet.

Nico gave him a sexy smile under the shade of a wide-brimmed hat he had set at a jaunty angle. "You want to speak of last night, maybe?"

Heat exploded now, and he shook his head to countermand what his face revealed. "No. Not exactly."

"Then what?" Nico leaned over and played his hand over Theodyne's leg.

The sensual touch hardened Theodyne's cock, making it less than comfortable to ride a horse. Theodyne chuckled. "You should stop or you'll do me an injury."

Nico laughed and removed his hand from tracing any farther up Theodyne's thigh. "You don't have to tell me now. It can wait until later tonight when we go down for sleep."

Theodyne doubted they would begin the restful hours with sleep. Not if the look in Nico's eyes was any indication. Anticipation was a ball of tension under Theodyne's breastbone. The two of them were now connected in a most fundamental way.

Theodyne tried not to think of it at all as they rode farther into the valley. Instead of making the turn that led to the town proper, they cut northward and followed a different road. All along the trail there was evidence the world no longer belonged to the living. A new order was beginning to take root and it saw the world through black, empty sockets.

A scent of rancid meat permeated the air and seemed to follow them for leagues. The horses grew restless, throwing their heads and pulling on the bits. If Theodyne didn't know better, he'd swear the necromancer had infected the countryside.

Theodyne listened for the elementals, but they were silent. He reined in his horse. The animal grew even more nervous. It shook its head and sidestepped a few paces, stamping at the ground in agitation.

"Nico, we need to leave this place."

Nico spun his horse to face Theodyne. "What's wrong?"

"The elementals have stopped speaking to me."

As if to emphasize the evil present in the glade, a murder of crows descended from the sky. Their black eyes missed nothing around them.

Anger, real and potent, flashed across Nico's face. "That death-dancing bastard has turned these innocent birds to his cause. He has no honor or soul."

Pedraus peeked his head out of the wagon flap long enough to catch a glimpse of the impending attack. He ducked back inside and came out with one of his curious little brown bottles.

He lifted the stopper and jerked his hand, sending the contents airborne. With a collective squawk, the crows dispersed and circled overhead as if trying to decide their next move.

"What was in that bottle?"

Pedraus gave a sniff. "A little something my father called *liquid scarecrow*."

Theodyne marveled at the concoction. Whatever was in the bottle did the trick, for even though the crows continued to follow, they did not come close enough to do any harm.

The miles rolled by, and with each landmark they passed, Theodyne felt a more pressing need to hurry back to Lancor. In their absence something had gone terribly wrong. He did not want to bring up the change he felt to Nico; it would only make the adept worry.

There had been too much upheaval since the night Jolen brought the message to the villa. Too many tears and rents in the fabric of what Nico held to be true, and Theodyne wished to protect him for a while longer. They would near the fault line soon enough, and with it, the tide of destiny would sweep them both out to sea.

If they didn't drown in an undertow first.

They stopped for the night near a river. It was not the same one they'd stopped at on the way to the school. This one roared as it moved by, cutting its way from the mountain and to the pasturelands. The elementals were alive in the water, burbling and waving their liquid fists as they churned in violence.

Theodyne longed to sleep on the bank and listen to their ancient song as they cut through the land, forging a wider path with each passing year. He might be able to learn what to expect at the villa.

Nico came down to the soft slope of the river's edge and laid a blanket across the ground. "Come here and get off the ground. You'll get your clothes all dirty."

Theodyne glanced up and smiled. The setting sun haloed Nico's dark hair, giving it crimson highlights around the edges, making him look like a fire elemental.

Theodyne reached up and dragged Nico down on the ground beside him. "I've been known to collect much more dirt on my clothes than this piece of land can offer. I think I'm safe enough."

Nico shot him a smile and stretched out next to him. He stacked his hands behind his head. "I have a horrible feeling of what we'll find when we return to the villa."

Theodyne glanced at Nico's profile. "I didn't want to be the one to say it. I feel the same."

"I have so much to answer for." Regrets dripped from Nico's words. His shoulders sat heavier, rounded inward as if dragging the pain into his soul.

"No, you don't."

"I should have seen the necromancers for what they were. Not imagined them as an ill wind."

Theodyne raised a brow. "Maybe, but you still have measurable influence with the clerics of Lancor. You're building them a new cathedral. That goodwill has to stand for something. Ask for an audience with the Holy See and discuss the necromancers with him. Perhaps you can form a temporary truce."

Nico turned to Theodyne, elbow bent and propping his head on his hand. "It's worth a try at any rate. Unless the Medovins have gotten to the clerics already."

"That goes without saying. However, I'd think not even the clerics will stand by and let a death dancer into the fold. They'd see it as unnatural and anathema. It goes against everything they teach from the holy book. To turn a blind eye is to suffer the worst form of corruption—that of the soul."

Nico leaned over and brushed his mouth over Theodyne's. "You amaze and confound me on every level. Now you have turned philosopher."

Theodyne brushed a bent knuckle across Nico's cheek, the surface rough with stubble. "I'm no more than I ever was—though I do know more about myself than I did when we started this journey."

"You may not have been born with title or privilege, or hold rank in the order of the Gold School, but you are my equal and more than my match."

Heat filled Theodyne. It was unlike any he'd ever known before. It wasn't the heat of desire, or lust—though he certainly felt both of those emotions. This was bone-crushing, breath-stealing love. Overwhelming and so big there was no room in his heart to contain it all.

Tenderly, as if bedding a nervous virgin, Theodyne began to love Nico, afraid that if he let his passion loose, it might smother them both. Instead, he held those emotions in check and kissed his way down Nico's throat, over his collarbones, across his chest and down. Theodyne unbuttoned Nico's shirt to reveal the soft dark hair that spread in a sexy shadow down his chest.

He flicked his tongue across each of Nico's copper nipples, eliciting a moan that made Theodyne hard as stone. He moved lower, reaching the lacings of Nico's pants. Nico lifted a hand and stroked the side of Theodyne's face.

This time was not hurried or desperate, but slow and gentle. Theodyne took his time and did not allow Nico to take control—not even when he started begging for mercy. Theodyne needed to bring Nico to the breaking point, knowing that if he did, Nico would finally say what Theodyne wanted so much to hear. The words he so hungered for.

Theodyne moved to Nico's side, rolling him so he lay on his belly in the bedding. Theodyne brushed Nico's hair from his ear and whispered, "Do not hold back your emotions. Live them."

Nico's fists knotted in the linens. "Ask yourself if that is what you really want from me."

Theodyne nuzzled Nico's ear. "More than you know."

Nico shook his head. His eyes closed.

With a heart filled with sadness, almost to the point of breaking, Theodyne prepared Nico to receive him. He rounded his hand along Nico's muscular flank, and spread Nico's full cheeks. The oil he used was a combination of sandalwood and a plant extract he'd found in his trunk. Theodyne had no idea how it had gotten there, or where it came from, but a single drop on his finger had heightened his awareness.

He hoped it worked for Nico the same way.

Theodyne rimmed Nico's anus with the head of his cock, leaning slightly forward to unleash a litany of truths he had no desire to hold inside. Nico's fingers crushed the blankets under him, but still he said nothing.

"Why do you deny me?" The words were torn from Theodyne's throat on a crack of emotion. If he was to be the only one in love, then he'd suffer the consequences gladly, but he'd not speak his heart again until Nico reciprocated.

As Theodyne drove inside Nico with steady thrusts, he waited to hear even a single exclamation fall from Nico's lips that proclaimed his feelings. There was nothing save the whispery words of the same arcane language he'd used the night before.

"Speak Dominicál Common, you great fucking bastard!" Theodyne pulled on Nico's hair, bending his head back. "I want to know what it is you say to me."

Nico grabbed for Theodyne's hand. "Listen with your heart and mind, not your ears, and you will know."

Theodyne wanted to yell that this was no time for cryptic remarks and philosophical games. He didn't. Instead Theodyne released his grip on

Nico's hair and twined their fingers together, holding Nico tightly—as if he never thought to let him go.

Why were these words so hard to understand when the primer had come so easily? It did not make sense. The harder Theodyne concentrated, the more elusive the language became, but never once did he let up on the steady cadence of his hips rocking sweetly into Nico.

Theodyne placed his free hand under Nico, skimming down the front of his body to encircle his cock with a tight fist.

Nico moaned and moved his face against Theodyne's. Only one clearly discernible word fell from Nico's lips before they plunged into the abyss. "Listen."

Theodyne did as told, but heard nothing save the savage beat of his heart and the labored breath as he tried to drag more air into his lungs.

Disappointment was an arrow to his side. Theodyne lay there with Nico, trying to understand why the phrases were so elusive. At length, he felt Nico relax and drift into slumber. Theodyne was not so moved to follow suit. He studied the wagon canopy and listened to the nocturnal animals as they called to one another. The rocks, grass, and trees were a remote mumble in the distance. They, too, had quieted for the night.

Perhaps the language was a mystery for a reason. Not due to Theodyne's lack of advancement in the order, but some other impediment. The necromancer? Perhaps. But that didn't feel right. He had still been able to unlock the *Eye of Truth* while under the influence of the death dancer.

Theodyne fell asleep with Nico in his arms and no closer to an answer.

Chapter Twenty-One

THEODYNE DIDN'T like the change of air in the villa. The moment he stepped inside, all the stones and plants began to whisper to him. Grape vines were very outspoken. He'd not realized how much until now.

The servants stared at him with accusing eyes. As if at any moment he would bring the wrath of the *prolate* down on them. Theodyne had news for them. He had no plans to go anywhere near Estobán Medovin—not after the encounter with the necromancer.

What he needed to do was return to his formal studies. They'd been neglected the past few weeks and though he'd gotten through quite a bit of the primers, Nico had not as yet tested him on the principles Theodyne needed to advance to the next level. But then, nothing about his movement through the school of alchemy had been orthodox. Was that even a word to use in conjunction with so esoteric a field?

Theodyne took one of the books to the little *plazo* where he'd read before. There was such a calming arrangement to the stone benches and flowering vines, he tended to lose all track of time and concerns.

Unfortunately, today the elementals would not leave him be. They were concerned by the changes to the villa in Nico's absence. None of them good.

Theodyne held the place in the primer with his finger and leaned his head back against the wall. He closed his eyes in an attempt to center his mind and concentrate only on the power of the sun beating down on him.

He was still a free man.

The constant reminder of his tenuous parole was heavy on his heart and mind. It took but a little slip or slight and he'd be back again before the *prolate* and on to a sentence of death.

Perhaps he should ask Nico if he wanted to leave the area—go somewhere to start fresh. If they did that, he'd allow Nico to remove the mark of past crimes from his face so as to leave this part of his life behind.

"I've got you now, you slick devil."

Theodyne cracked an eye open and watched as the cook, Molari, came at him with a cleaver raised as if he meant to use it. Theodyne rolled off the bench and landed looking up at the sun's glare behind Molari's head.

"What are you about? Are you trying to kill me?"

Molari lowered the cleaver. "I should. You, in the master's graces and doing him a grave disservice behind his back. He was wrong to bring you into his house, and you planning to steal from him the entire time."

A prick of conscience lanced Theodyne's heart. "I've stolen nothing."

"Stop lying. We know for a fact you did. We've heard the tales of how you sneaked his most prized possession out of the villa, shortly after you came here." Molari gave a sage nod as if Theodyne had already been condemned of the crime.

"I did no such thing and any man who says otherwise is a liar."

"We will see about that. Soon as I find the master, I'm going to tell him all, and he'll throw you out on your ear. Better yet, I should call the *prolate*'s men and have you arrested before the master is any the wiser."

Theodyne picked himself up from the tiles, brushing dirt from his clothes. "You think that's going to work for you? Think he's going to thank you for going over his authority and squealing to the *prolate* like the coward you are? Try it. We'll see how long you last in this household once you've done that."

"Your threats don't scare me none. You were a fraud when you came here, and you'll be one when you leave to meet your justice."

Theodyne lost his bravado. He *was* a fraud. That was a truth he could not deny; however, he'd never once claimed he'd lived his life piously. He'd damn sure never tried to hide his crimes. The record of his conviction was there on his face.

"We'll let the master decide. It's the least you owe him for giving you a position in his house with wages and a place to live. Do not try to pretend you rise to a noble cause when we both know this is nothing more than a case of vengeance. And a petty one at that." Theodyne picked up the primer where it had fallen to the ground.

No sense in hanging around outside. Now even his favorite place to get away from people had been compromised. What he really wanted to do was find Menarch and strangle the fucker.

Theodyne sent a mental picture out to the elementals, showing them Menarch's age-wrinkled face, asking if any of them had seen the man at the villa.

Every brick, every stone and tree relayed to him that they had. The whispers grew louder, more intense. The elementals were unhappy to have played host to such a man in the master's absence. He smelled of evil.

No matter how hard Theodyne tried, he could not get them to explain what they meant by that statement. A human's idea of evil and an elemental's might be vastly different. To grain, the smell of a burnt harvest might be evil. To a tree, the scent of a woodman's sweat might be evil. There was no telling the gauge by which they measured the evil of a human heart.

Theodyne would say this much—they had pegged it in Menarch, though he wasn't so much evil as he was single-minded when it came to his talents. The fact he'd egged Theodyne on to steal the *Eye of Truth* proved there was at the very least mischief in his soul. But what if from that mischief grew darker, deeper emotions? Theodyne had noticed a change in the man—or some element within his character unnoticed before. It was worth discovering the source.

He had to find out what had transpired while he was away, and he couldn't do that here at the villa. He'd have to venture into the city proper—but first he needed to confess his original mission to Nico.

Theodyne searched the villa without any success and finally returned to the *plazo* to wait for Nico to come to him.

THERE WERE changes in Lancor all right. Subtle ones. Small and delicate enough to balance on the edge of a knife, but also sharp enough to cut if the need arose. Matters at the villa were somewhat better, though not even the power of Nico's influence could transmute the gray of pewter to the shine of gold.

The mood of the servants was subdued. An underlying tension seemed to permeate the grounds. If they weren't careful, they'd rot the grapes on the vine and spoil the wine that sat fermenting in the casks.

Nico left the servants to unpack the carriage and went on a walk of his property, feeling the elements for any imbalance that might explain the shift in energy. All seemed in order. The vines were healthy and flourishing, but would not be for long if the negativity continued. He had to find the cause and correct it before the year's crop was lost.

He stood beneath a blazing sun, absorbing the rays and channeling his energy along the beams, trying to see if there were any rips in the local fabric. There was nothing there. No essence of the necromancer.

Nico continued his walk, taking care not to miss any of the many small gardens or walkways used for contemplation. There was nothing to cause alarm or raise suspicion. All was as it had been the day they'd left.

And yet it had changed completely.

The buildings and fields might look the same, but the positive energy that had initially drawn him to the land had evaporated. It was a shell now. Nothing more than a place to lay his head at night.

If the problem wasn't external, then it most assuredly had to be intrinsic. Nico started back to the villa and noticed Theodyne sitting on the stone bench on the *plazo*. His face was raised skyward, his eyelids closed.

Nico dropped down on the bench next to his lover, content to wait until Theodyne broke the silence.

"Your house is ill, Nico."

"I know, but I haven't a clue as to the source. I found no trace of the necromancer or his ilk."

Theodyne cracked one eye open and glanced at Nico. "It isn't something as esoteric as a necromancer that infects your house. It's the knowledge that those who live here feel they have been wronged."

"How do you know this?"

"Because I came here initially under the guise of stealing the *Eye of Truth*. I fear my former associate, Menarch, has been here several times since we've been away."

Nico's heart slipped and fell. Cold suffused his body, making all his limbs numb. "What has that to do with my house? You were with me."

"According to the elementals that inhabit the villa, he was here to cause dissent among your servants and search for the *Eye of Truth* on his own. When his search proved fruitless, he told your staff I stole it." Theodyne gave a shrug of his muscular shoulder. "I had no idea what it was until we were ensconced at the school. By then I had no intention of going through with the challenge. Hell, for what it's worth, I gave up that mission when you offered me the apprenticeship."

Nico's breathing eased a bit. He slid his arm around Theodyne's shoulder and pulled him close. "Let me handle the staff. I promise they will never question your honesty again."

"Nico, they have every right to question me because of their loyalty to you." He moved into Nico's embrace. "They haven't had the chance to get to know me the way you have. Or as well."

"Is that all the elementals told you?"

A look passed over Theodyne's face. "No."

"Are you going to enlighten me?"

"I'm not sure what good it would do."

"And why is that? Do you think I won't defend what is mine?"

Theodyne shook his head. "No. It's not that. Far from it. I just know where this is headed and I'm afraid, for me, it's not good."

"Why? Theodyne, love, talk to me." Fear did a bottleneck in Nico's throat.

Theodyne looked off across the vineyards to the far horizon. "There are rumors that nobles have been missing important objects and jewels from their safes. Since my release from Pallonia, I am at the head of the suspect list, or so say the elementals."

"Impossible. You haven't even been in town."

"To a group of nobles who already know me, who have lost much to my talent, it is nothing to see me put away again. To Estobán Medovin it is a final way to get rid of me. He is not likely to let the matter go away with a few coins."

Nico blew out a breath and stood. "Have there been formal charges drawn up?"

"Not that the elementals have heard."

"Then we leave it for now. If the nobles want to fight one of their own, then they can try, but they will get nowhere. You were with me and had an entire school full of adept-level alchemists as witnesses."

"That isn't going to matter to them. It surely didn't matter to Molari. He came after me with a meat cleaver, claiming he was going to go to the *prolate* and not consult you on the matter."

"The filthy beggar." Nico pulled his arm away and crossed both over his chest. "How far has the matter gone? Within the house?"

"If I'm getting threatened with a cleaver, pretty far, I think."

"Right." Nico stood. He had some excess energy to work off, and righteous boiling anger. "I will tell Pedraus to gather the servants. Come, we will face them together."

Theodyne followed him through the house and to the study, where they waited for the household servants to come before Nico.

"Stand behind me with your hand on my chair. Yes, just so. It will show that you have my confidence and my protection." Nico gave Theodyne a smile. "Once I speak with them, it will all be fine. The tension will evaporate and you may concentrate on your studies. As for the *prolate*—I shall go visit him in the morning."

Pedraus ushered the servants into the office and took a place at the door, allowing none of them to exit until Nico had finished speaking. Not that any of them might be so bold, but it was better to be safe than take a chance.

Nico waited, letting the silence and his displeasure spin out before he opened his mouth. Let them wonder for a few moments why he'd called them before an audience. Let them stew in the knowledge the rumors had not failed to reach his ears.

Once the servants began to squirm in nervous anticipation, Nico steepled his hands and looked over his fingers at them. He stared at Molari. "It has come to my attention that members of this staff have accused my apprentice of stealing my property. What proof have you of such a crime?"

Molari's lips moved in indignation. "You will believe anything the thief tells you."

"Yes. I trust him implicitly. He told me candidly about the scheme that brought him here and the name of the conspirator. I also know for a fact the item which he is accused of taking left with me, in my personal belongings, when we traveled to the school."

Molari paled and bowed his head in shame. "I did not know. I beg your forgiveness, my lord."

"Did it not occur to you to wait until all the information was at hand before taking the word of one unknown to you? That is, if this Menarch is indeed unknown to you." Red suffused the cook's cheeks. "So you do know him."

Behind Nico, Theodyne tensed. The hand on Nico's shoulder gripped a bit harder than before, as if he was holding on to his temper by the anchor Nico provided.

Enlightenment came as a dark dread crept over Nico's soul. He waved his hands to the other servants. "Begone with a warning. Do not think to undermine my authority in this house by dealing in rumors and innuendoes, then spreading them as fact to the authorities. It will not serve you well." He pointed at Molari. "You stay."

The others looked back at him with worry. None of the servants had ever seen Nico in such a temper. The fact he was a fair and just employer who never spoke a cross word to any of them was enough to make even the stoutest of servants fearful.

The door closed with a quiet click. Pedraus once again put his age-stooped body between the servant and the exit.

"Now you will tell me in great and minute detail how exactly you know the thief Menarch." Nico did not change positions or do more than blink, waiting for Molari to spill what he knew.

The cook wiped his hands down the sides of his soiled apron. There were splatters of blood from a slaughtered animal and flour from a pastry. Sweat made wet rings under his arms and dampened his forehead. Heat in the kitchen was a constant companion, and it wore on Molari like cheap clothes.

"I… I met Menarch years ago. It was a game of chance and I won enough money to not only buy back my indenture but to leave my situation behind and find a new one. I traveled the whole of the country, and everywhere I stopped, I met with Menarch. I thought it curious that he should take the same route, though even I had no notion of where I headed.

"At each stop we played more games of chance. Some I won, others I lost. None of the payoffs were as big as the first one, and in the tallies of wins and losses, I have to say I probably started losing more than I won, but if I should only regain my stroke of luck...." He stopped here and shook his head. Regrets carved deep lines around his mouth. "When I settled here in Lancor, I worked for a noble house—the House of de Rivo, the great and powerful cousin of the Medovins."

Nico feared he knew where this was headed but wanted to hear the words from Molari's mouth. He wasn't a heartless man. People made bad decisions and errors in judgment all the time. Wasn't he only lamenting earlier that he'd done the same when not looking for the necromancers, though the signs were all around them?

Molari mopped his forehead. Sweat now ran down into his eyes as if the confession had turned the office into one of his ovens. "Every spare coin I received, I spent trying to make the bank I did on that first game. What started as a want to better my station ended an obsession."

"Has it ended?" Nico asked quietly. "The changed patterns on the silver, the lowered quality of the food at my table—both suggest you've been skimming from the household coffers to feed your problem."

The more Nico thought about it, the more he resented it. Not merely for the fact the bastard had stolen from him, but because he had the audacity to accuse Theodyne of the same and worse. However, the most damning connection had not been laid bare yet. He waited for Molari to admit what Nico already knew from what *wasn't* said.

When Molari remained silent, Nico nudged. "Are you forgetting one rather significant detail in that story?"

Molari shook his head in denial. "No. I've told you everything."

"Not everything. You have failed to mention that if it weren't for you, Menarch would have never known about the *Eye of Truth*. You were the one to put him on the trail in the first place, and since perhaps you were too afraid to take it yourself, Menarch came up with a scenario where you'd both keep your hands clean of the deed, while accusing an easy target."

Molari held up his hands in protest. "No. It didn't happen that way."

"Then how did it happen?"

"I needed to pay off my debts with Menarch. He holds several markers in my name. He asked for information in return for clearing the marks. That is all."

"What kind of information?" The request was too vague to glean any solid evidence from it. Nico needed more to tie the attempted theft of the *Eye of Truth* to Theodyne's former associate.

Molari rubbed his head. He squinted as if the low light suddenly hurt his eyes. "I don't remember."

Nico felt a shimmer of warning. He reached out and sifted through the energy coming from Molari, but felt nothing close to the sickness of the mind of the necromancer.

There was nothing there. It felt rather... blank. Not as if his mind had been stripped, because the void invariably became filled with ideas and memories pieced together from the fabric the person still maintained. This was more like a dark cavern of which Nico could not see the bottom or judge the depth. It did not seem to affect Molari's other faculties.

"Very well. I will investigate this further. Please return to your duties."

Molari gave a sheepish nod and left the room.

Pedraus shuffled to stand before the desk. "Should I go into Lancor and find this Menarch?"

Theodyne removed his hand from Nico's shoulder. "No. I'll go."

"Are you sure? I would think it unsafe for you at this time."

"If I am taken—and I fear I may be—you can use your influence to see me freed. And besides, I doubt Menarch will talk to you."

Nico grabbed Theodyne's hand. "I would rather not go that route and risk your life in such a manner. I almost lost you once, I won't again."

Heat rose to Theodyne's golden eyes, making them flash like the heart of flame. "Then how do you propose to play this out? We need to know why Menarch decided to go after the *Eye of Truth*. When he first told me about it, I thought it merely his sad lust for treasure. As a thief, I can understand that need for the one item forever out of reach. The one that will be large enough to quit the game."

"Is there such a thing? I thought thieves did it mostly for the thrill and the glory." Nico smiled briefly. It was hard to imagine Theodyne moving among society's most famed houses and wealthiest families. He must have been something to behold with his fine clothes and his looks unspoiled by the branding of his crimes.

It was a harsh thing to think of a man he loved. Theodyne was so much more than the sum of his looks. There were moments when Nico did not even notice the scar burned into his lover's flesh. It was as if his love had rendered the mark invisible.

Theodyne raised a brow. "What?"

"Nothing. Trying to decide our next steps. We must tread with care. If what I saw in Molari's mind just now is any indication of what we face here in Lancor, it's an entirely new form of control. Or at least a very refined one." Nico rubbed his hand around his mouth. Stubble grated against his palm, making a scratching noise in the ensuing quiet.

"Is he infected by the necromancers? I thought you said you didn't feel them around the villa?"

Nico narrowed his gaze, staring at the door Molari had exited a few moments before. "I'll have to check the archives. Their attempts at mind control can take on many different forms. Just because I didn't feel the hallmark of a necromancer, doesn't mean one hasn't grabbed hold of Molari."

"Or Menarch." Theodyne started from the room.

"Where are you going?"

"To consult with the elementals again. I think I might not have asked the right questions the last time."

When the door swung closed, Nico rested back in his chair. His head had begun to pound.

"My lord, I fear... no, that's not right," Pedraus began. "I have a feeling we are running out of time. There are wolves at the gate, and it is only by the grace of some divine power that young Theodyne hasn't been taken yet."

Fear pulled and tugged at Nico's heart. "They won't take him. They can't. I won't let them. He's done nothing wrong."

"There is a common misconception among the citizenry. No matter how long a man spends in prison, they never will believe his sentence paid in full. Those in Lancor—in the great houses who have felt the sting of Theodyne's skill—will say '*once a thief, always a thief.*'"

Pedraus spoke sense and logic. His wisdom was as deep as any well. He'd served Nico from the cradle as he'd served Nico's father before that. Nico trusted the faithful servant. The words more weighty for the speaker.

And that troubled Nico more than anything.

What was he going to do? Forbid Theodyne from going outside or stepping foot off the villa land? There was no way he'd restrict Theodyne in such a way, even if it were for his own good.

Violent pounding came from the front door.

Pedraus started to go answer it, but Nico stalled him. "Only let them in if they have a writ signed by the *prolate.*"

Pedraus gave a head bob and left the room. Nico leaned back in his chair, his stomach roiling at the tension he felt coming from the hallway. Whoever had come to his door had brought with them massive amounts of negative energy. It was like the tidal surge of an angry sea, cresting on the shores of his home and wiping out all the positive protections.

Pedraus came back into the room and handed Nico a piece of paper. An arrest warrant for Theodyne Thespacian on the grounds of stealing jewels from the Countess de Riva.

That bitch!

He was going to answer this charge for Theodyne. Nico doubted the former thief even knew the Countess. However, she was the *prolate*'s cousin.

Nico stood and met the *prolatic* guards in the entranceway. He handed the arrest warrant to the guard leader. "You do not want Thespacian. You want me."

The guard swallowed hard. "But my lord, you were not named. The Countess—"

"Is lying."

"My lord?"

"Let me accompany you to the *prolate*'s palace, and I will speak to the Medovin myself. As a titled lord, he owes me that much consideration."

Nico grabbed his hat and a cloak and followed the guards out into the setting sun. Anger rose up to choke him. There was no reason behind what the *prolate* planned to do to Theodyne other than pure revenge. Well, they'd see about that when Nico showed up in place of his lover. Then again, taking something away from Theodyne might serve as an alternate punishment.

There were so many lands and much property to consider, plus the people in his employ who would no longer have means to support themselves.

Nico turned to Pedraus and gave a small nod. The servant returned the gesture, knowing the significance of the moment. They'd discussed this pass at length many times over the years. Now the preparations would begin in earnest.

"Nico! Wait!"

Theodyne stood on the threshold, eyes golden and wild. His heart was there for Nico to see so plainly. "Don't do this. Not for me."

He gave a sad smile. "For you, I'd do anything."

He allowed the guards to lead the way.

BY THE time they reached the *prolate*'s palace, full dark had fallen. Torches lit the way. The flickering flames caused the shadows along the walls to grow into grotesque forms. Monstrous in size and shape, they bore no resemblance to the people who cast them. Another of the necromancer's tricks? A little something to unnerve Nico before he went before the court, or only the simple play of light along the contoured stones?

It mattered not.

He was taken directly to the court, where Estobán Medovin sat in his formal robes of state. His cousin and another man sat on either side of him. The one on the left dressed in no official manner Nico knew. The robes were dark gray and rotted at the sleeves. A cowl came up to hide the face in bitter darkness. This was not the same necromancer he and Master Oberon had seen in the Agia crypt, but another one. Power leaked from the death dancer's essence like a festering wound. Influence filled the room, permeating all who stood in the chamber—all but Nico. He was made of stronger fiber than any Medovin in history.

At Nico's appearance, Estobán Medovin stood and pointed at the guard leader. "This is *not* Thespacian."

"No, sir. It is Count Nicodemus de Valencia. He says he is the one you want."

Medovin's angry gaze flicked to Nico. "Oh, really? And you suppose the court or the complainant do not know who wronged them?"

"No. I know because it was another who came to me for a consultation on the necklace the Countess claims to have been stolen."

"A consultation? Of what matter?"

Nico gave Medovin a wry smile. "Exactly."

Confusion spread across the *prolate*'s face. His cousin gave a discreet throat clearing that captured the *prolate*'s attention. Cesare leaned over and whispered in Estobán's ear.

The *prolate* straightened. "We will hear your version of events."

"Does it matter? I am the one directly involved if I say I am."

"You are truly an odd man if you believe I'll place you in jail in your lover's stead." Medovin gave a knowing smile. "I *have* heard the rumors."

"And I've attempted to hide nothing of my relationship with Theodyne. He hadn't even arrived at the villa when my client was there."

Then a thought struck him. Had they both been set up? Theodyne for taking the necklace he had no knowledge of, and Nico for doing the work in the first place. Theodyne had been sent there by Menarch, who knew of Molari and the *Eye of Truth*. Was it so far of a stretch to think that Desdemona diGarza and her cousin the Countess might have been agents of the Medovins as well? At this point, Nico believed most sincerely there was nothing to which the *prolate* wouldn't stoop. At least under the direction of the necromancer.

Nico looked into the eyes of the *prolate* and that of his cousin. There, deep inside the swirling mists of memory, was the same rotting flesh he'd seen in those affected at the school. Now, how to play this? He needed to tread very lightly, use the most delicate touch.

Should he attempt to disengage the necromancer when the death dancer sat only a few feet away from his puppets? Surely that was a most dangerous proposition. Still, Nico had no choice and very few articles with which to work.

In the spirit of a true valiant, Nico committed body and soul to stopping the necromancer and plunged into the act.

To outward appearances he did nothing more than take a step forward, but the deed was akin to stepping off a dock into the icy waters of the frozen North. Every muscle and joint of his body seized with cold. Movement and perception slowed. Reactions became dreamlike—as if he no longer had control of his physical self.

And he without the blood of an elemental.

No! He would not die this way. Would not face his ancestors knowing he had failed when the world needed him the most. Like a drowning man searching for the bottom of the lake in order to push himself to the surface, Nico dug deep and bent air to push the necromancer's influence away. The concussion rippled outward like a cannon blast, sending debris upward and outward.

The Medovins looked to their benefactor with shocked faces as the necromancer stood from the dais, his arms raised in a promise of retribution.

Did they expect Nico to wither under their master's unholy power? They were badly mistaken if that was the case. He'd never let the fate of the city-states land in such evil hands. Nor remain. The problem was how to keep the necromancer from opening a portal and escaping.

The sharp point of a blade rested directly on his spine. Nico turned his head. A guard held his spear level. One good shove and Nico would be either dead or paralyzed. Neither was a good option.

Nico glanced at the blade and smiled. Did the necromancer not understand that *form* meant everything? That the Grand Matter was not impressed by such human weapons? They were as sand beneath an alchemist's feet—and even sand had its place in the material world.

With no more than a thought, Nico envisioned the blade stuck in a fire and heated until the metal turned molten and dripped on the floor. The guard staggered back a few steps, unable to believe his eyes.

"Seize him!" Cesare Medovin was on his feet, directing the guards as if they were his own personal army.

The guards surrounded Nico. He lifted his hand and made a pushing motion. Their staffs disintegrated, turning to sawdust before being blown away on a breeze.

Odd. The windows were all closed. Nico turned. The necromancer had his arms raised, calling forth wind from the ether. This wasn't just any force of air, but one that penetrated the body and struck right at the bones.

It became harder for Nico to raise his hands in order to direct the action. Slowly, as if his spirit were liquid and his body a sieve, he began to leak away.

Dearest ancestors! The necromancer was trying to steal his soul while his heart still beat. This was not what he'd found in the students, not even the influence he'd felt within the Mcdovins. This was murder most profound.

No. Nico would not allow his very essence to become trapped in some ethereal prison designed by the death dancers. It was not the way of alchemy. The adepts believed in the right of ascension. To travel to the next plane of existence, and for the soul to evolve was to move forward. Thus was the core of their beliefs.

Balance.

The heavens and earth revolved around balance. Without it, all was lost.

Nico held on to his consciousness, trying desperately to remember what it was to be whole. To live inside a three-dimensional body. He clung to the memory as tenaciously as an eagle did its prey, gripping the small, squiggling entity in its great curved talons.

He felt his body failing, falling to the floor.

This could not be happening. Nico was stronger than this, had trained his entire life to manipulate all kinds of physical matter—was there nothing he could use as defense against the call of death?

One by one, Nico concentrated on the particles that composed flesh and blood. Metals and salts. Sulfurs and gases. Each unique and precious in their makeup.

Granules began to fall from the necromancer as he advanced on Nico. Nico did not know how long he could hold out against the pull on his soul. Every beat of his heart grew slower, signaling doom.

The necromancer stood over Nico, and finally he saw what was beneath the cowl. A horrible visage stood highlighted in the dancing torch flames. What had once been a man was now nothing more than a fleshless skull. Eye sockets were empty caverns that stretched into infinity. This was no necromancer, but death itself, standing before Nico to deliver final and lasting retribution.

The alchemists had never thought to beat death, but to embrace it and go gladly when the time had come. This was not right!

Death was a natural function of the world. Part of the divine order. *So in life, so in death.* The *Eye of Truth* spoke at length on the subject. Death was *not* evil. It simply was another state of being.

Nico mustered up the last of his waning strength and tugged hard on the particles. The necromancer stumbled forward, not expecting the resistance. Pieces of his robes began to fall like a dirty rain, showering Nico in the filth.

The piles of debris vibrated. Faster and faster they moved, heading toward each other before combining into one big mound. Winds began to stir the sloughing, sending them into a swirl as when Nico built a globe. Only this time the materials did not make a sphere and Nico did not control the alchemy.

From the fabric of the necromancer, another had risen. A complete and perfect copy of its sire loomed over Nico. Bony hands were stretched outward. Fingers clenched around Nico's throat. Darkness came, and he had no more energy or defense against them.

They had orchestrated his demise well.

Chapter Twenty-Two

PAIN GNAWED on Theodyne's insides. Every crash of the necromancer's power against Nico descended like a lightning strike. The heavens themselves wept, and the elementals were in a blind rage.

He'd left the villa with his pockets stuffed full of the storm globes. Nico had cautioned they were dangerous devices, and now was as good a time as any to find out.

The air elementals carried him on currents faster than he could have ever run. The *prolate*'s court loomed ever closer. The windows displayed the battle that raged within. Lights danced and flashed. Winds rattled the glass in the panes. Shadows grew like hideous monsters living inside the palace.

Theodyne reached into his pocket and held tightly to the storm globe in his hand—a little extra insurance for what he might face. But face them, he would. For Nico.

As he moved by a torch, he pulled it from the wall and held it aloft. Inside the flame he saw the dancing eyes of a fire elemental.

"How would you like to burn hotter and brighter than any flame ever known?"

The fire elemental rose, grew white. It leaned toward the heavy doors, closed against intrusion. Guards stood at the ready, lances crossed to bar his way.

"No one is allowed in during court session."

"Can't you hear what is happening inside? There is a war being waged, and you stand there and do nothing save waste the air you breathe." Theodyne blew on the flame, giving it an explosive outward force. It was just enough impetus to make the doors explode off the hinges.

The fire elemental crackled with laughter.

Theodyne surveyed the destruction, and his heart bled. Nico lay on the floor. He didn't appear to be breathing. His face was waxy and pale as two necromancers stood guard over his body.

"You may have your lover's corpse when you turn over the *Eye of Truth*." The voice issued from both necromancers in an evil chorus.

Anger burned from the well in Theodyne's soul where all the hatred he'd ever felt had festered like an abscess. It was more than he could stand, more than he had ever tried to hold back.

Nico would never want the *Eye* turned over, not even for his own soul.

Theodyne tossed the storm globe. It hit the tile flooring and shattered, unleashing a storm as violent as any he'd ever seen. Rain pelted him. Hail as big as hen's eggs hit the floor and bounced in an angry staccato. Lightning zigzagged through the room. Guards ran and ducked for cover. Still more rushed inside to see the unbelievable spectacle.

Theodyne raised his hands and let the power of the elements work through him. The sensation of being ripped apart from the inside brought his head back and mouth open on a shout born of pain and fury.

"Never!"

He clasped his hands together and the concussion shook the ground beneath their feet. The walls trembled. Hunks of the ceiling began to fall in around them.

Theodyne dove for Nico. He covered the fallen adept, giving his back to the raining debris. The elementals kept the bulk of the pieces from hitting him, but the dust still landed in his hair like a dirty shower. The rain continued, turning the mortar to mud.

This close to Nico, Theodyne noticed life. It was small, barely detectable, but there nonetheless. He ran his hand over Nico's cheek. "Nico? Wake up." He had to shout to be heard over the raging storm.

Nico's eyes moved back and forth behind his closed lids, as if he was trying to come awake but failing. From all indications, he was continuing to fight the battle in his unconscious state.

What had they done to him?

Theodyne looked up and focused all his rage on the necromancers. Flames erupted from the wall sconces; fire elementals sprang to life at the call to arms. They flew through the air in a ribbon of color and heat. The electric arcs of lightning organized and found targets. The necromancers moved in unison out of the way, shifting on agile feet, trying to outrun Theodyne's vengeance.

The fire elementals continued their attack, not letting up until the necromancers danced within the twirling robes of flame. Unholy screams were rent from the voids where their faces should be.

This time they would not escape their fate.

The necromancers hit the floor, rolling around and contorting in pain. The stink of rot and burning flesh filled the room. They smelled as any other would while dying through incineration. It was the common denominator.

All men lived. All men died.

Even death dancers.

With the necromancers extinguished, the fire elementals diminished and the storm quieted—their revenge was complete.

Theodyne's had yet to be spent.

Under the dais sat two quivering forms. Estobán and Cesare Medovin had crawled under there to hide from the carnage. Theodyne stalked up the stairs and reached under the table to pull Estobán out by his robes.

He lifted the *prolate* up by the collar and shook him. "See what you've done? See the destruction your greed and corruptions have wrought?"

Estobán blinked up, as if waking from a long, hard slumber.

"Theodyne?" Estobán glanced at his former lover as if he did not remember the grand entrance Theodyne had made or the battle that had raged all around him. He lifted his hand as if to touch the scar on Theodyne's cheek. "Your face?"

Theodyne leaned out of reach. "A souvenir from your temper tantrum when I left."

Estobán visibly swallowed. "I never meant...." He glanced around Theodyne. "Is that Count de Valencia? What happened here?"

Theodyne threw Estobán into a chair and stepped back. "Are you trying to tell me you don't remember consorting with the necromancers? Or maybe Cesare would care to enlighten us on his involvement with them?"

Cesare crawled out from beneath the safety of the dais. A chair lay broken into splintered wood in front of him. He rose to his feet, brushing bits of dirt and what looked like sawdust from his robe of state. "I have no idea what you mean."

"Do not lie to me. I saw you with the necromancer in Delaneux. There were two of them inside this room with you. I have no idea what game you are playing, but you jeopardize us all."

With dignity and a nose lifted into the air as if he smelled something foul—and no doubt he did, with the stink of charred death dancer on the air—he leveled a gaze at Theodyne. "I have never once dealt with such abominations. He speaks in lies, but then, what do you expect from a common thief? The necromancers are nothing more than myth."

Theodyne's head pounded with rage. His eyes hurt with the blood that pumped behind them. "I may be a thief, but I've damn sure never been common."

Estobán looked around the room, lost. "This place is a shambles. Are the guards all dead?"

At the moment, Theodyne didn't give a damn about the guards. The only person he cared about was Nico.

A moan rose from down on the court floor. Nico was waking.

Theodyne hurried down the steps and bent over his lover. He lovingly brushed his hand over Nico's forehead. "Nico? Nico? It's Theodyne."

Nico's eyes slowly opened. Words came from his lips in a litany of thin whispers. They were the same ones he'd uttered while they'd made love. This time was different though—this time Theodyne understood.

"I love you more than air and sun. You are the water, light, and salt of my soul. May the Gods bless and keep you always."

Tears blurred Theodyne's vision. He bent and brushed his mouth against Nico's lips. "I love you too. You are all that and more."

Then Nico came fully awake, his mouth pressed to Theodyne's in thankful benediction.

When they broke the kiss, Theodyne moved away, giving Nico room. "Can you sit?"

"I think so." Nico put words to action and sat up, moving stiffly and guarding his side. He winced and gave a grunt of pain. "I think I may have injured my ribs."

"We'll have you seen to." Theodyne turned and looked at the Medovins. "See what your scheming has done to him? You will pay for this."

Nico shook his head. His hand rested weakly on Theodyne's arm. "They knew not what they were doing. They had fallen under the necromancer's influence, as did our students. Their guilt is not of their making."

Theodyne did not know what to say. His rage had no outlet now— save for the remains that floated like ashes carried away by the winds.

Estobán rose and came forward. His hands rotated palms up in a gesture of supplication. "Please, Theodyne. I have no idea of what you accuse me. I only now feel as if I've woken from a very strange and dark dream. There are pieces there, flashes, but no solid memory."

What was Theodyne to say to that? He was so willing to believe Jolen and the others, knowing that his own mind had been invaded and controlled by the necromancers; why was it so hard to trust that Estobán had gone through the same ordeal?

Estobán took a few steps closer. "What have I done in my slumber?"

Finally Theodyne brought his shoulders down in a feeling of resignation. "What have any of us done under their influence? It's what we do from here on out that matters."

"Do you believe they will return?" Estobán addressed the question to Nico.

"I have no doubt in my mind. They were after an alchemical relic: the *Eye of Truth*. It is our most holy text. Having failed to gain access to it but in the bits and pieces stolen from our students, I believe they will try again." Nico was still ashen-faced, but his words were strong.

There was a moment or two of silence, then Nico continued. "I fear if they fail here, they will go to our neighbors to the North and East. With the *demigoge's* health failing, the church will soon be in turmoil, and the city-states will be ripe for takeover. I hate to admit it, but I fear Master Rhone was right. There will be a time soon when the alchemists will be asked to choose sides. I only hope it is far enough in the future for us to mount a defense."

Theodyne didn't doubt that for a minute. He glanced over at Cesare. He was the weak link in the chain. Unlike Estobán, there was no sorrow or remorse in his actions—only righteous indignation. It made Theodyne wonder just how deeply the man was involved in the intrigues.

Nico rubbed Theodyne's arm in a loving touch. "We must stand together if we are to defeat them for good."

Reluctantly and at length, Theodyne nodded. He didn't like working with Cesare, but he could put the past behind him and offer his hand and service to Estobán. For Nico and for the city-states.

Theodyne lifted his hand in friendship to his former lover. "We have to make a plan."

Estobán nodded and offered his hand to Theodyne. "I will stand with you."

Nico raised his hand to place over theirs. "As will I."

They turned as one to stare at Cesare. He rolled his eyes and came forward, placing his hand on the three of theirs, completing the pact. "As will I."

Theodyne tried not to let Cesare's reluctance undermine the moment. He planned to hold both Medovins to the promise.

Together they would change the course of history and protect the city-states from the necromancers. He didn't know how or when, but they would. They had to.

It was proclaimed so in the *Eye of Truth*.

Glossary

adept—Highest level obtained by alchemical master.

Adepts' Council—Body of ruling alchemical adepts who preside over matters pertaining to the Gold School.

aerothant—Product of union between human and air elemental.

Agia, Ignatius—*Prolate* of city-state of Calabris. Head of the House of Agia; also referred to as the Agia.

alchemy—The search for enlightenment through the study of science, theology, and the esoteric, and how it relates to the natural world.

aquathant—Product of union between human and water elemental.

Bertolini, Oberon—Adept-level alchemist.

cardgran—Highest level of cleric in the Dominicál city-states. Make up council who elect a new *demigoge*.

city-states—Provinces/principalities in country of Dominicál. They are as follows: Auflaven, Bellor, Bonsuret, Brixton, Calabris, Devani, Dharakhan, Flurian, Nequan, Pliern, Romanta, Sadonia, Trumolo.

Delaneux—Largest town in city-state of Calabris. Seat of the Agia family.

damsk—Silver coin.

Dante, Mecurian—Founder of the Gold School; ancestor of Count Nicodemus de Valencia.

demigoge—(pronounced: de mí gōche) Derived from the word demagogue; supreme religious head of the Dominincál city-states.

desan—A Holy See—Highest cleric of a city-state; however, is one step below a *cardgran* in the clerical order.

Donando, Headmaster—Headmaster of Gold School.

Eye of Truth—Sacred text of the alchemists, a book of immense power. Contains both codex of laws, spells, and incantations, and rubbings from the original Emerald Tablet—the basis of all alchemical study.

etherealthant—Product of union between human and spirit elemental.

gint—Brass coin.

Grand Matter—Also called Prime Matter; universal substance of which everything springs; origins of life.

guitern—Instrument, cross between harp, guitar and mandolin.

Holy See—See *desan*. Highest clerical authority in a city-state. Terms Holy See and *desan* are used interchangeably.

Krutarch, Master—Adept who wrote keyed primer.

Lancor—Largest town in city-state of Sadonia; seat of the Medovin family.

Medovin, Cesare—Estobán's cousin.

Medovin, Estobán—*Prolate* of Sadonia; head of Medovin family, also referred to as the Medovin. Theodyne Thespacian's ex-lover.

Meripen, Jolen—Journeyman of the Gold School.

necromancers—Also called death dancers; can raise or speak with the dead. Greatest foes of the alchemists.

necromon—Title of esteem and respect given to head necromancer.

plazo—Small garden or gathering place within confines of an estate, usually decorated with colorful stones.

prolate—Ruler of a city-state, also head of his family.

pyrothant—Product of union between human and fire elemental.

slew—Copper coin.

spagyrics—Alchemical term; act of breaking down a substance than putting it back together in its highest form.

terrathant—Product of union between human and earth elemental.

Thespacian, Theodyne—Former thief, now an apprentice in the Gold School.

tonza—Gold coin.

Valenica, Count Nicodemus de—Alchemist adept. Direct descendant of Mecurian Dante, head of Gold School.

CASSIE SWEET lives and works from her home office in the New Jersey Highlands, where she shares space with her over-affectionate Golden Retriever and artist husband. Her writing takes her to many destinations, both real and imagined. You can catch her on Twitter under her other writing personae @MKMancosKScott and on Facebook under Kathleen Scott/MK Mancos Author Page.

http://www.mystickat.com/

GATEKEEPER

RAYNE AUSTER

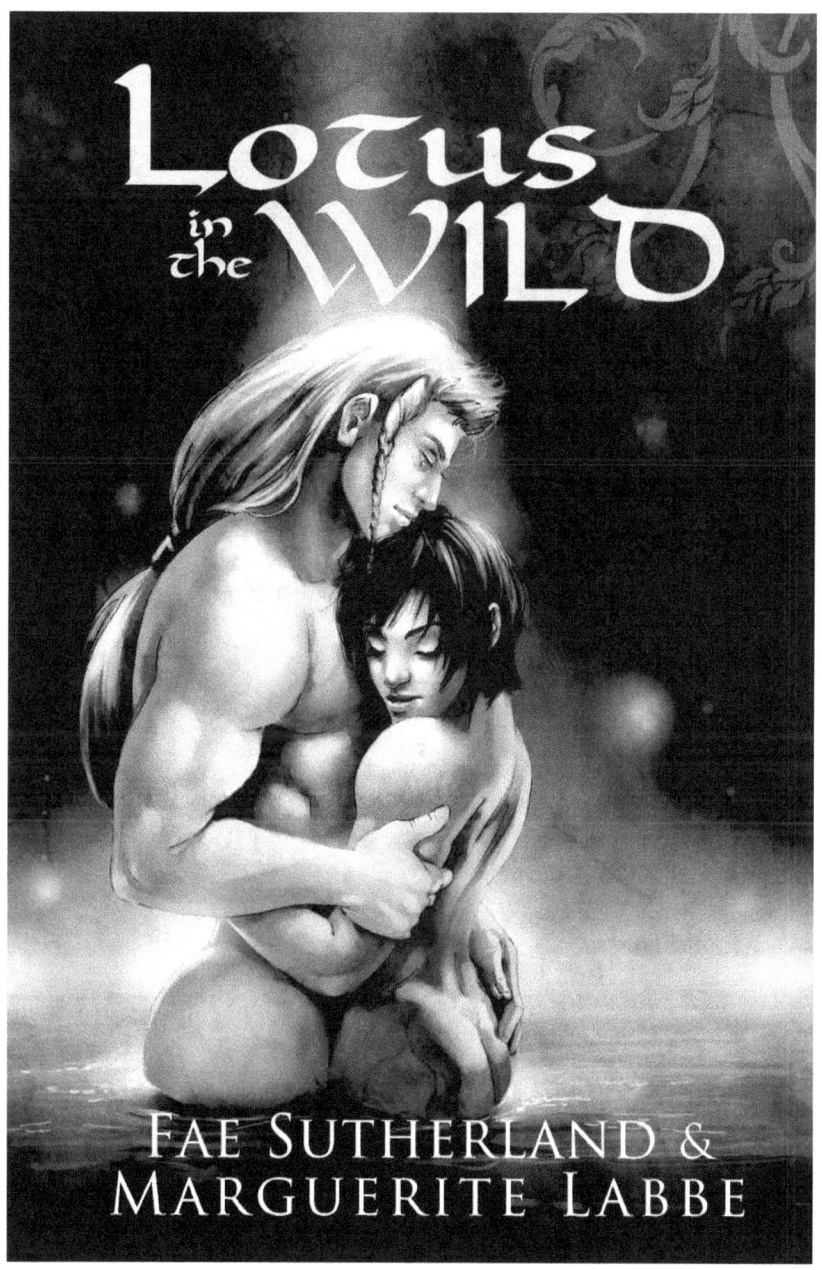

www.ingramcontent.com/pod-product-compliance
Lightning Source LLC
Chambersburg PA
CBHW051630260626
47170CB00004B/1108